To Save a Dictator

A TIMELESS story

by

Rusty Bradshaw

What readers are saying about Rusty Bradshaw's books.

The Rehabilitation of Miss Little

Captivating!!

This story is very well written! Rusty does such a great job describing the scenario, he doesn't suck you in - he absorbs you! You feel like you are among the characters. And you have to keep reading to find out what drives the people to do what they are doing. I hope Rusty keeps writing! I look forward to reading another book by him!

Awesome book!

This book was highly recommended to me, so I bought it. I'm so glad I did! I'm not much of a reader, but this book was hard to put down; it kept my attention from start to finish. It's a great story, kind of sad about what she went through, but a good ending. I can hopefully look forward to more books from this author!

Moist on the Mountain

Awesome!

Another good book from the author! Love his writing. I got the book for myself, finished it in a couple of days. I was so interested in the story, it was hard to put down.

Fun book to read

Keeps you interested, and you don't want to put the book down until finished.

Gorge Justice

The Best 1 Yet

As I've said before, I'm not a reader, but after reading the first two books by Rusty Bradshaw, I thought I'd read the third. This book is his best yet. I finished it in three days! It made me cry, made me sad, get angry, and happy. It's worth reading!!

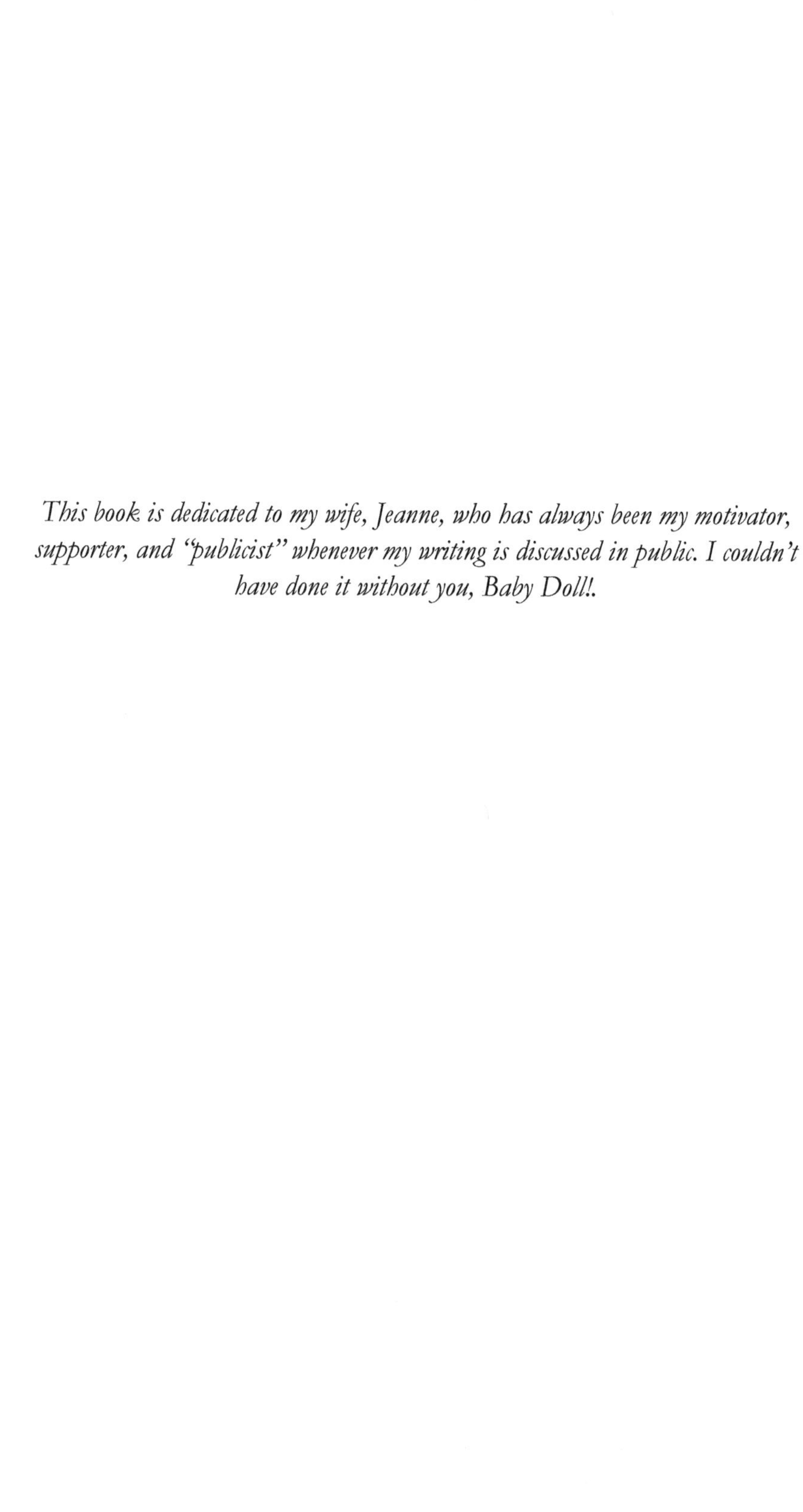

This book is dedicated to my wife, Jeanne, who has always been my motivator, supporter, and "publicist" whenever my writing is discussed in public. I couldn't have done it without you, Baby Doll!.

PROLOGUE

Peter Wilson was excited by the news of his second child. He was the father of a fine daughter, and now the possibility of a son filled his mind.

As he walked along the sidewalk, a trek he made hundreds, even thousands, of times, he thought of his extended family in Chicago. How pleased his mother would be to hear the news. She was so delighted when Mary Ann was born that she almost came out to California to live with him and Gwen, and their new daughter. Maybe this time, she would come.

The world was different from when Peter was born in 1983. Now, children were almost throwaways at just about any age. There were so many children on their own because of broken marriages, divorce and homelessness. When Peter was born, children were welcomed, and in fact, a must in most marriages. The divorce rate was lower, and families worked harder to stay together, no matter how tough things became.

It was not quite like when his parents were first married, and certainly not like his grandparents' time. But when he and Gwen decided to start a family, society was still a favorable place for children.

Peter's walk took him through many back alleys. In this day and age, he didn't even need to walk. Streamlined cars zipped everywhere, and anyone could afford one, no matter how poor they were. In fact, Peter owned three of them. But he liked the exercise. Besides, today he wanted to walk and think of the developing child. Would it be a son or another daughter? Would it be healthy? What kind of future was in store for the little one once brought into the world?

Thinking about his new child, though, did not take his mind away from the true purpose of his adventure out of the house. He was headed to his office. A multi-room, single-story collection of offices in the somewhat out-of-place strip mall in the industrial area about a mile from home.

Peter Wilson was a stockbroker. It was a small investment company he started five years ago when the American economy was booming. He started with just himself and a secretary. But in the first three years, business was so good he added two associates and two more secretaries, who now insisted on being called administrative assistants.

In the past two years, business at Wilson Investments began to level out. He maintained his clients, as did his associates, but new clients were few and far between. On this early Saturday morning, he was on his way to meet with his associates to talk strategy for getting the business back on an upward trend.

Pausing at the office door while pulling the keys from his pocket, Peter felt a chill. It was a warm June morning, so he wondered if there had been a chilly breeze filtering inland from the Pacific Ocean a few miles west. But he gave it no more thought as he turned the key and swung the door open.

As Peter pulled the key out of the door, stuck it in his front pocket, and looked up, he was met by an unfamiliar office.

He looked around the room and saw a counter that ran the width of the room with a small half-door in the middle. Behind that, there were four desks spread out through a wide open space. Lining the walls were filing cabinets. This was not the small reception area with a receptionist's desk to the right that he had seen daily. His company's building included several separate private offices for his associates and their assistants. They were accessed by a small hallway down the middle of the building. There was no counter and no half-door in the center.

"Who are you?" Peter heard a stern voice say. "And how did you get a key to this building?"

Peter was suddenly aware of other people in the room – five men in uniforms. The one who had spoken was walking toward him through the half-door in the counter. It was not lost on Peter that while the tall blond man walked through the opening, his right hand rested on the butt of a pistol in a holster on his hip.

The man's uniform was all black, and he wore black knee-high boots polished to a fine shine. On the right breast of his uniform shirt was an embroidered eagle with its wings spread wide and upward. On the left breast was a small band of multi colored patches above a black Iron Cross bordered in silver. On each collar were two white embroidered symbols that looked like small lightning bolts squared off at the ends.

"Tell me how you got in here," the man shouted as his hand tightened on the pistol's grip.

Suddenly, like a quick-draw artist from the Old West, the man had the gun pointed at Peter's chest. Peter recognized it as a Luger P08 from some World War II-era movies he had watched. The uniformed man gestured with his left hand to the men behind the counter, and two of them came forward and took Peter by each arm and led him toward the back of the building. They came to a door, and it was opened by one of his escorts, and they all walked through the doorway.

They emerged in a room filled with computers, control panels, and consoles. Three men stood directly in front of them.

"Put him in a cell," the man with the gun, right behind Peter, ordered, and jabbed the barrel into Peter's back.

Peter did not know how long he had been in the cell. The men in uniforms had taken his wallet, keys, watch, and cell phone. He glanced around to try and get his bearings. The cell they had thrown Peter in was small and had only three walls. The remaining side had no wall, no bars. It was criss-crossed with red beams of light. A low, steady hum echoed off the walls.

He rose from the steel cot and walked toward the light-crossed opening. As he touched the light pattern, there was a crackling sound, and pain shot through his body. The jolt startled him, and he was partly thrown and partly stumbled backward, and he fell on the cot.

Still a bit confused, he got up and tried again. But this time, he only lightly touched the light beams with a fingertip. He received a light shock, but enough to make him jerk his hand back. He looked at the beams and tried again. This time, he thrust his entire arm into the beams, but it was thrown back with such force that it felt as if someone was trying to rip his arm off. He sat on the edge of the cot, rubbing his arm that was completely numb from his fingertips to just above the elbow.

With pain throbbing in his shoulder, he sat back down on the cot. He tried to make sense of what happened to him in the last few minutes. Was it minutes, or had it been hours, or even longer? He was not sure.

As he tried to make sense of the situation, he heard a door open, then close, and he heard the sound of boot heels hitting the bare concrete floor. Then two back-uniformed men stepped in front of the cell. Neither of the men was anyone he had seen so far.

"What is your name?" one man asked, as the other pulled a pencil and small hand-sized notepad from the front pocket of his uniform trousers.

Peter shook his head.

"As I've told you already, my name is Peter Wilson," he said slowly. "I own Wilson Investments. This is my company's office building. I came here to talk to my associates."

"Describe your office," the questioner ordered.

Peter gave him a detailed description, right down to the color the walls were painted in each room.

"I know that's not what it looks like in here," Peter said. "The only explanation I have is that you guys came in here last night and switched my office to this."

It was hard to believe that such a transformation could be made in just one night. But it was the only option that made sense. The frustration on the questioner's face was clear. His partner with the notepad remained poised to write, but he had yet to put pencil to paper.

"And why would we do such a thing?" the questioner asked in a raised voice. He then reached to his left and pushed a button on a small control panel on the wall, and the criss-cross of lights at the front of the cell disappeared, and the humming stopped. The questioner quickly stepped into the cell and right up to Peter, still seated on the cot. Grabbing him by the collar, the man jerked Peter to his feet and pulled him so close their noses were nearly touching.

"You will give us the information we want," the uniformed man yelled. "It will either come easy or not so easy. That will be your choice."

He pushed Peter back down on the cot.

"You are a spy against the Reich, and we will find out why you are breaking into our office here in the Western Province," the man said as he paced back and forth in front of the cot.

The hair on the back of Peter's head and his arms stood straight up when he heard the words "spy" and "Reich." He knew enough history and saw enough movies to know the meaning of them both.

"What do you mean 'Reich'? We are in the state of California in the United States of America," Peter asked cautiously.

The man stopped his pacing, grabbed Peter's shirt collar with his left hand, and jerked him to his feet again. He raised his right hand and swung it open-palmed at Peter's head. He instinctively raised his left arm to ward off the blow, but was only slightly successful. The man's arm continued its arc, only being misdirected enough that his hand slapped Peter in the temple rather than the full face.

Peter's attempt to defend himself enraged the uniformed man, and he shook Peter violently. Then, with his victim momentarily off balance, he sent his right arm, with a balled fist this time, crashing into Peter's left eye. He directed another punch at Peter's nose, which immediately started to bleed. He was then thrown back onto the cot.

The attacker stepped back, looked at the blood on his knuckles, and pulled out a white handkerchief from his right breast pocket with his left hand and wiped his right hand clean. He looked at Peter, lying motionless on the cot, with disdain.

"You will tell us what we want to know," he said calmly. "And then you will die."

Peter had no doubt this man meant what he said. But his mind was reeling with what had happened to him in the last…what was it, minutes, hours, days; he could not remember.

Without taking his eyes off Peter, the man raised his right hand and snapped his fingers. The man with the notepad, still standing just outside the cell, motioned with his left hand for someone to come forward.

A tall, slender blond woman walked into the cell. She wore a uniform much like the others, only cut for a woman's figure. She had a small pouch at her right side, secured over her left shoulder with a leather strap. From the pouch, she retrieved a syringe and a small bottle containing a colorless liquid. She plunged the needle into the bottle and pulled back the plunger, filling the syringe.

Peter's heart rate quickened, and his whole body tensed. It didn't take a genius to figure out their intention. They planned to inject him with something, either to force him to give them information he did not have or worse, to just eliminate him. Neither possibility appealed to him.

With no real plan in mind, just knowing he had to avoid that needle, Peter jumped up and took one step to the right to go around the man who had struck him. But he was ready for an escape attempt. He gave Peter such an uppercut punch to the gut that the air went rushing out of his lungs. As he tried to regain his breath, Peter began to get faint, and he fell back on the cot.

He could see, through increasingly blurred eyes, the female officer moving closer to him with the syringe at the ready.

Very faint light started to slip through Peter's eyelids as they began to flutter. Within seconds, he was able to slow the flutter and open his eyes just a sliver. All he could see was bright white light. He closed his eyes again, waited a few seconds, then tentatively opened them. This time, he got them halfway open.

He began to hear noise filter into his ears. It was little more than faint background noise and a loud ringing at first, but slowly he began to recognize it as voices. Those voices seemed hauntingly familiar.

Once again, he closed his eyes, squeezing them as tight as he could, and held them that way for a few seconds. As the ringing in his ears began to subside, the voices he heard became clearer. He recognized his associates, Stephon Weiler and Candace Buford. He quickly opened his eyes.

The white light assaulted his senses, but it was not as bright as before, and he could make out Stephon's and Candace's faces, although not in total focus.

"Hey, man, you're back," Peter heard Stephon say.

The more he let his eyes adjust to the light, the more he could see the looks of puzzlement and concern on their faces.

"What happened?" Candace asked.

Peter reviewed his most recent memories – coming to the office, finding it so changed, the uniformed men, the cell, the woman with the syringe. Even as he relived it in his mind, it seemed impossible. Maybe he had dreamed it – maybe for some reason, when he got into the office, he had passed out for some reason and dreamed it all.

He was not ready to answer Candace's question just yet.

As his eyes cleared more, he looked around. He saw that he was on the floor in the storage room of the office. There were the shelves with office supplies, a spare desk and chair, and some cleaning supplies.

Stephon and Candace still squatted in front of him, but he could now see past them to the other side of the room. There was the door to the room, just as he remembered it. But for an instant, a vision of the cell flashed through his mind.

But it still seemed too unreal to put into words.

"Did you hit your head or something?" Candace asked.

Just as the words left her mouth, someone could be heard coming in the front door of the office complex. Stephon got up to see who it was. He returned shortly with two paramedics.

As the medical team examined him, they peppered him with questions. The questions about his medical history he answered readily. But he held back when they asked him what happened.

"I don't really remember," is the only answer he gave.

"What medications are you taking?" one paramedic asked as he looked into Peter's eyes with a penlight.

"None," he responded.

"Are you sure?" the paramedic asked.

"Nothing prescribed, just some vitamin supplements," Peter told him.

The paramedic beckoned to his partner to take a look at Peter. After he had done so, he checked a second time. He then turned to the other paramedic with a quizzical look on his face.

"Barbiturates?" he asked. His partner nodded his head, but both were puzzled.

"How did you get barbiturates into your system?" the first paramedic asked.

Peter had heard of that kind of drug. But he had never taken any kind of drug in his life, neither prescribed nor illegal. And he was a teetotaler -- no alcohol whatsoever.

Peter started to say he did not know how such a drug could get into his body. But then he remembered the tall, slender female officer with the syringe. As incredible as it may seem, he decided it was time to tell his story.

CHAPTER 1

Wyatt Logan lay on his right side facing the wall of a bedroom that was not his own. Through the windows, even with the curtains drawn, the rising sun began to brighten up the room.

He had awoke a few moments earlier, but lay still, turning events over in his mind. He could feel on the back of his neck the steady, shallow breathing of a sleeper.

Lucy Preston, also lying on her right side, was pressed up against Wyatt so tightly he could feel her breasts, covered by the loose-fitting satin negligee, flattened against his bare back. Her left arm was draped over his side with her hand pressed firmly on his chest.

He let his memory travel back to January 1941, when the "Lifeboat" team traveled back to Hollywood to foil a plot to steal the only copy of the film "Citizen Kane." In a lush hotel, Wyatt and Lucy ended up in bed together and consummated the feelings they were each having for the other. It was a sweet moment in their lives, one he liked to replay whenever possible.

Unfortunately, that also led to the memory of discovering Jessica, his wife, who was killed in 2014, was still alive, saved from death by Rittenhouse to serve its own ends.

But following another year of traveling through time to keep Rittenhouse from disfiguring history, Wyatt and Lucy had finally admitted their love for each other.

As Wyatt lay there savoring his closeness with Lucy, he knew things had morphed into what he had hoped for almost from the moment he met her.

Six months had passed since the Lifeboat team, aided by a future Wyatt and Lucy and an Advanced Lifeboat, went back in time to resurrect Rufus Carlin, a Mason Industries programmer and the team's pilot, after he was killed on a mission to the 1848 California gold rush. It was also during that trip that Homeland Security Agent Denise Christopher, working in 2018, was able to finally dismantle Rittenhouse.

Connor Mason's time-traveling Mother Ship was stolen by Garcia Flynn, an Eastern European-based ex-National Security Agency asset, and a small group of associates. While the rest of the group's motivations were centered on Rittenhouse, a mysterious organization whose roots dated back to the early days of the United States, Flynn hoped to use the Mother Ship to change history so that he could save his wife and daughters, who were killed.

Rittenhouse had actually funded Mason's research and development of the time-traveling machine for its own ends. The organization's present-day members wanted to go back in time to change American history to allow Rittenhouse to control the country.

During the mission in 1937, the Lifeboat team came to believe that it was Flynn who wanted to destroy the U.S. "in the crib." But his aim was to prevent the Hindenburg explosion in New Jersey, so the airship would be destroyed on the return trip to Germany with some important Americans aboard, traveling to the coronation of Great Britain's King George VI and Queen Elizabeth.

However, Lucy, Rufus, and Wyatt hijacked the zeppelin shortly after a successful landing at Lakehurst Naval Air Station. After a short scuffle aboard, the ship blew up due to a stray bullet from one of Flynn's henchmen, but everyone aboard survived, although a photojournalist who originally survived the disaster was killed. In the chaos that ensued, Flynn gave Lucy a journal he claimed she wrote and encouraged her to ask Agent Christopher about Rittenhouse.

Lucy then learned that the man who raised her was not her biological father because that man married the granddaughter of a Hindenburg passenger. She pressed her mother on the issue and, after some denials, was given an address to visit. When she knocked on the door of the house, it was answered by a man who confirmed he was actually her father. He also revealed he was a leading member of Rittenhouse, which meant Lucy was connected to that organization.

When the Rittenhouse threat is eventually eliminated, the time machine Mother Ship was disassembled. But Agent Christopher decided to keep the Advanced Lifeboat intact and in mothballs at their hidden bunker in case someone else came up with another way to travel through and change time.

Since then, there had been no ripples in time to address, and the Lifeboat team was able to pursue their lives.

Rufus and Jiya Marri, another Mason Industries programmer, restarted their relationship and began discussing plans for establishing their own tech business together. Connor Mason, former head of Mason Industries, who started the time machine project, began rebuilding his company, and continued to consult with Agent Christopher and helped monitor the timeline for disturbances.

As for Wyatt and Lucy, they spent as much time together as they could. Lucy wanted to return to teaching history, but positions were hard to come by while schools were in session. She looked forward to summer when there would be openings and had, in the past two months, been making applications as positions became available.

Wyatt remained in the Army's Delta Force and was on call for Agent Christopher. However, the six months since the last trip in the Lifeboat, he had drawn no assignments for Delta Force but maintained his regular Army duties. Despite being assigned to housing on the base, Wyatt spent most of his nights at the house Lucy used to share with her mother, Carol, who turned out to be a Rittenhouse agent and was killed in 1848 San Francisco, and her sister, Amy, who disappeared from the timeline following the team's first trip back in time to May 1937 to reset the timeline of the Hindenburg airship disaster in New Jersey.

Amy's fate was never determined, and Lucy, who at one point coerced Agent Christopher and Mason to help her bring back Amy in exchange for her participation in their efforts to stop Rittenhouse's interference with history, eventually gave up her efforts to restore her sister to the present timeline when the Mother Ship was destroyed.

Wyatt felt Lucy's hand start to slowly move up and down his chest. Then he felt her body snuggle up even closer to his.

Lucy had become very comfortable with this new turn in their relationship. In the last six months, she had opened her home to him. It was slow at first. They had not even slept together the first month. But as time went on, they became closer, and it was more and more comfortable as the days went on.

"I never get tired of this," Lucy purred into his ear. "I feel so alive and safe with you."

She squeezed him even tighter, if that was even possible. Wyatt enjoyed the moment, then rolled over on his left side to face her. His right hand caressed her face and brushed the dark auburn hair away from where it had fallen over her left eye and tucked it behind her ear.

"Lucy, I have loved you since the day I met you," he said softly.

They embraced wholeheartedly, held it for several seconds, then embarked on a long, sensuous kiss.

Standing at the stove cooking eggs, bacon, and hash browns, Lucy reflected on the past two-and-a-half years. Getting pulled into the time travel project to help restore history had been a shock at first. But the more she worked with Connor Mason and Agent Christopher, the more real history she got to experience.

When Rittenhouse was taken down and she decided to go back to teaching history, Lucy was excited about using her first-hand experiences in the past to enhance her approach in the classroom. It would take some imagination, of course, since she could not tell her students she had actually been involved in the incidents she was talking about.

She could hear the snickers now if she did share that she had traveled back in time.

"Ms. Looney Tunes was at the Alamo. She looks pretty good for her age."

"Ya think she can introduce us to Marilyn Monroe?"

"Is Clark Gables as much of a hunk as he seems to be?"

She was happy to keep the secret of her time travels to herself.

But her desire to go back to teaching was driven by providing a learning experience that students would not get in any other history classroom. So it was taking a little work to come up with a curriculum that would be different than other classes but still not include discussions of her adventures in the past.

And then there was her life with Wyatt.

Prior to the first venture into the past, Lucy had been so engrossed in her career as a history professor that she had little time for relationships. She had dated, but no one man could measure up to that love of history.

After traveling to 1937, Lucy returned to find herself, in addition to her mother, suddenly cancer-free and her sister erased from history, engaged to a man she did not know. While she tried to make that work, it never did. And just as she started to let her feelings for Wyatt rise to the surface, Jessica returned from the dead.

But through it all, Lucy had always loved Wyatt and longed for a life with him. And now it was reality.

"Boy, that smells good," she heard in her ear as she felt his strong arms circle her from behind. "And so does the cook."

Lucy reveled in the moment, not really wanting it to end.

"Why, thank you, gallant sir," she said dramatically as she dished up his breakfast, then turned to face him. She planted a short kiss on his lips as she handed him the plate.

Reluctantly, Wyatt broke from the embrace and went to the dining table. Lucy followed after rinsing the pans and utensils and dropping them in the dishwasher.

"So, what do you have planned for the week?" Wyatt asked. His schedule was set, another week of Army exercises.

"Well, so far, just hoping to get calls for interviews," Lucy answered.

She nibbled on some of the fruit she had cut up for herself before cooking Wyatt's breakfast.

"I hope you get what you are looking for," he said.

Lucy was focused on securing a teaching position, but she was also thinking past that milestone. She wanted to know what her future with Wyatt would look like. It was something that had come up in the last six months, but no serious discussion was had, and no decisions were made.

In those discussions, the word "marriage" was never spoken. But it was on both their minds. Because of his experience with Jessica, Wyatt was a bit reluctant. But he certainly could imagine a blissful life as Lucy's husband. Lucy also envisioned a wonderful life as Wyatt's wife. But she, too, was reluctant to enter into a marriage in general and, because he had been hurt before, with Wyatt in particular.

But after six months of being together, nearly every private moment he was not occupied with his Army duties, Lucy was feeling the time had come to bring it to a head.

"Wyatt, I'd like to talk about…"

"Lucy, there's something I think…."

The simultaneous aborted statements took them both by surprise, but they quickly recovered. They smiled at each other. This was not the first time they had been thinking the same thing at the same time.

"You go ahead," Lucy said.

"No, you first," Wyatt answered.

She dropped her eyes to the tabletop and smiled, a slight blush filled her cheeks.

"Well, I wanted to talk about our future together," she said slowly.

She looked up to see Wyatt formulating a response. As his mouth opened to speak, his cell phone, lying face up on the corner of the table, began to ring. He glanced over at it, then back to her, then suddenly did a double-take. Wyatt stared at the phone for a couple of seconds, picked it up, and faced it toward Lucy. The caller ID read "Agent Christopher."

Jiya sat at her work station in the second bedroom of her small apartment. After the team stopped going on regular missions, she set up the work station at home. She and Rufus had agreed to work with Connor Mason as he rebuilt his company. Since he had no offices at the time, setting up at home was a practical idea.

In the meantime, Connor had established offices for his company a few months ago. They were modest, compared to what he had before the Rittenhouse adventures, but it was a start. Jiya and Rufus worked in Connor's offices, but she decided to maintain her home work station so she could work after hours when inspiration came to her.

She had been at the computer since three o'clock in the morning, not being able to sleep. It was like that some nights. Jiya had developed visions of the future not long after the Mother Ship was stolen and Lucy, Wyatt, and Rufus began traveling back through time in the Lifeboat. Jiya's visions started after she had to go along on one of the missions, and each time she got a vision, she became semi-catatonic.

While she had learned to control her visions of the future during her time in the mid-1800s, there were times when she could not tell whether her dreams were visions or just plain dreams.

This morning, she had started working on a Mason Industries project – rebuilding the company's base for multiple location connectivity – but after a while, she turned her attention to a personal matter.

She and Rufus had talked about running their own tech company. They had both gotten their start with Mason Industries, and they still had a loyalty to him, despite all that had happened in the past two years, but they both felt it was time to branch out on their own.

Since they had renewed their relationship, such as it was, after he was brought back, they believed they wanted to work together for their own future. So as she sat at the computer now, she was looking at the start of a business plan she had begun writing a week ago. But her focus was not much on the plan at the moment.

"What kind of relationship do we have?" she thought.

Jiya was madly in love with Rufus, and she was convinced the feeling was mutual. But it was something of a platonic relationship. After professing his love for her six months ago, Rufus had reverted to his former approach to Jiya – the standoffish, quiet, shy Rufus. They had yet to have sex, and neither did they spend the night at each other's homes.

Jiya had also been a bit shy about her feelings for Rufus in the beginning, but she opened up about it as time went on. And her time in mid-1800s San Francisco had made her quite a bit bolder.

So Jiya wanted this relationship to advance at a faster pace.

She was trying to decide the best way to broach the subject with Rufus when they saw each other later that day, when her phone buzzed on the desk. She looked down and saw "Agent Christopher" in the caller ID.

Rufus' eyes fluttered open. He was lying flat on his back in the middle of the double bed in his studio apartment. He rolled his head over to look at the clock. The red digital lights read seven-thirteen in the morning. He sat up in bed quickly.

"What the hell," he said aloud and grabbed the radio clock.

Sure enough, the alarm had been set properly for five in the morning. He had slept through the annoying loud buzzing of the alarm until it automatically shut itself off after fifteen minutes.

Rufus shook his head, trying to knock the sleep out of his brain. He slowly began to remember.

He had been up until one o'clock in the morning working on the mathematics of a program for Mason Industries on his tablet. The intricacies of the program were escaping him, but he was determined to work it out. When he finally did, he was exhausted and asleep as soon as his head hit the pillow.

Now, as he worked his way out of bed and into the bathroom, he was trying to figure out why he was having so much trouble with the program. It was a simple algorithm and should have taken him only a couple of hours to write. As he got into the shower and started soaping himself down, it came to him.

His thoughts on the program had been interrupted by his brain and feelings having a little battle. It was about Jiya and their relationship.

He loved her; there was no question about that. But he was trying not to get too close too soon. They had been through a lot in the last two years. He wanted some time to process it all, make sure it was all behind them, and see whether Jiya really did feel for him as she claimed, or if it was a closeness born from their shared experiences and dangers.

As he dried himself off, he convinced himself that his feelings for her were the real thing. Now he needed to determine exactly where she was coming from. And he wanted that to happen soon.

They had been talking about starting a business together. Rufus knew full well that to be partners in a business was a very large commitment. He also knew that couples working together was tricky business, and owning a company together would be a further complication.

Rufus Carlin did not like complications. And he had had enough in the last two years to last him a lifetime. Complications in a romantic relationship that was also a business partnership could be explosive. He'd seen enough of that in the last two years as well.

As he walked into the living/kitchen area of the apartment, he saw on the nightstand that his phone was blinking. He picked it up and saw there was a voice message from Agent Christopher.

Chapter 2

Working their way down the ladder, Lucy first followed by Wyatt both felt the memories flooding back. But they each took them in differently.

Lucy replayed the missions with each step since opening the bunker hatch with an emotional bias. For her, each mission -- from the Hindenburg crash to the Alamo, from Charles Lindbergh to learning she was connected to Rittenhouse, from the Salem witch hunts to Rufus' death and rebirth – was a way to restore Amy to her timeline.

Wyatt's military-trained mind saw them merely as one mission after the other.

When they stepped off the ladder and began walking, hand in hand, toward the far end of the long bunker, they passed the living spaces they had made their temporary homes for a year.

Lucy's and Wyatt's thoughts during this walk turned to their feelings for each other, how they had grown over that year, and the obstacles they had to overcome to finally admit their feelings to each other. Wyatt briefly thought of Jessica and their short-lived reunion. As it turned out, Jessica was also a Rittenhouse agent. During the mission to bring back Rufus, Flynn killed her.

But those thoughts were pushed aside. He preferred the thoughts that centered around Lucy.

They glanced at each other and smiled, with the knowledge that all those madly in love have, that they are aware of what the other is thinking.

When they looked ahead, they could see the computer terminals used to track the Mother Ship. There were two people seated in front of them, facing the terminals. Surely, they had heard the hatch open and close. But they continued to look at the information on the terminals.

Past them, Lucy and Wyatt could see the Advanced Lifeboat.

The round structure with the interlocking rings at 45-degree angles above and below the hatch was parked in an alcove that was cleared of all other equipment and furnishings. They both recalled the rattling noise and the shaking inside the Lifeboat when those rings began to rotate, ever faster, as they prepared to make a time jump. Despite the number of trips they had taken, it always unnerved Lucy.

The wear and tear on the machine was clear. The future Wyatt and Lucy had made more than a hundred time jumps in it before going back to help restore Rufus to the timeline. That endeavor called for only a few jumps, but all combined, the scars of travel through time remained on the metal surface of the Advanced Lifeboat.

But somehow, it looked cleaner, sharper than they remembered it.

As Lucy and Wyatt got within a few feet of the bank of terminals and the two occupied chairs there, one chair swiveled around, and there sat Agent Christopher.

"Hello, you two," she said. "It's been a while."

In the first ninety days after the "save Rufus" mission ended, Lucy and Wyatt had visited the bunker a few times to visit Denise, who, with the help of Connor, kept a constant vigil on the time tracking equipment. Even though Rittenhouse had been taken down and the Mother Ship destroyed, Agent Christopher did not want to let her guard down, lest there be other time incursions.

But after those first visits, Lucy and Wyatt began to focus on their own lives and on each other. There was little time for visits.

Denise rose from the chair with the half-check smile that showed itself rarely during the past two years. She went first to Lucy and gave her a hug.

"It's so good to see you," Lucy said into her ear. "Sorry, it has been so long."

Denise broke the embrace and put both hands on her shoulders.

"I miss seeing you, but I understand," she told Lucy, then glanced over at Wyatt. With a cock of her head, she walked over to him and held out her hand.

Wyatt glanced at Lucy with a puzzled, maybe even a hurt, look. He then extended his own hand. Denise took it and pulled him toward her, then wrapped her arms around him.

"After all we've been through, you think a handshake will do?" she asked with a chuckle. When she pulled back, she could see a slight blush on his stubbled face.

"Hello."

Not one to be overly emotional, unless it was about himself or his former company, Connor Mason remained seated at his terminal, never taking his eyes off the monitor.

Lucy and Wyatt looked at each other, again sharing the same thought. They then looked at Denise, who rolled her eyes. Oddly enough, she was thinking the same thing.

"I hate to break up old home week, but we have a serious problem here," Connor said, still staring at the computer monitor.

Denise, Lucy, and Wyatt turned toward Connor and walked up behind his seat.

"He's right," Agent Christopher said. "That's why we called you all here."

"All of us," Lucy asked, with a hint of anticipation.

"Yes," Denise said. "We called in Rufus and Jiya as well. They should be here soon."

After two years of dealing with time jumps and Connor's sophisticated equipment, even though he was more trained for the action part of the work, Wyatt recognized what he was seeing on the monitor.

"Is that what I think it is?" he asked.

"Yes, it is," Connor answered. "And I must say I'm mildly impressed."

Wyatt was a little irritated with the sarcasm in Connor's voice. He knew the company executive — or former executive, he reminded himself with a little satisfaction — had a healthy dislike and distrust of the military. But it stung his ego anyway.

But in contrast, there was a bit of pride that he actually knew what he was seeing.

"These readings are what we saw whenever the Mother Ship was powered up," Connor said.

Wyatt couldn't help thinking the remark was aimed at him because Connor really didn't believe he recognized what he saw on the monitor. But Wyatt pushed his irritation aside.

"How could that be?" Lucy asked. "The Mother Ship was destroyed."

"It was," Denise confirmed. "I oversaw the disassembly myself."

She went on to explain that all the components that contained time travel programming were blown up so they could never be duplicated. The shell of the mother ship was broken up into smaller pieces, and each piece, except one that Rufus had secretly kept, was melted down and sent to a steel processing plant to then be used only in United States warship construction.

The Advanced Lifeboat was, of course, right in front of them. The original Lifeboat, after some quick repairs and refurbishing, was used by the future Lucy and Wyatt to return to their own timeline once Rufus was back in his own.

"And there's no need to worry about anyone who made the improvements to the Advanced Lifeboat," Agent Christopher said. "Everyone, except the future Wyatt and Lucy, who were in on that, is in this bunker…"

They all heard faintly the hatch at the other end of the bunker open then close again.

"…or soon will be."

Now there were three people at the computer terminals. Rufus and Jiya were deep into calculations and comparing readings they were seeing and those recorded of the Mother Ship's activity. They had worked silently, except for short asides to each other and Connor from time to time, for almost an hour.

While they worked, Denise chatted with Lucy and Wyatt, catching up on what had been going on in their lives over the past four months. There was little need for her to play catch-up with Rufus, Jiya, or Connor. They had been at the bunker almost daily, in shifts, to monitor the equipment, and Agent Christopher had plenty of chances to chat about their lives.

Suddenly, there was an animated three-way conversation at the computer terminals. Denise, followed by Lucy and Wyatt, rushed over.

"Look, these readings look almost exactly alike," Rufus was telling Connor. "But notice they are not identical."

He adjusted the monitor to enlarge one section.

"There is the slightest fluctuation right here," Jiya said, pointing her finger at one line of code.

Connor stared at the monitor for a few seconds.

"Yes," he finally said. "It is miniscule, but it is there."

He leaned back in his seat and thought for a few more seconds.

"But it is so slight, it could be an anomaly in the system," he said. "This could be a glitch that we just didn't notice in the Mother Ship code."

Rufus shook his head vigorously. He held out his hand in a "show 'em" gesture to Jiya. She punched a few keys on her keyboard, and a series of lines of code popped onto her monitor. They all looked identical.

"These are all the times we monitored the Mother Ship when it was powered up in the two years it was operating," Jiya explained. "There is not one glitch in any of them."

She punched a few more keys, and one more line of code appeared at the bottom of the series. At first glance, it looked like all the others. But then Jiya put her finger at a certain point on the bottom line. Connor sat forward in this chair and looked closely.

"This is the track you saw just today," Jiya said.

Connor looked at the line for more than a minute. His concentrated look turned slowly to puzzlement, then to irritation as he looked toward Agent Christopher.

"You said every bit of equipment that had programming in the Mother Ship was blown up," Connor said.

"That's right," she answered. "I supervised the disassembly and demolition myself."

"Every...single...piece," she added with emphasis.

"Then this means there is another Mother Ship out there," Wyatt said. He looked at Connor. "You said the Lifeboat – the original one – was the only other prototype."

All could see the irritation tightening Connor Mason's face. He had not always been truthful with the others, including holding important details back. But that was all in the beginning, before Rittenhouse had taken over his company. But since then, he had been totally open and honest with other members of the team.

"The Mother Ship and Lifeboat were the only working models," he said. "There were two mock-ups that had no electronics in them. But those were confiscated and then destroyed."

With an almost pleading look, he turned to Agent Christopher for confirmation. His facial expression took on more of an "I told you so" appearance when she nodded her head.

"Then how do we have a working time machine out there now, apparently getting ready to take a trip in time to do who knows what?" Lucy asked.

Connor heaved a heavy sigh, looking at the others as if they were missing the obvious.

"Things like this don't happen in a vacuum," he said, motioning to the Lifeboat and the equipment around them. "The Germans and the Japanese were working on atomic bomb projects as were the Americans during World War II, all obviously independent of each other."

He could see the looks of acceptance on the faces of the others. But he just had to drive it home a little more.

"There are plenty of things that put these ideas in people's heads," he said while doing an Internet search. A lengthy list of movies, books, and television shows about time travel popped onto the screen. "This idea didn't just pop into my head out of the blue. Jules Verne was my earliest inspiration."

Agent Christopher was quick to step in. She needed to keep the team's focus where it belonged, not on a tit-for-tat argument about who was to blame.

"That is understood," she said. "But what we have to do now is figure out whether we're talking about a new time machine, who has it, and what they plan to do with it."

CHAPTER 3

Paulina Howser was born into a lower-middle-class family in Casper, Wyoming. Her father was a science professor at Casper College, and her mother was an elementary school teacher.

The parents had moved to Wyoming two years before her birth, as they were not finding quality employment in their respective professions in the southern United States. While the civil rights movement in the country was more than 20 years behind them and the Civil Rights Act outlawing employment discrimination based on race, color, religion, sex or national origin was passed in 1964, some parts of the country were slow to grasp the concept, particularly the former Confederate States of America from the country's Civil War in 1861-64.

Wyoming is known as the Equality State, but it was still mostly, aside from the various Indian reservations, a "white" state in the 1960s and 1970s. The state began to see more people of color come in during the 1960s, but mostly as athletes for the University of Wyoming, particularly its football team.

The Cowboys were starting to build a winning program under head coach Lloyd Eaton. He began to recruit black players for their speed, and it paid off. Wyoming became a powerhouse until the Black 14 incident, when some black Cowboy players wanted to wear black armbands during a game against Brigham Young University to protest the Mormon Church that prohibited blacks from entering the priesthood.

Eaton suspended the players, and the Wyoming football program plunged into obscurity.

But the state's community colleges picked up the mantle and recruited black players for their basketball teams.

When Paulina's father, George, considered a job at Casper College, he researched the state's educational system and found the story about the Black 14. He nearly withdrew his application, but decided to press on when his research showed an increasing number of black residents in the years since the 1969 University of Wyoming Black 14 incident. He decided the state was living up to its name.

He eventually got the job and, when he and his wife, Carol, settled in Casper, she was able to get her first teaching job.

Paulina was followed by two other siblings, and the family flourished. Education salaries in Wyoming's largest city were not on par with some other states, but they were enough to give the Howsers a good life.

Paulina did well in elementary school, as did her siblings. But once she got into Natrona County High School, she began to outpace her classmates. By her senior year, she was in the top three in her class. While her grades were top-notch in all courses, she excelled in the sciences. Not surprising, considering her father's influence.

Paulina received a number of college scholarship offers. She chose the one from the California Institute of Technology in Pasadena. Again, she thrived and received her degree in mechanical engineering.

It was during her time at CIT that she refined a project she first envisioned during high school in the squat shadow of Casper Mountain.

Not only did Paulina Howser thrive in the sciences, but she also had an affinity for history. That interest spanned all the disciplines of history – world, national, regional, and all others, including family history.

The interest in family history started when she was in fourth grade, when her class was given an assignment to construct a family tree. As was her practice, a trait she took into adulthood, she put everything she had into it, including reaching out to far-flung family and even the Mormon Church, reputed to have the most complete genealogy records in the country.

The result was a 30-page report complete with charts and maps that blew her classmates' projects right out of the water.

It was that report that gained her tremendous respect from her teachers and school administrators, and resentment from most of her classmates. It was also that respect, as well as the resentment, that pushed her to perform even better in the years to follow.

Paulina was one of the few blacks in America who could trace their ancestors back to 1619, when the Dutch brought the first slaves from Africa, landing them in Jamestown, Virginia. Details were sketchy, but Paulina learned that her first ancestors in America worked as indentured servants who, after several years of work for their master, earned their freedom.

It was shortly after that that the trail went cold for a while.

It popped up again briefly in 1698, showing that the original families that would eventually produce her parents had moved to the Pennsylvania colony. The next record she found was in 1723 for both family branches, still in Pennsylvania but in towns on the colony's western edge. Several more records were found in 1744 and 1775, both in the same location as before.

Their next move was to what would become, in 1792, Kentucky. But before it did gain statehood, the maternal branch of the family moved to the area that would, in 1803, become Ohio. Traces of the two family branches were lost again until 1858, when the maternal family branch appeared in the Oregon Territory. The paternal branch popped up again in 1860 in Kansas.

While the maternal side had a head start, it appeared both family branches were headed west, just ahead of the country's expansion in that direction.

From the hit-and-miss records she was able to discover, the men on both sides of the family tree were, without exception, manual laborers, and the women tended the homes. Not surprising for those times, husbands and wives tended to stay together throughout their lives. And they continued to stretch the family line, with each marital union producing at least three children, sometimes many more.

Eventually, the two family lines that led directly to Paulina's parents settled in Southern California. It was there that her two sets of great-grandparents, and later her two sets of grandparents, were born.

Her paternal great-grandfather, Lucious Howser, was the first in the family line to serve the United States in the military. With a wife and young son, Floyd, at home, he enlisted in the Army shortly after the Japanese attack on Pearl Harbor on Dec. 7, 1941. A year later, a great-uncle, Joseph Blanchert, joined the Navy.

Lucious later went to flight school and was eventually assigned to the Tuskegee-trained 99th Pursuit squadron and served in North Africa before being transferred to Italy. It was there in 1943 that Lucious was shot down and did not survive the crash.

Joseph, following his initial training, served as a cook on several vessels in the South Pacific before being transferred to the battleship *USS Colorado*. In November 1944, the ship participated in the Battle of Leyte in The Philippines and was struck by two Japanese Kamikaze aircraft. Joseph was among 19 killed in the attacks.

Paulina's family lines were touched three more times by war – in Korea, Vietnam, and Iraq. In each case, the family members survived but had horrific injuries.

It was this part of her family history, combined with her reading of books like "The Time Machine," A Connecticut Yankee in King Arthur's Court," "The End of Eternity," and others, that helped spawn an idea that she hoped would spare her family members the death and disabilities they suffered.

Paulina sat at the computer monitor, looking out at the Time Pod, her name for the machine she created in hopes of saving members of her family. Standing on five thick steel legs, one with a ladder welded to it, was a large sphere. A hatch opened outward above the leg with the ladder. The sphere was different shades of gray as it was a patchwork of different steel plates that Paulina and her three assistants were able to find at various scrap yards.

Looking through the open hatch, Paulina saw a different look inside. The bulk of her expenditures were on state-of-the-art electronic and computer equipment. That's why the outside looked like an old car that had been in many accidents and had various sections replaced but not repainted.

Gathered behind her were Bobby Anderson, Glenda Ballinger, and Ivan Radinski, the three people she had brought into the project. She was able to pay them a modest salary each, but they were also in it for the science.

Paulina had done all the design work herself and had the parts and materials purchased over a six-year period after she earned her final degree. It took her about six months to locate the people she needed to help her, and in the past year, they had assembled the Time Pod. They had just finished the power-up test, and all readings looked perfect.

"Now we need to take it for a little test run," Paulina said, continuing to stare at the machine.

"What did you have in mind?" Glenda asked.

Paulina thought about it for a few seconds.

"It would need to be something small, but something that will prove that we were back in time," she explained, still looking ahead.

Ivan moved toward the pod and turned back to face them when he was at the hatch.

"I'll take it back just a few days and do something here in the lab that will show I've been there," he said.

Ivan and Paulina both knew how to pilot the pod. Glenda and Bobby were learning. But in reality, it was all theoretical until they actually made a trip back.

Paulina stood and walked to him. She placed a hand on his arm.

"No," she said. "I'll make this first trip alone. I don't want to risk it not working and lose you."

"Any of you," she added, turning her head to look at the others, then back to Ivan.

"But that's exactly why it can't be you," Ivan said. "If something goes wrong and you don't come back, none of us has your intimate knowledge of the design to build another one."

She started to protest, but he cut her off before she could get a word out.

"Yes, I know the specifications are there in the computers," he said. "But they don't include your instincts, your intuition that came up with the changes we made along the way."

He reached up and took her hand from his arm. He turned and climbed into the pod, closing the hatch behind him without another word. Paulina knew he was right and moved back behind the bank of computers.

The warehouse that was their laboratory began to reverberate with a sound reminiscent of a turbine engine warming up. As the sound reached a peak, there was a boom in the warehouse as if a dozen bass drums were struck at once – and the pod disappeared.

Paulina and her comrades stared in amazement for seconds that stretched into minutes. Less than five minutes later, the boom sounded again, and the pod reappeared. The hatch stayed closed, and they feared the worst. Suddenly, there was a clank and a hiss, and the hatch swung open. Ivan, on his belly, pulled himself out and tumbled down the ladder.

All three of his colleagues ran to him and saw that he was in some pain and could not speak clearly. But they could tell he was coherent because he waved them away and slowly got to his feet. Bracing himself on Bobby's and Glenda's shoulders, he walked to a couch nearby and plopped down. He gestured in a manner that told the others he just needed time to recover and he would be fine.

"I went back only a week," Ivan explained. "I went in at night when I knew no one was here."

Bobby still held the shattered pieces of the coffee mug that Ivan had broken while in the lab on that first test run.

"So we were right about side effects to going back into our own times," Paulina said.

It had taken almost an hour for Ivan to no longer feel the tearing pain he felt in his head and joints. After the pod materialized in the warehouse parking lot a week past, he went into the lab and broke the mug on the concrete floor. On his way back to the pod, he began to feel the pain. It increased as he set the coordinates to return to he present-day lab, and by the time he returned, it was almost unbearable.

"So we'll have to avoid our own timelines," Paulina said. That ruled out going back to help her cousin, who was injured during the war in Iraq.

They made two more test trips, one to 1965 in which Ivan piloted and Bobby rode along in the pod built to carry two people, the other to 1955 with Paulina at the controls and Glenda riding along. On Ivan's trip, they put a white cross at the edge of the lab parking lot, and it was there when they returned to the present.

Paulina's trip entailed a little more. She believed breaking or placing objects in the past was one thing, but altering the future was another altogether.

She traveled back to Glenda's hometown at the time a new high school was opening. The administration decided to select Lions as the school mascot. However, before the decision was announced, Paulina and Glenda conducted a clandestine effort to change the minds of the administrators. When they returned to the present, the school's mascot was the Bears.

Paulina was then ready to make some bigger changes in history. She and Bobby traveled to Italy in 1943, and she tracked down her great-grandfather. On the day of his fatal mission, she told him who she was and that if he flew the mission, he would die.

"You are a fool, girl," he said. "There is no way you be tellin' the truth."

As he started to head out of the tent to go to the flight line, she grabbed his arm. He gently took her hand and pulled it away.

"Besides," he said. "I've been assigned to this mission, and there ain't no way I can go to my CO and tell him I can't fly because my great-granddaughter told me I would die. I'd be locked up in the booby hatch."

Paulina watched in despair as Lucious boarded his plane and prepared for takeoff.

She and Bobby made a second trip; this time, she tried to seduce Lucious to make him miss the mission. But he would have none of it. A third attempt, in which she appealed to his commanding officer, claiming Lucious was the father of her baby, was also unsuccessful.

"Even if that is true, young lady, I cannot just pull him off the mission just for that," he said. "I'd then have most of the squadron parade girls in here claiming they are the fathers of babies."

Disheartened, she spent the next three days in seclusion. With the Time Pod, she thought it would be easy to make the changes in her family's history to save her relatives. The test runs had proven that history could be changed. But it turned out to be harder than she thought.

But on the fourth day, she came into the lab with a new light in her eyes. Her team saw she was reinvigorated.

"I figured out how to help my family," she said with unbounded enthusiasm. "We're going to stop these wars from even happening, starting with World War II."

CHAPTER 4

While Rufus, Jiya, and Connor hunched over their computer monitors and calculators and Denise busied herself with phone calls to her superiors, Wyatt and Lucy decided they needed some alone time.

They walked hand-in-hand away from the equipment area and toward what had been their living quarters in the bunker. They walked in silence until they got to what had been Garcia Flynn's room. Standing at the door looking in, they could see it was much the same as it was when he left it for the last time.

Wyatt could not help but remember when he was certain there was a romance building between Lucy and Flynn. He remembered how angry and, yes, jealous he was. He also remembered how close he had come to losing her.

He also recalled how badly he felt seeing the photo of Flynn's body after it was discovered dead in the past, shortly after he killed Jessica on her original death date, then spent so much time watching himself with his family. He had sent the Advanced Lifeboat, which included an autopilot installed by the future Wyatt and Lucy, back to the present, knowing it would strand him in his own timeline. While he knew about the side effects, he did not know that being in such close proximity to his past self would accelerate them.

Wyatt looked at Lucy to find she was already looking at him. He knew instinctively she had been thinking the same thing.

They moved down the corridor and entered what had been her room, which was also as she had left it. They sat side by side on the bed.

"Well, before we were so suddenly interrupted this morning, you wanted to talk about our future together," he said after they sat in silence for a few moments.

Lucy blushed and looked down at her hands folded in her lap.

"I did," she said sheepishly. "I know how I feel about you, and I'm pretty sure I know how you feel about me. I just think it's time to talk about where we are going," she added after a few seconds' pause.

Wyatt was silent for nearly a full minute. In that time, Lucy was afraid to look away from her hands. She recalled all too well how much Wyatt had missed Jessica, and how overjoyed he was when it was discovered she had been brought back to life.

But she felt him get up from the bed, and suddenly he was kneeling in front of her. He put his finger under her chin and lifted her face so they were looking eye-to-eye.

"Lucy Preston, will you marry me?"

Lucy felt the air go rushing out of her lungs. She sat there with her mouth open. Suddenly, as she felt light-headed, she realized she had not taken a breath in a while. She gulped in several long breaths to fill her lungs full of air.

"Oh my god," escaped through her lips.

Wyatt's eyes remained in a solid lock with hers.

"This is not the best time or place, and I did leave an important part of this at your house," he said.

The air went out of Lucy's lungs again, and she nearly collapsed into his chest.

"I'm sorry," he said. "I didn't mean to scare you. Maybe this is too soon."

Lucy vigorously shook her head against his chest, but she was struggling to get any words out. He started to speak again, and she held up her right hand, palm facing him, then held up her index finger.

"Just let me catch my breath," she managed.

She took a few deep breaths until her head cleared. She then raised her head and put her hand on his cheek and rubbed the stubble, savoring the sandpaper-like feel on her delicate skin.

"I didn't want to rush you into anything," she said. "I just wanted to talk. You know, in all these months we have had so much time together, but we really haven't talked about where we are going with this."

Wyatt took her left hand and cupped it in both of his.

"In the last six months, I have thought of nothing else but the day I could be your husband," Wyatt said. "I have been trying to figure out how to bring it up. I was going to bring it up this morning, just when Denise called."

Lucy leaned forward so her forehead touched his.

"All these times when it seems like we're sharing the same thoughts and this is the one thing that doesn't get shared," she thought.

"I know, right?"

Lucy jolted upright, sure she had heard Wyatt's voice in her head. He gave her a puzzled look, then they both broke down and laughed.

It was at that moment that Agent Christopher appeared in the doorway.

"We need you two to come see something," she said in a serious enough tone that it got Wyatt's and Lucy's attention immediately. They got up and headed for the door.

"Did I interrupt anything important?" Denise asked as they went past her and headed for the computer consoles.

"See here, where there's this little blip in the line, and again here," Connor pointed to the graph displayed on the monitor. "That is different than the power up we saw before, and it's a lot like what we saw when we tracked the Mother Ship's movements."

He, along with Rufus and Jiya, turned to the other six eyes staring at the monitors. The scientist and his colleagues could tell by the deer-in-the-headlights look on their faces that it had not been fully understood. Jiya and Rufus gave them sympathetic looks, but Connor's expression was one of frustrated disgust.

"In all this time we've worked on this, they still don't get it," he thought.

Rufus spoke before Connor could even formulate a sarcastic remark.

"What we see here is that this new time ship has made a jump," he said.

"Where did they go, and when?" Agent Christopher asked.

Jiya jumped in to answer.

"That's an odd thing," she said. "They went to exactly the location from where they started. But they only went back a few days."

"And they returned to the present less than five minutes after they arrived in the past," Rufus added.

Lucy, Wyatt, and Denise looked at each other in puzzlement.

"Why on earth would they only go back a few days and come back so quickly?" Denise asked. "It doesn't seem possible they could have achieved much, if anything."

In their two years of time travel adventures, she, Lucy, and Wyatt had always dealt with people who were trying to use the Mother Ship to change history to suit their own desires. Anything before Flynn stole the Mother Ship, they had nothing to do with. In fact, they knew very little about that period; only what little they learned from other members of the team.

"It is clear they are testing the machine," Connor said with the same frustrating disgust he displayed earlier.

He, Jiya, and Rufus took turns telling the others about the extensive testing that had been done with the Lifeboat, as it was the first prototype, and then the Mother Ship. That testing included a number of power-up tests followed by numerous jumps back in time, beginning with short trips that became longer with each one.

Jiya shuddered when she recalled that testing period. She also remembered when she started getting the visions after having to take a trip to the past during the Lifeboat team's attempts to stop Rittenhouse and her visit with former Mother Ship pilot Stanley Fisher in the institution. While she was later able to control her visions, they still bothered her.

In the next two days, the team followed two other time jumps by the mysterious new machine. The first was to 1965 and the second to 1955. While they were also able to track the locations of the jump, they could detect no historical changes.

However, while monitoring the third jump, which was to a small town in Indiana, Lucy was following events of the time and location through records and news reports of the period. She was glancing at a newspaper story about the new local high school and how officials selected Lions as the sports teams' mascot. As she was about to move on to the next item, the word Lions faded and in its place came Bears.

A few days later, the team followed three more time jumps, over a three-day period. Each trip was made to the same time and location – a small military airfield in Italy in 1943. Stationed at the airfield were the famed Red Tails of the Tuskegee-trained fighter pilots of the 99th Pursuit Squadron.

Lucy's monitoring of the 1943 news focused on that unit. But she had no clue what she was looking for.

CHAPTER 5

It had been a week since the team watched the last of the three trips to Italy by the mysterious new time travelers.

Agent Christopher arranged with the Army to have Wyatt assigned to her on a more permanent basis, so there was no need for him to go to the base. He moved his belongings into his old room in the bunker and spent his days and some of his nights there. Lucy was also there most days, and when Wyatt wasn't sleeping at the bunker, he was at Lucy's house.

Rufus and Jiya also spent their days at the bunker monitoring the computer readouts. They did spend the night there once, but did not want to make it their home again.

To make sure the equipment was monitored for any other time jumps, Agent Christopher set up a rotating schedule so that at least one person was there during the night. She learned what to watch for so she could be part of that rotation, and no one needed to be there overnight more than twice per week.

During the first time Wyatt and Lucy stayed the night at her house, they had the chance to talk about Wyatt's proposal in the bunker. With all the attention paid to the new time travelers, neither had thought much about the fact that while the proposal was made, there had been no answer. Once things cooled off, that lack of an answer hung in the air like a bad smell.

They sat on the couch in the living room after watching the movie "Jurassic World: Fallen Kingdom," something they had not been able to see when released because they were too busy time traveling. They sat in silence for a few minutes. Wyatt was the first to speak.

"So, we have a little unfinished business," he said.

Lucy was a bit puzzled for a moment, until he stood, took something out of his pocket, and went to one knee in front of her. Once again, the air rushed from her lungs.

"Lucy Preston, will you marry me?" he said, extending his hand, exposing a diamond ring. They both glanced at their cell phones, sitting on end tables on opposite ends of the couch. When they remained silent, they looked back at each other and giggled.

After a moment, Wyatt looked deeply into her eyes, then glanced down at his extended hand and the ring there, then back up at her face. She took a deep breath.

"Oh, Wyatt, nothing would make me happier than to be your wife," she said.

But the lack of the word "yes" in her response gave Wyatt pause. Lucy could see the hesitation, maybe even hurt, in his eyes.

"I really mean that, Wyatt," she said quickly. "And if you had had the chance to ask that day in the kitchen, I would have said yes without hesitation or regret."

She took another deep breath and noticed Wyatt's expression had not changed.

"I would have said yes the other day at the bunker if Denise hadn't come in when she did," Lucy said. "But now after what's been happening the last couple of weeks…."

Wyatt began to retract his outstretched hand. Lucy grabbed his wrist and pulled it back to its previous extension.

"Oh God, Wyatt, don't think this is me saying 'no,'" she said, a tear starting to form in the corner of her left eye. He reached up with his free hand and gently wiped it away, his expression softening a bit.

"What if we end up doing all that time jumping again?" she asked. "Will we have time for us?"

Wyatt knew what she was saying, and he expected it from her. He had thought about it and had some reservations about making this commitment to her with the potential of time travel lurking in the background. But he let her speak.

"What if one, or both of us, gets hurt real bad, or worse?" she said. "What if we end up changing history in a bad way because of the way we feel about each other?"

Wyatt had an answer for the latter.

"That changing history part, we've been there already, and I don't think we've damaged history in a way that hurt us or anyone else, that we know of," he said. "As far as getting hurt, we've faced those risks before, and we came through them."

Lucy, still holding his wrist to keep his arm extended, could feel her resolve crumbling.

"It would be quite a bit different than before," she said. "Then we were hiding our feelings for each other. Look what happened with Jessica."

She regretted saying it as soon as it left her lips, but she still knew that it was a valid argument.

Wyatt's expression this time showed a deep hurt at the mention of Jessica's name. Not so much because of memories of her it brought into his mind, but because of memories of what he had done to the team with his actions. He tried to pull his arm from her grasp, but she held his wrist tighter.

"Wyatt, I'm ready to make this commitment to you," she said as she plucked the ring from his hand and held it up in front of them both. "I want this so much."

His expression brightened a bit.

"Yes, Wyatt, I want to marry you," she said, releasing his arm and putting the ring on the ring finger of her left hand, surprised that it fit exactly.

She could see the tension in his body relax a bit.

"But we have to proceed carefully," he spoke her thoughts.

Lucy began to tear up again, and Wyatt moved to sit next to her on the couch. He wiped the tears away as gentle as a mountain breeze.

"I understand what you are saying," he said softly. "But I am willing to take the risk. You are so worth any risk."

Lucy blushed again, and they embraced.

"I'm not in a rush," Wyatt said when they broke the hug. "We can take this as slow as you want."

"What we need to do is see how things go with this new traveler," Lucy said. "But that doesn't mean we can't do some planning along the way."

Wyatt looked down at the ring on her finger.

"Maybe we shouldn't tell the team just yet," he said. "So maybe you shouldn't wear that for a while."

Lucy pulled her hand to her chest and covered it with her other hand.

"No way, Wyatt Logan," she said forcefully, but playfully at the same time. "I am proud to be your fiancé and I don't care who knows it."

"It might make things awkward," he said.

"So let it be awkward," she answered, and grabbed him in an emotional hug.

The team was in the middle of a brainstorming session, trying to make sense of the new time travel trips they had monitored.

When they first gathered, Jiya nudged Rufus and motioned with her head for him to look at Lucy's left hand. When he saw the ring, he took in the significance immediately. Agent Christopher also noticed the ring, but gave no indication that she had. Connor saw it after all the others, but as his attention was focused on the scientific and nothing else, he dismissed it as not important.

"These first three trips are clearly test runs," Connor said. "They wanted to see if the machine would actually take them back in time."

He pointed to the first of three side-by-side screenshots on the main monitor.

"This one, because it was only a few days back, was probably just to see if it would go back," he explained. "They may have even tried to do something that would show, when they returned to the present, that they had been in the past."

Lucy was busy researching at another computer station, but was taking in every word.

"But I have really studied things for the last few days and haven't found anything in history that was changed, large or small, from that first jump," she said.

"It didn't have to be anything most people would notice," Rufus put in. "It could have been something only they would notice."

Connor nodded.

"The next jump tells me something, but it also comes with questions," Connor said.

He pointed to the second screenshot.

"In this second trip, they go back more than 40 years," he said. "It is possible there is someone in their group making these trips who is in their 40s, but I doubt it." He looked at Jiya, and she knew instantly what he was thinking.

"So you're saying they figured out after only one trip that they couldn't travel within their lifetimes?" she asked.

"That's not possible," Rufus interjected. "It took us numerous test trips before we figured that out after Stanley started feeling the pain and seeing the visions."

He saw Jiya shudder and close her eyes tightly. Rufus reached out and put his hand on hers. He could feel her shake, but it subsided with his touch.

"So I would say that something got out to alert them to be aware of this," Connor said, with an accusatory look at Agent Christopher. She shook her head with a stern look on her face, and he reluctantly accepted that.

"Well, whether it was from the government, Rittenhouse, the institution where Stanley is, or even from my own former company, something got out and they found it," Connor said, emphasizing the word former as if to absolve himself of personal guilt.

"I haven't found anything changed about their second trip, but there was that high school mascot change on the third trip," Lucy said, still staring at the computer monitor.

They all agreed that the first three trips were test runs. But it was the next three trips that were stumping them all. Why would this new time travel team conduct four tests, including the power up, then make three trips to the same time and location within a three-day period? Everyone agreed those last three trips were not tests. But the question was, did the other travelers go back to observe history, or were they attempts to significantly change history?

But what could be accomplished by going to a small airfield in World War II Italy three different times?

"What if they went back the first time to try and change one thing, but it didn't work, so they went back again, and again, when the second time didn't change what they wanted?" Lucy asked, still staring at the computer screen. "If it wasn't to change history, only to observe, why go back to the same place and time? You would think they would go elsewhere."

The rest of the team looked her way, and there was silence for a few seconds. Noticing Lucy slowly turned her head to face them.

"I've been studying this airfield they went to and the military units that were stationed there," Lucy explained.

With modifications Connor, Rufus, and Jiya had made to the equipment in the past six months, the team could, in theory, have access to historical records before and after time jumps. In theory, because there had been no time jumps to test it. Lucy had been using those adjustments and believed she could prove the theory.

She explained how she had studied all aspects of the airfield and the servicemen there. She discovered two significant issues.

First, unit logs and records before the first jump and after each of the three jumps to that area showed some differences in personnel. Just about everyone's lives, except one, had been changed in minor and major ways, ranging from reprimands to injuries to deaths that had not happened in the original timeline.

The only exception was a Red Tails fighter pilot named Lucious Howser. He died after being shot down on a mission in all the versions of history.

"He died on the same day, in the same way, on the same mission, in the same plane," Lucy said. "There were no variations."

"And what's the second thing?" Agent Christopher asked.

"In each history where there was a jump, there were notes in unit logs that a woman who did not belong there was on the base," Lucy said. "There was no such mention in the logs in the history before the jumps."

Wyatt could tell there was something else. "Go on," he said.

"During the third jump, there is a notation in the commanding officer's log that the woman tried to convince him that she was pregnant with Lucious' baby and she wanted him taken off the mission for that day," Lucy said. "But he also noted in his final report after the war that was the one and only time he had ever seen the woman."

"She was trying to keep that pilot from flying on the day history records that he died," Wyatt said. "That means she wants to change that man's history, to keep him from dying."

Everyone in the room recognized the significance of the revelation.

It was Agent Christopher's night to watch the equipment. Lucy was also in the bunker, continuing her study of the significance of the three visits to the airfield in Italy. Wyatt was also in the bunker, but he had retired to his room an hour before, having tired of waiting for Lucy to finish her work.

At one point, Lucy rubbed her eyes and sat back in her chair, looking to take a break from staring at the monitor and the flow of information there.

"So, what's with the bling?" Denise asked, with a knowing tone.

Lucy blushed a little and glanced down at her finger with the engagement ring.

"I think you know," she replied, wondering where Denise was going with the inquiry.

"Well, I believe I do," Denise answered. "But I still want to hear the details."

Lucy explained what had taken place in recent weeks between her and Wyatt in regard to their future together. She was very detailed when explaining the two proposal sessions.

"I can't say it's a big surprise," Denise said after hearing the whole story. "The surprise, really, is what took you guys so long."

Lucy was glad to be doing this one-on-one with Agent Christopher. It made it easier for her to talk about it since she wasn't enthralling the whole group with the tale.

"Everything with the time traveling, then Jessica, then it all coming to an end – or so we thought," Lucy said.

Denise smiled and leaned back in her chair.

"I am excited for you both, of course," she said, which raised the goosebumps on Lucy's arm. "But if we end up back in the time travel thing again, how is that going to affect you two?"

Lucy read into the inquiry just the opposite – how will it affect their performance in the time jumps?

"We have talked about it," Lucy said after a moment's thought. "It is something we are a bit concerned about. But what we've been through already indicates we will handle it just fine."

Lucy's assessment was based on her belief that there were no more Jessica skeletons in Wyatt's closet, and hers were gone with the changes in the timelines they had already made. Her mother's death during the 1800s mission, the fact that she had given up her quest to bring Amy back, and the end of Rittenhouse.

Denise gave a small nod and said nothing more on the subject. She continued to have her concerns, of course, but wasn't ready to make an issue of it unless something came up. After all, there had so far been no time jumps from the new group to pull her team back into the fray.

As that thought passed through her mind, the alarm went off on the computer she had been monitoring. She leaned forward and took in the information. Lucy joined her at that station, looking over her shoulder.

They both saw that the new travelers had made a time jump. The date on the readout was October 5, 1916, and the location was Bapaume, France.

"This is more than just a test jump," Lucy said as she wrote down the information and returned to her computer terminal.

Agent Christopher immediately began sending text messages to the rest of the team, including Wyatt, who was just down the corridor.

CHAPTER 6

During their two years of time jumps, the Lifeboat team used a cache of clothing and equipment from different periods in history. Most of the items were purchased by Connor Mason from various sources, including movie studios and museums. After the first year, when the team moved to the bunker, Agent Christopher salvaged what she could after fire destroyed Mason's facility, and she added to it when she could.

While Wyatt and Rufus were busy finding appropriate clothing, now kept in a large storage area in the bunker, for the jump to 1916, Lucy was searching history for any significant events on October 5, 1916, in or near Bapaume, France. It was toward the end of the four-month action that was the British and French first offensive in the war, commonly referred to as the Battle of the Somme.

The offensive had been a long stalemate of trench warfare in which very little ground was gained and lost by both sides. In fact, the village of Bapaume changed hands three times from the war's first year to its last. In 1916, it was the Germans who had control of the village, but the British and French forces weren't far away.

While there were several skirmishes in the area early in October, the only event of historical significance that turned up in all Lucy's searches was that Adolf Hitler, future dictator of Nazi Germany but then a corporal in the German army, was wounded on October 5, 1916 in the village of Le Barque, just a few miles south of Bapaume.

Lucy was certain this was the reason the travelers had gone to that time and location in history. But the reason was puzzling.

From the most benign, perhaps the travelers were there simply to observe. Maybe they were researchers and wanted to gain more detailed facts about the incident.

But Lucy's experience with Rittenhouse and that organization's efforts to change history to its favor told her there was something else afoot.

But what?

Since Hitler survived this and other wounds during World War I, and numerous assassination attempts in the years thereafter, she was not ready to believe the travelers were there to ensure he stayed among the living. History had already established that.

Her next theory was that they had gone back to try and implant themselves upon him in some way to create a sense of trust they could use in later years.

But to what end? Perhaps to direct him to make alternative decisions in critical times in history. Just where that could lead, she was still trying to puzzle out when Wyatt joined her at the computer consoles.

"What are you thinking?" he asked. She explained her findings and theories so far.

With his military-trained mind and knowledge of military history, Wyatt expanded upon Lucy's historical influence conjecture.

"There are certain decisions Hitler made during World War II that, if made differently, could have changed the course of the war," he said. "They could convince him to delay the invasion of Russia, go ahead with the invasion of Britain, and, with special knowledge, how to succeed with that. Or, they could convince him to start earlier and concentrate on developing the atomic bomb."

"There is another possibility," Connor's voice behind them startled them both. They had been so lost in their own conversation that they didn't notice he had come in and stood behind them in silence almost from the beginning of their discussion.

"What if they went back to kill Hitler, which would then erase World War II from history?" he asked.

Wyatt saw the look of hope on Lucy's face.

"That would eliminate the huge loss of life," she muttered.

Wyatt was not as hopeful.

"I suppose that is a possibility," he said slowly. "But I'm not so sure that would work out that way."

Lucy and Connor both began to object, but he continued.

"The turmoil in Germany after World War I was so great that anyone could have risen to power; it just happened to be Hitler," he said. "While his death in World War I would have been of little significance at the time, with him gone in the aftermath of the war, someone else, just as sinister or worse, could take power and take the world to war anyway."

"Or it could be someone more benevolent," Connor said with conviction.

Wyatt shook his head.

"That is doubtful, considering the feeling in Germany after the war," he said. "Look at what happened with the Weimar Republic." He was getting a little irritated with Connor's apparent lack of historical knowledge. "It wasn't Hitler who started what became the Nazi Party."

Connor gave an annoyed smirk and sat down at one of the computer terminals.

"I know all that," he sniffed. "But if these people are going back to influence Hitler, they would also be prepared to influence others."

This time, it was Jiya, who had heard much of the conversation as she slowly walked from the bunker hatch down the corridor to where they were standing, who put in her two cents.

"And if they can do that, we wouldn't have that terrible war in our history," she said.

Wyatt and Connor began to speak, but Lucy cut them off.

"I think I can tell you first-hand what can happen when history gets changed," she said. "I lost my sister." She glanced at Wyatt. "He got his wife back, then she had to die again to bring Rufus back."

Lucy could see the hurt eating at Wyatt as she spoke, and she could feel it in herself.

"I think we need to treat this like another Rittenhouse attempt to change history for their own ends," she said sternly. "And it's up to us to protect history."

"I agree," Agent Christopher said as she and Rufus joined the group.

They all looked at each other. The looks they exchanged indicated everyone was in agreement, although reluctantly from some. Wyatt, Rufus, and Lucy went to change into their period clothing. When they returned, they climbed the ladder into the Advanced Lifeboat, Lucy trailing the trio. She turned and looked back at her colleagues.

"And so it begins," Denise said, referring to her earlier private conversation with Lucy.

When she sat in her seat and began strapping in, Wyatt looked at her and held out his hands, palms upturned, and his look asked the question, *"What was that about?"*

Lucy gave a slight wave of her hand, and he understood they would talk about it later.

Rufus manipulated the controls, and they felt the usual turbulence of the Advanced Lifeboat in motion through time.

When the Advanced Lifeboat's journey through time began, inside the bunker, Jiya, Connor, and Denise suddenly disappeared, replaced by several men and women dressed in green-gray uniforms. On the left sleeve of each was the German eagle worn by officers during World War II – minus the characteristic swastika.

The Advanced Lifeboat hatch opened, and the occupants found themselves in a large barn. Cows and horses looked out at them in wonderment from their stalls, but luckily, there were no people inside.

Lucy had chosen the barn because of its size, large enough to hide the Advanced Lifeboat, and its proximity, just about a mile from the village of LeBarque. They traveled back to October 4, 1916. Wyatt wanted the extra time to recon the situation and to get there ahead of any possible changes in history. The barn was also in an area that records showed was away from the next day's military action and safe from any shelling for at least a week.

Wyatt, dressed in a German army captain's uniform and carrying a leather case containing maps and forged documents to identify them and explain their presence on the battlefield, exited the Advanced Lifeboat first. Lucy followed, then Rufus, both dressed in civilian clothing.

"I need to secure this barn," Wyatt said. "You two stay here until I come back."

Rufus' confusion and fear were evident.

"What if you don't come back?" he asked.

Wyatt smiled, both in amusement at his friend's consternation and masking his own concern. They had been in dangerous situations before, including combat, most notably at the Alamo, and survived. But Wyatt also knew how unpredictable things are in war.

"I'll be OK," he said, then looking to Lucy. "I will."

She smiled knowingly as Wyatt turned and left the barn.

"He is so aggravatingly calm," Rufus fumed after he was gone. Lucy smiled and put a hand on his shoulder.

"Trust me, under that calm front, he's like a duck on a pond," she said. "On the surface, he seems as cool as a cucumber. Under the water, he's paddling furiously."

Rufus just shook his head as he sat down on a half barrel. *"Why does that not make me feel any better?"* he asked himself.

Within an hour, Lucy and Rufus heard Wyatt's voice barking orders in German, one of five languages he spoke fluently, outside the barn. Then he walked inside, shutting the door behind him.

Lucy ran to him and threw her arms around him. He responded, but broke the embrace when he saw Rufus look away nervously. Lucy glanced around and saw the same thing and blushed a little.

"Sorry, Rufus," she said.

"Oh no, go ahead," with a wave of his hand, then motioning to an empty stall. "But if it goes any further, you need to get a room."

Lucy and Wyatt looked at each other and smiled.

Wyatt then explained that he secured six privates to guard the barn. He convinced their commanding officer that he was charged with testing a new weapon hidden nearby, and he needed the men to guard it. He also told the officer that because the weapon was top secret, under no circumstances were the guards to go inside the barn. The forged documents he brought, though done hurriedly in the bunker, were sufficient for the deception.

He had also asked the officer about Lance Corporal Hitler, who by this time had distinguished himself on the battlefield as a dispatch runner. He told the officer he had heard of the corporal's exploits and wanted to meet him later, and was told where he was stationed.

"So what's the plan?" Rufus asked a little testily. "Do we go tell him we're here to keep him alive so he can become the biggest genocidist in history?"

Wyatt sighed. He understood where Rufus was coming from. He, too, wanted Hitler eliminated. But he also could see the logic in Lucy's argument that he must be kept alive, if killing him was the travelers' aim, to keep history on its current path.

"No," Wyatt said calmly. "What we need to do is surveil him so we can stop anything that is contrary to history as we know it."

"It's what we have to do," Lucy said, trying to be supportive.

Rufus shook his head.

"I know I should understand," he said. "After all, you guys tell me I was killed during one of our trips and you brought me back."

He took a long, deep breath.

"I'll do what you say we have to do," Rufus said. "But I don't have to like it."

Wyatt and Rufus sat in the passenger seats of the Advanced Lifeboat while Lucy slept in a requisitioned bedroll just at the bottom of the hatch. She was sleeping quite soundly despite the occasional pop of a star shell or thud of a mortar. Her almost 24/7 research on the travelers and their prospective time jump had been exhausting.

Wyatt had agreed to stand the night watch after getting several hours' sleep while Rufus and Lucy kept an eye on things. Rufus was supposed to be sleeping while Wyatt was on watch, but sleep was not coming easy to him.

Wyatt sat looking out the hatch, watching Lucy's shallow breathing while she lay motionless, except for a slight twitch at the sounds of the infrequent shells outside. Rufus had kept his focus almost exclusively on Wyatt.

"So, I had to do some recalculations for increased weight on this jump," Rufus finally broke the silence.

Wyatt turned to look at his friend and saw that he was pointing to the ring finger on his left hand. It took Wyatt a few seconds to comprehend the gesture, then he glanced at Lucy and saw her left hand exposed, the engagement ring standing out.

"What's up with that?" Rufus asked.

Wyatt looked back at his fiancée.

"I don't think it's been a secret how I feel about her," Wyatt said. "It was time to make the commitment."

He looked back at Rufus.

"And what about you?" he asked.

Rufus squirmed in his seat a little bit. Sharing personal thoughts, especially of this kind, was not in his nature.

"I'm just not there yet," he answered, hoping that would end the conversation. But he wasn't that lucky.

"Why not," Wyatt asked.

"I'm just not," Rufus said a little testily. But Wyatt wasn't going to let him off the hook.

"Oh, come on, man," he said, leaning forward in his seat. "I've seen how you two look at each other. It's also no secret that there is something there."

Rufus decided to play along, although still guardedly. Maybe he could discover something in the conversation.

"You think you see something from both of us, not just me?" he asked.

Wyatt rolled his eyes.

"It is so obvious, I can't believe you haven't noticed," he said.

"I notice," Rufus answered, a little offended. "I'm not completely stupid about things like that."

"So what's the holdup?" Wyatt asked.

Rufus considered the question for a few moments. He wasn't ready to spill his guts, but he needed to get at least some of it off his chest. At the same time, he figured he might get a few tips if he opened up a little bit.

"Is it just because of what we've gone through?" he asked. "Will it be the same without all this turmoil of time travel?"

He had not intended to reveal quite that much of his doubts, but once he opened his mouth, the words came pouring out.

"You know what I mean about people being in tense situations being drawn to each other," he said, trying to soften his earlier words.

"Yeah, I know the psycho-babble about that," Wyatt said. "But it's mostly bullshit. People feel how they feel. Circumstances have very little to do with it."

While Rufus mulled that over in his mind, Wyatt had another thought. Because of his own experience, he didn't think it could be true, but then again, anything was possible.

"Have you ever had a relationship with anyone before?" he asked.

Rufus was taken by surprise by the question. Wyatt could see the reluctance to talk about it on his face, but he gave him time to think about it.

Rufus fought hard not to fire back a quick answer that would make him look stupid, like less of a man, or give Wyatt the wrong idea about his sexuality. While he had no problem with people of the same gender being in love, and even having sex, he did not see it as his life view. And like most people who feel that way, his first reaction was to make sure he was not labeled as gay.

But the fact was that Rufus had been, from an early age, focused on science; he was a geek through and through. Personal relationships had not been a major part of his thinking growing up and in early adulthood.

Like most virile men, he certainly noticed attractive women. But like most geeks, he was awkward in social situations and a bit clumsy in his approach. For that reason, he did not approach women to whom he had an emotional, or even physical, attraction.

Sure, there had been infatuations, and a couple of women had approached him. But they amounted to nothing. But those details were not something he wanted to share with Wyatt – or anyone, really.

"Nothing serious," he finally answered.

"Are your feelings about Jiya serious?" Wyatt asked. Rufus nodded without hesitation. "How do you know?" Wyatt continued his questioning.

"When I am around her, she is pretty much all I think about," Rufus said. "It hasn't been that way with anyone else."

Before Wyatt could fire his next question, Rufus went on.

"That leads to distraction," he said. "That has happened over the last two years."

"What do you mean?" Wyatt asked.

"There have been times I put her welfare above the missions we have been on," Rufus explained. "That is dangerous, not just for her and me, but for all of us."

Rufus again stopped Wyatt before he could speak again.

"If I make a mistake and someone gets hurt, I couldn't live with that," he said.

Wyatt chuckled a little, but not because he found what Rufus said humorous. He could tell, though, that was how Rufus took it.

"I know exactly how you feel," Wyatt quickly said. "Do you know how bad I felt after you were killed in San Francisco? It was all because of my fixation on Jessica."

Rufus' expression changed from annoyance to understanding, then empathy. Wyatt went on.

"Don't think Lucy and I have not had those same doubts," he said. "Once the prospect of more time jumps came up, we talked about this very thing. How would we react? Would our feelings for each other put missions – or history – in jeopardy?"

He looked back out the hatch at Lucy's still slumbering form.

"But what we have for each other, and the future we can build together, is worth the risk, we believe," he continued. "It's something we have to keep a handle on, be very careful about if this time traveling thing continues beyond this."

He could tell Rufus was deep in thought.

"That may not be the case with you and Jiya," Wyatt said, but quickly added, "And it may very well be. That is something the two of you have to decide."

He reached over and patted Rufus' leg.

"Now, get a few hours of sleep so I can do the same before we have to go out there," Wyatt said, motioning his thumb toward the barn door.

"You want me to get sleep after loading that on me?" Rufus thought.

But within a second, he found sleep. It wasn't the most restful, but sleep it was.

CHAPTER 7

The Lifeboat trio stood close together in a trench just outside LeBarque the next morning. The stench of mud, sweat, blood, and gunpowder assaulted their senses. They were in a position about fifty yards from the bunker entrance, where Lucy's research indicated Hitler was wounded.

Wyatt wanted to be able to observe the future dictator before and after the wounding, but wanted to do so from a distance. It was more of a defense against him taking action to kill Hitler himself. As much as he wanted to, he trusted Lucy's urgings that they preserve history as it had already happened.

There was another reason for the distance from the subject. According to historical records, Hitler was wounded by a shell splinter as he stood in the bunker entrance. Wyatt wanted to keep himself and the others far enough away to avoid any of them getting hit by splinters. Of course, there was no guarantee that there would be no other projectiles in the area where they stood.

When they first arrived about an hour earlier, Wyatt continued with the cover story he had devised and shared with the others. He told commanders in the trench he wanted to observe Hitler as he was being considered to be part of the tests of the new weapon they were supposedly responsible for.

While the presence of a black man and a woman on the battlefield raised some eyebrows, Wyatt explained that Rufus was his personal footman and Lucy was part of the team that developed the weapon, his only explanation of which was that it could give the Germans an advantage of huge proportions on the battlefield.

The forged papers he carried in his leather field pouch were a great help in convincing those who questioned them. His identity papers identified him as Captain Wolfgang Hochstetter, Lucy's alias was Sigrid Valdis, and Rufus went by the name James Kinchloe. The names were Rufus' idea, taken from the old television series "Hogan's Heroes."

The trio had seen Hitler come out of the bunker several times since their arrival, which coincided with the start of a charge toward the British and French lines. As a dispatch runner, Hitler was in the trench ready to take any messages to the command center behind the lines and then to bring messages forward.

At the first sighting, Rufus and Lucy did not recognize him. They were looking for the familiar face dominated by the square, Charlie Chaplin-style mustache. But the man they saw had a fuller growth on his upper lip, even coming to a bit of a point on each end. It was rumored that he favored the mustache look because it was a similar style to that worn by Fredrich Wilhelm Viktor Albert, better known as Kaiser Wilhelm, the German emperor and king of Prussia until his abdication in 1918. The rumor went on to say that after the Kaiser abdicated, Hitler was so disappointed and disgusted with the man that he clipped off the ends of his flourishing mustache and adopted the Chaplin style for the rest of his life.

But Wyatt recognized him immediately and whispered, "That's him." Since then, they had been on the alert.

Suddenly, a shell burst on the ground just across the trench from where Hitler stood. The Lifeboat trio ducked down at the sound of the blast, and when they looked up again, they saw Hitler sitting down on the plank flooring of the trench, writhing in pain. Wyatt saw blood on his trousers near his groin.

Wyatt slowly moved forward, motioning for the others to follow. Two soldiers tried to stop them, but Wyatt sternly ordered them to allow them to pass. By the time they got near him, two soldiers had Hitler upright, and they were carrying him as he put his weight on their shoulders on either side of him down the trench away from the Lifeboat team.

Wyatt quickened his pace to keep up. As they reached a wooden ladder out of the trench, Wyatt rushed ahead and went up, and turned to offer his hand to help.

"We'll take him from here; you return to your duties," he ordered.

Hitler took his hand, still feeling the pain, and Rufus, scrambling up the ladder, followed by Lucy, took his other arm and put it around his shoulder for support. Rufus took some comfort in the fact that Hitler was suffering such pain.

"At least I can see him like this," he thought. *"Not quite enough, though, to make up for what we're going to allow him to do."*

As the men got Hitler to the top of the trench and Lucy followed, they began carrying him away toward the rear area. After about two hundred yards, they saw a truck and took him to it. They hoisted him into the back and got in with him.

"Take us and this man to the nearest aid station," Wyatt ordered the driver, who was sitting behind the wheel.

"But I am waiting for a platoon to take to the front," he responded.

"Take us to the aid station," Wyatt yelled.

The truck immediately began to move forward.

Using portions of Hitler's uniform, Wyatt field dressed his wound. It wasn't critical, but because of the location, it was plenty painful. When he tightened the dressing, Wyatt couldn't resist making it a bit rougher than necessary. He found that the pained look on Hitler's face wasn't meeting the level of satisfaction he had hoped for.

Wyatt's hand moved to the pistol on his hip. But he felt a soft hand touch his, and he pulled it away. He glanced back and saw that pleading look on Lucy's face. He refused to look at Rufus, who he was sure was cheering him on.

But he did get a little more satisfaction watching Hitler react to every bump the truck hit. Vehicles of that era had little or no suspension, so every little indentation or pebble in the road bounced their occupants around roughly.

As the truck pulled up to the aid station and the Lifeboat trio began to help Hitler to his feet, a black woman and a white man appeared at the tailgate and opened it. When Wyatt saw them, alarm bells began to go off.

For starters, Wyatt knew it was unusual enough to have a black person and a woman on a World War I battlefield. While there were black people in Europe, they were a small percentage of the population, and they had not been integrated into the armed forces.

The next alarm was their clothing. What they wore did not match the period in time. It looked more like they came from the 1960s or 1970s.

When she saw the couple, the same alarm bells went off for Lucy. She gave a warning look to Wyatt, and he acknowledged it.

"We can take the corporal from here," the woman said in French as she and the man started to climb into the truck.

"That's OK," Lucy answered in the same language. That was another alarm bell. Why would a French woman be behind the German lines?

But now the woman was right in front of Hitler with what appeared to be a medical bag.

"Just let me give him a shot of morphine, then, to ease the pain," Paulina Howser said as she pulled a syringe from the bag. "Can you expose his wound, please?"

As she reached for the dressing, Lucy saw the syringe in Paulina's hand. It was made of glass and had a plunger. However, syringes in use on World War I battlefields looked more like tubes of super glue with a needle attached.

Lucy swiftly grabbed each of the woman's wrists and gave Wyatt a glance that called for help. He took hold of the woman's right hand that held the syringe while Lucy took it from her. Wyatt then drew his pistol, a period Luger, and pointed it at the man.

"Get out," he said in English.

The man slowly backed out of the truck, and Rufus followed. He gave the man a quick check for weapons and found a Glock handgun in his waistband. He took it and pointed it at the man's chest. Wyatt motioned for Lucy to let the woman go, and he waved his gun, indicating she should get out of the truck as well. Before leaving, Lucy opened Wyatt's field pouch and carefully placed the syringe inside. Everyone but Hitler and the driver was now outside the truck.

"What were you trying to do?" Lucy asked Paulina. She did not answer. They all stood looking at each other for a moment.

"Sie sind nicht Deutsch," Wyatt heard Hitler say calmly, and he turned to face him, rotating the gun to point at him.

"Neither are you, but what difference does it make?" Wyatt hollered into the truck, knowing Hitler was actually an Austrian who petitioned to join German emperor Kaiser Wilhelm's army.

As Wyatt spoke, Rufus turned his head to face Hitler. Bobby Anderson jumped on the opportunity.

He reached out and slapped Rufus' hand that held the Glock. His arm swung toward the truck, and he lost his grip on the weapon. It bounced off the sideboard and clattered to a halt near where Wyatt crouched. He looked around in time to see Bobby grab Paulina's hand and lead her away at a dead run. Rufus and Lucy both began to give chase.

"No," Wyatt yelled. "We can't afford to go after them."

He turned back to Hitler.

"We are not German," he said in German. "My name is Henry."

"What are you doing here?" Hitler asked.

Wyatt glanced around at Lucy, who wore that pleading look again.

"Just be happy that we were," he said, then helped him to his feet.

The three eased him out of the truck just as three orderlies came out of the aid station.

"Take this man, he is wounded," Wyatt ordered in his best German.

As the orderlies took him inside, supporting him on their shoulders as he hopped along on his non-painful leg, Hitler turned his head back at Wyatt.

"Danke schon, Henry," he said.

Wyatt started to raise his hand to wave, then caught himself. He was already starting to feel sick as he realized the opportunity that he had just passed up.

When the Lifeboat powered down and the hatch opened, Rufus rushed out before Wyatt and Lucy could get their safety straps off. They looked at each other. Lucy's look asked the question, *"What was that about?"*

"I'll tell you later," he said as he stood up, grabbed his field pouch, and helped Lucy begin the descent out of the Lifeboat. Once out, she had a spoken question.

"Why did you tell Hitler your name was Henry?"

He was a little surprised. He did not realize anyone had heard that part of the conversation.

"I don't know," he said. "I kind of felt like I had to say something."

"But why make up a name?" she asked.

"I don't know, I just didn't want him to know my real name," he answered.

"Why Henry?"

"It was the first name that popped into my head," Wyatt answered. "It was one of my uncles' name."

They walked over to the computer consoles where Agent Christopher waited for a briefing. While Connor was sitting at one of the terminals, Jiya and Rufus were nowhere to be seen. Before Lucy or Wyatt could say anything, they heard Connor, sitting at one of the terminals, clear his throat.

"I think you might be interested in this," he said. The three of them moved to his station.

"I just came across this when I was looking for any historical changes due to this jump," Connor explained.

Agent Christopher, Wyatt, and Lucy looked at the headline of the Google search on the screen.

"The man who spared Hitler's life in World War I."

Wyatt and Lucy gasped together, sure the tale at the aid station was revealed. Connor clicked on the link, and the story appeared.

It was Hitler's own account of how, after being wounded in the thigh near LeBarque, France, in 1916, he was limping back to his own lines when he walked right into the sight line of a British soldier with his rifle pointed right at him. The Brit noticed Hitler had not raised his own rifle, so he lowered his and waved Hitler on. Hitler waved back and continued on his way.

He was telling the story to British Prime Minister Neville Chamberlain in 1938 when he was in Germany to negotiate what became known as the Munich Agreement. Chamberlain noticed a portrait in Hitler's office of a British soldier in World War I carrying a wounded comrade.

"He was the most decorated soldier for Britain, winning the Victoria Cross, Distinguished Conduct Medal and Military Medal, among others," the article quoted Hitler as telling Chamberlain. "Perhaps when you return, you would be so kind as to give him my regards. His name is Henry, Henry Tandy."

Lucy and Wyatt looked at each other in astonishment.

"This article never came up in searches before the jump," Mason said.

When he left the Lifeboat, Rufus took Jiya by the hand and led her down the corridor to what had been his quarters. When they were inside, he took her other hand in his and faced her. The serious look on his face was also tinged with pain. Jiya braced herself for bad news, but just what it could be, she had no clue.

"Jiya, I love you," Rufus began. "I want to spend my life with you."

Her heart seemed to skip a beat. This was certainly not what she expected, but it was not an unpleasant surprise.

"I love you, too, Rufus, but..." He cut her off by giving her hands a gentle squeeze.

"I know that, but I've got to wonder why," he said, and gave her hands another squeeze as she started to respond. "I'm not much of a romantic, and I'm not in a position to be able to support you in the way you deserve."

"Support me?" Jiya asked as she disengaged her hands from his. "Like having me barefoot and pregnant, a housewife, while you're out bringing home the bacon?'

She turned her back on him for a moment, then whirled to face him again.

"I don't need your financial support, I can take care of myself," she said a little angrily. "The support I need from you is that you are there for me, stand beside me in all things."

She paused a moment. The pained look on Rufus' face made her soften her irritation a little.

"Clearly, I'm not doing a very good job of that," Rufus said. "And I don't have a ring to put on your finger."

Jiya almost laughed out loud, but choked it back for fear of hurting him further.

"Do you really think that's what this is all about, a ring?" she asked.

"Well, you did make a point of getting my attention on Lucy's," he answered, now confused. "Seemed like a hint to me."

This time, Jiya couldn't control herself and giggled.

"No, it wasn't a hint. I just wanted you to see it," she said, moving toward him until they were almost nose-to-nose.

"Well, if you don't want to get married, what do you want?" Rufus asked.

"You," Jiya said, throwing her arms around him. "The rest we'll figure out as we go."

"Nothing has changed," Glenda said as Bobby and Paulina climbed down the ladder from the Time Pod. "Everything is just like it actually happened."

"I know," Paulina said angrily. "There were people there that stopped us."

"Germans?" Glenda asked. Paulina did not answer, just walked past her to the office in the warehouse.

"No," Bobby said. "We were behind German lines, but these people spoke English."

Ivan moved away from his computer terminal and rolled his chair closer to the trio now gathered near the pod.

"Are you saying there were British people behind German lines?" He asked. "And they just randomly happened to be in a position to stop you from getting to Hitler?"

Bobby shook his head.

"They were in the truck that brought him to the aid station," he explained. "When Paulina tried to inject him, they somehow figured it out, and a woman grabbed her arm and took the syringe."

"A woman?" Glenda asked.

"Yes, and there was a black man with them," Bobby answered.

"There was someone else?" Ivan asked.

"A man dressed as a German captain," he answered. "He and the black man spoke English, and the captain spoke to Hitler in German."

The three of them stood in silence for a few moments. Glenda broke the silence.

"So, does that mean we've failed?"

"This time," Bobby said.

The others looked at him with questioning expressions.

"No, we're not done with this," he said. "Paulina says we'll try again. But we have to be better prepared."

He told his colleagues they needed to do more research into the periods into which they were going. For one thing, the clothing they had purchased from the thrift store before the jump had clearly not matched what Rufus and Lucy had worn. It made them stick out like sore thumbs. For another, they had to have more details about the specific times they would visit.

"And we believe those other people being there was no accident," he said. "We think someone else is traveling in time."

CHAPTER 8

When Lucy, Wyatt, and Rufus were debriefed by Agent Christopher, she took extensive notes. When she learned of the syringe the mystery woman tried to use on Hitler, she had it sent to the FBI crime labs in Quantico, Virginia, for analysis.

She also took specific note of who the other time travelers could be. Lucy reported that as Bobby grabbed Paulina's hand to lead her away, he said, "Paulina, we've got to get out of here." She protested only briefly by trying to pull her hand away from his, but his grip was stronger.

Agent Christopher found it significant that they had at least a first name to work with.

She also provided Lucy, Rufus, and Wyatt with a bit of information from her perspective on the time jump.

"Just as the lifeboat left, I felt this kind of chill," she explained. "Or maybe it was a feeling that something was somehow different."

She further explained that the sensation seemed to last a few moments and then disappeared. When she regained her senses, she looked at Jiya and Connor, expecting them to say they felt something similar.

"They didn't say anything, but the way they looked at me and each other, I got the distinct impression they felt something too, but didn't want to say anything because they didn't quite know how to explain it. That's exactly how I felt."

This was the first time she had discussed it openly. Lucy and Wyatt had nothing to offer.

"Maybe it was just adjusting to starting this all again," Wyatt said, trying to dismiss it.

The debriefing gave her the double task of testing the material in the syringe and having it fingerprinted, along with having Homeland Security personnel do a search of all black women with the first name of Paulina.

In doing so, she was careful to give a cover story for the research she was asking government agencies to perform. It was easy enough, as Homeland Security was focused on terrorist activity, so any terrorist-related investigation would go largely unquestioned.

Agent Christopher did not want the government to be fully involved. The lessons from the Rittenhouse experience were that just about anyone was corruptible where time travel was concerned. Only a small handful of people outside the bunker knew of the Advanced Lifeboat's existence.

In the past year of their previous time travels, the Lifeboat team was confined to the bunker, with any forays outside strictly controlled. The exception was Wyatt's clandestine expedition after receiving a message from the wife he thought at the time was dead. That proved to be a disaster.

But now Agent Christopher was confident the bunker team was trustworthy. That is why all were allowed to come and go as they pleased with no restrictions.

However, she was careful about what was shared with Connor Mason.

While he did consult with Agent Christopher and helped her monitor the timeline after they had brought Rufus back, his time spent on that was very part-time. He spent much of his other free time trying to restart his company. It wasn't easy, but he was determined to do so.

But now that the team had a new threat to time to deal with, less of his time was spent on his company and more on the Lifeboat team's efforts. In the past weeks, the time spent on his company swiftly shrank to nearly nothing. He was beginning to resent that.

Agent Christopher could see that in his increasingly surly attitude. Recalling his cooperation with Rittenhouse, though it was a bit reluctant, she worried that in his frustration and bitterness about being taken away from his efforts to rebuild his company, he might share something about the project – something she wanted to avoid at all costs.

But he was still vital to the project, so she had to find a way to appease him but keep him out of the critical information loop as much as possible. For that reason, when she debriefed the team about the trip to 1916, Connor was the only member of the team not included in the meeting. She also decided that any time Connor was in the bunker, she would make sure she was there as well.

Several days after the debriefing, during one of Connor's night shifts monitoring the timeline, Agent Christopher was working on some unrelated Homeland Security research. Not a word between them had been spoken in hours, and she wanted to break the monotony.

"How are things going with your company?"

Agent Christopher's intent was just to have a conversation. But as soon as the question was out of her mouth, she knew it was the wrong thing to ask. She immediately saw it confirmed by the angry look on his face.

"I really wouldn't know, since I'm here most of the time." His sarcasm was cutting, and though she expected it as soon as she realized the inappropriateness of her question, Agent Christopher was stung by his response.

But she did her best to conduct damage control.

"I'm sorry, Connor," she said. "I know we're taking a lot of your time. But this is important to so many people, we are trying to use all the resources we can."

"And my company is important to me," he shot back.

Now her awkwardness was replaced with anger. The possibility that history could be changed and people wiped out of existence was, in her mind, a bit more important than anyone's selfish desires.

"Connor, when I compare that people could be just done away with in the blink of an eye to your precious company, my choice is crystal clear," She said.

Connor's look softened a bit, but only a bit.

"I understand the significance of what this team is doing," he said, looking back at the computer terminal. "Who do you think started all this?"

He let the implications of his words sink in to Agent Christopher's mind. He knew that by creating the time travel machines, he had gotten the ball rolling toward his company's demise. He was also aware that some of his questionable decisions along the way sealed its fate.

But the pain was just as real as if it had come at someone else's hands.

"Agent Christopher, you have a family, do you not?" Connor asked after a brief pause.

She nodded her affirmation to something he knew very well.

"Well, I do not," he began. "I put my life into my work; I left no time for marriage or children."

He looked around at the equipment and the Advanced Lifeboat in the bunker.

"My business was my family, my children," he said. "And I've seen my family injured, taken apart, little by little. This is all I have left."

Denise began to understand the depth of Connor's loss. She stood up from the computer and walked toward him.

"Rebuilding my company is a way of getting my family back," he said.

"But it wouldn't be the same," she said as she stood at his left shoulder. He nodded slowly.

"If I lost my family, I don't know if I would want to try and rebuild it," Denise went on. "I don't know if I could stand to have a family that was not what I had worked so hard to build."

Connor looked up at her. His expression was no longer one of anger, but now his face exuded understanding. But there was a hint of hope there.

"But starting over gives one a chance to re-examine their past mistakes, a chance to get it right the next time," he said.

Denise put a hand on his shoulder.

"Perhaps you don't have to rebuild to have that second chance," she said. "You have an opportunity at a new 'family' right here."

The resentment in Connor that had been receding as they talked began to bubble again.

"How can I be part of this family when I am not even trusted?" he asked. Agent Christopher could see where this was going.

"Even before Rittenhouse fell and in the past six months, I've been left out of certain things," Connor said. "Just look at this last trip. You all discuss it behind closed doors, and here I was alone with the machinery."

Denise considered his words in silence for a few moments. He was correct; she had been deliberately leaving him out of the operational details. But she had also believed his interest was more in the technological and less in the missions. She focused more on his mistakes and the alcoholic binge he went on after Rittenhouse bombed his company headquarters, but pushed out of her mind how he was revitalized after helping save musician Robert Johnson from Rittenhouse in 1936.

"Point taken," she said. "You can't be a part of the 'family' if you are treated like just a gadget in the toolbox."

She pulled out a chair from a nearby terminal, sat down facing him, and began to brief him on the team's 1916 trip to save Adolf Hitler.

Two days later, the entire Lifeboat team, including Connor Mason, was gathered around the dining table in the lounge area of the bunker, brainstorming.

"What was in the syringe you brought back was a massive dose of the Marburg virus," Agent Christopher said as she laid a document on the table. "This leads to bleeding throughout the body and later to organ failure and death."

She let that sink in.

"Normally, this would take some time, but the virus wasn't identified until 1967, so doctors in 1916 would have no idea how to treat it," she explained.

"She wanted us to remove his field dressing, so I think she was going to inject it directly into the wound," said Wyatt, who had seen his share of battlefield wounds during his military career. "He would have already started to have an infection with the unsanitary conditions, so this probably would have worked much faster."

"So she wants him dead," Rufus said. "And that's a problem because…?"

Lucy pulled up some information on a laptop in front of her and turned it to Rufus for him to read. It gave the results of the changes in history made when Hitler died in 1916 as a result of Paulina's injection before the team put history back on course.

Even with Hitler eliminated, a group of Germans formed a political party that eventually seized political power through much the same means as the Nazis, but this time in 1930. They followed much the same path as the original history, except that they did not enter into a European war until 1942, at a time when the German military was stronger and more focused on goals. The war ended in 1950 with Germany controlling all of Europe, including Great Britain, North Africa, and half of the Soviet Union.

By 1960, the Germans and Japanese had squeezed the United States nearly dry with blockades on both coasts and economic sanctions, blocking those countries free of German control from supplying America with the goods it needed. The Germans and Japanese jointly occupied the country.

Rufus slowly turned the laptop back toward Lucy with a resigned look on his face.

"Because we changed history back, no one here realized it, but the Germans even used this bunker as a scientific research center," Lucy said.

"So no matter what, he has to stay alive until history has him dead in his own bunker in April 1945," Agent Christopher said.

"How do we know these people won't try to change history in another way?" Wyatt asked. "There are so many ways it can be done if the aim is to eliminate the Germans from the world domination equation."

"We don't really know for sure," Agent Christopher said. "But it seems clear with their three attempts at the Red Tails base that they focus on single events."

"They are not experienced in time travel," Connor said. "They are making some of the same mistakes we did in the beginning." He looked at Jiya.

"Their pattern follows ours almost perfectly, except what they are doing is accelerated," she explained. "It's like they are in a hurry."

"And when you are in a hurry, you take shortcuts," Agent Christopher said, using her criminal investigative experience. "That leads to mistakes."

She reached into her briefcase and pulled out some more documents and laid them on the table. "Like this," she said.

One was several pages of names, all with the first name Paulina. The second was an FBI fingerprint search.

"There were fingerprints on that syringe," Agent Christopher said. "They matched one of the names on that long list in a background check for a job application to a technology firm."

Connor's ears perked up at that. But Agent Christopher shook her head, "*Not yours*," she mouthed. She could see the relief on his face. At least he couldn't be connected to this.

Lucy grabbed the FBI fingerprint search and read the name Paulina Howser and learned she was a black woman who earned a master's degree in mechanical engineering from the California Institute of Technology. She had also earned a second master's in quantum theory. There was also a photo attached to the report.

Lucy showed the photo to Rufus, then Wyatt. They each nodded in turn.

"That is the woman we saw try to inject Hitler in 1916," she announced.

Agent Christopher sighed.

"So now we know the what and the who," she said. "What we now need to figure out is the how."

"To do that, it sure would be helpful to know the why," Jiya said.

Connor gave an exasperated grunt.

"It seems obvious she wants to eliminate World War II from history," he said.

"But why just that?" Lucy asked. "If I were in her shoes, I would want to eliminate war altogether. Why not go back to the beginning of time and find a way to eliminate all wars?"

She looked around the table, but saw only unknowing stares.

"Because she can't," Lucy continued. "It is far too complicated. You might be able to eliminate one, but unless you follow up with every single armed conflict, you're not going to stop them all."

She paused for a moment.

"And not all these conflicts are interconnected," Wyatt said. "If one major war is eliminated, how do we know one of the smaller ones might end up taking its place as a major one?"

"We also know from our own experience that history is harder to beat than we think," Rufus said, with a nod to Wyatt, acknowledging his experience with Jessica.

"No," Agent Christopher said. "This is something more personal."

At that remark, Lucy shuffled through her notes and found what she was looking for.

"The three trips she made to 1943 were about that Red Tail pilot," she said. "His name was Lucious Howser. I think he is a relative who died, and she is trying to bring him back."

"And her direct attempts did not work," Wyatt said. "So she's trying to eliminate the entire war, hoping that will do it."

They all seemed pleased with themselves that they had solved the puzzle. All but Agent Christopher, that is.

"But we've still got some work to do," she said. "The best thing we can do is try to be prepared for her next jump, so we've got a bit of a head start. So we need to figure out when that would be."

All heads turned to Lucy. She looked at each one in turn as she gathered her thoughts.

"Well, this is just a guess, since we don't yet have a pattern to follow, but I'd say she is going back to times when there was some threat to Hitler's life, probably to make it easier to kill him," she said.

She pounded away at the laptop keyboard to do some searches. When she found something, she put her index finger in the air.

"He was wounded again in October 1918 in a gas attack," she said, looking up at the others gathered all around the table.

"Great, let's do what we can to prepare for that," Agent Christopher said. "But if she doesn't jump there, let's extend that theory out and build a timeline of where else she might go."

Chapter 9

Building a timeline for prospective time jumps was no easy task. There were so many possibilities when Hitler's entire life was considered. There were a number of ways he was in harm's way throughout the years until his actual death at his own hands on April 30, 1945.

Lucy focused on incidents in his life where his life was directly in danger, starting with the 1918 gas attack and through five recorded assassination attempts.

She included other incidents where he might have been a potential assassination target or in a line of fire, like the 1923 Beer Hall Putsch and the 1934 Roehm Purge. There were also assassination plans and attempts made both in Allied countries and Germany itself. These, like a poisoned bouquet of flowers thrown into his car during a parade and a small dog deliberately infected with rabies, either failed or were abandoned as unworkable.

The list of possible jumps was a long one with so many variables. But she was trying to be thorough.

Fortunately, she had plenty of time to research. It had been weeks since they returned from 1916 France, and the other time travelers had not made a jump. Everyone wondered what was keeping them from going back for another attempt to kill Hitler.

"Maybe they gave up once they saw there were other people following them back and stopping them," Jiya said, not really believing it herself.

"No, if they've invested so much in this effort, they aren't going to give up so easily," Agent Christopher said. "They'll eventually be back at it."

With that, the team ended the discussion and everyone scattered back to their lives, with the exception of Agent Christopher, who remained in the bunker to monitor the equipment. She even let Connor leave. She felt he deserved it and, while she still had some reservations about his trustworthiness, she was willing to give him a little slack. If for nothing else, to test how trustworthy he really was.

No one got to enjoy their evening off as a call from Agent Christopher came while Wyatt and Lucy were on a rare dinner date. They quickly finished their dessert, paid the check, and rushed to the bunker.

"Are we going back to France?" Lucy asked as soon as they got to the bunker. Rufus, Jiya, and Connor were all there when they arrived.

"Nope, we're going into the heart of the beast," Rufus said.

"Germany," Wyatt said.

"Not just Germany," Agent Christopher said. "But near where the Nazi movement really got started."

Everyone looked her way.

"Munich," she said.

"The beer hall," Lucy said, barely audible.

During an attempt by Hitler and his Nazi followers on Nov. 8, 1923, to overthrow the Bavarian government that failed, the following day, a group of about 3,000 Nazis and supporters marched toward the Marienplatz, the city's center. There was gunfire, and some of his followers were killed and wounded. Hitler was not hit by gunfire. On the first volley from Bavarian police in a narrow alley, Max von Scheubner-Richter, a Nazi district leader marching to Hitler's left, was struck in the head and fell to the street. Hitler stumbled over his body and wrenched his shoulder in the process.

As the march broke up following a second police volley and short reply from the Nazi marchers, a small car rushed up and Hitler was ushered inside. Because there was a warrant out for his arrest, even prior to what became known as the Beer Hall Putsch, he was taken to a hiding place.

In her preparations for different possibilities, Lucy discussed each with Wyatt for his military perspective. This particular incident was a most dangerous one to be involved in, he advised her.

"We would have to be right in the middle of all that," he said. "They are in a closed-in place, and the odds of one or the other of us getting hit are way too high. Even if these other travelers aren't military trained, common sense would tell them the same thing with even the most casual study of the incident."

However, they devised a plan that put only Wyatt in the middle of the Nazi column. He also planned to wear a Kevlar vest to protect himself from stray bullets.

"Wearing a helmet would be out of the question, so I'll have to take my chances with a head shot," he told Lucy. She was not happy about the prospect.

But all that went out the window with Agent Christopher's next pronouncement.

"We pinpointed the location where they took their time ship," she said. "They are near a small village called Uffing, about 44 miles south-southwest of Munich."

The name of the village was familiar to Lucy, but she wanted to make sure. Sitting at one of the computer terminals, she did a few searches and found her answer. She turned to the others.

"After the putsch failed, Hitler was taken to this village," she explained. "He had a German-American friend named Putzi Hanfstaengel who had a cottage just outside Uffing."

She stopped to think, then turned back to the computer. Finding more information, she turned back to the others.

"Two days later, the police came and arrested him," she said.

"My guess is the other travelers went there to kill him," Wyatt said. "I've been in that area. It is fairly developed now. I suppose in 1923 it was way out in the country. They wouldn't be noticed."

He looked at everyone in turn.

"Can we pinpoint this cottage?" Wyatt asked.

Lucy did a little research and, through a genealogy search on the Hanfsaengel family, found the cottage location as it was in 1923. She printed out a map and handed it to Rufus so he could use it to set their coordinates.

"The travelers went there the early afternoon of the putsch," Agent Christopher said. "I assume they went to prepare at the cottage for Hitler's arrival."

"We should get there a few hours ahead of them," Lucy said. "That way, we can be there when they arrive, and that will be the end of that."

Wyatt was not so sure.

"After 1916, I'm sure they will be prepared for us," he said, taking the map from Rufus and studying the terrain. "I have a better plan."

He shared that plan with Lucy and Rufus as they found their attire for the trip.

Peter Wilson was excited by the news of his second child. He was the father of a fine daughter, and now the possibility of a son filled his mind.

As he walked along the sidewalk, he thought of his family in Chicago. How pleased his mother would be to hear the news. She was so delighted when Mary Ann was born that she almost came out to California to live with he and Gwen and their new daughter. Maybe this time, she would come.

Thinking about his new child, though, did not take his mind away from the true purpose of his adventure out of the house. He was headed to his office. A multi-room, single-story collection of offices in the strip mall about a mile from home.

Peter Wilson was a stockbroker. It was a small investment company he started five years ago when the American economy was booming. He started with just himself and a secretary. But in the first three years, business was so good he added two associates and two more secretaries, who now insisted on being called administrative assistants.

In the past two years, business at Wilson Investments began to level out. He maintained his clients, as did his associates, but new clients were few and far between. On this early Saturday morning, he was on his way to meet with his associates to talk strategy for getting the business back on an upward trend.

Pausing at the office door while pulling the keys from his pocket, Peter felt a chill. It was a warm June morning, so he wondered if there had been a chilly breeze. But he gave it no more thought as he turned the key and swung the door open.

As Peter pulled the key out of the door, stuck it in his front pocket, and looked up, he looked around the lobby he knew so well and was struck by things that were different than he remembered them from the day before.

To the left were chairs lining three walls of the ten-foot by ten-foot area with a coffee table littered with magazines. To the right was a counter, behind which were places for two receptionists. In the middle was a hallway going to the back of the building with offices on each side.

These were the sights that greeted him each day when he went to work. What he did not see every day, hung on the left-side wall facing him, where a flat screen television had been mounted, was a five-foot by seven-foot flag, wide red stripes horizontally on top and bottom with a wide white stripe in between. In the center and slightly overlapping each red stripe was a black cross pattee. On the front of the half-wall counter, where he expected to see his company's logo, was a large eagle emblem with the bird's wings outstretched and a small cross pattee gripped in its talons.

"Who are you?" Peter heard a stern voice say. "And how did you get a key to this building?"

Peter was suddenly aware of an attractive but stern-looking woman behind the counter. The blond woman was tall, about six feet, and was quite shapely. Peter could not help notice the P08 Luger pistol in a holster at her hip. The woman wore an all black uniform. On the right breast of the uniform shirt was an embroidered eagle just like the one on the front of the counter. On the left breast was a small band of multi colored patches above a black iron cross bordered in silver. On each collar were two white embroidered symbols that looked like small lightning bolts squared off at the ends.

"Tell me how you got in here," the woman shouted as her hand tightened on the pistol's grip.

Suddenly, like a quick-draw artist from the Old West, the woman had the gun pointed at Peter's chest. With her free hand, she reached down and pressed a button on the telephone on the desk.

"Hauptman, please come to the lobby," she said without taking her eyes off Peter.

Within seconds, a man exited one of the offices and walked to the lobby. Dressed in the same type of uniform as the woman, but with a few more medal ribbons on his chest, he stepped up to Peter and looked him over from head to toe. He then looked at the woman behind the counter.

"He came in with a key," she said.

"And where did you get this key?" the officer asked Peter.

"This is my office," Peter said firmly, but with a little fear creeping in.

The officer looked at him for a moment and then backhanded him across the face. Peter's first instinctive reaction was to strike back. As he started to bring his arms up, he heard the woman bark, "Halt!' And he froze, remembering the gun in her hand.

The officer quickly grabbed Peter's wrist and twisted him around with his arm behind him. The officer pushed up on the arm, making Peter grimace in pain.

"Even though there are so few of you left, you Juden are still so arrogant to think we will listen to your lies," the officer said as he started pushing Peter down the hallway. They came to one of the offices, and the officer pushed Peter inside roughly. He tripped over a chair and tumbled into a corner facing the wall.

"What the hell are you talking about?" Peter asked as he began to roll over into a sitting position facing the office door. He was astonished to see two of his associates looking in at him with looks of wonder.

"We heard a commotion and came in here and found you sprawled on the floor," Candace Buford said, a little put out with Peter's tone. "Are you drunk?"

Peter blinked his eyes several times, trying to get his good senses back. He slowly got to his feet.

"Not drunk, but I'm not sure I'm really feeling well," he said softly. He then told Candace and Stephon Weller about what he had just experienced.

"And I have this feeling of déjà vu that this, or something like it, has happened before," he said, after finishing his tale.

His associates looked at each other, then back at Peter.

"We need to get you checked out," Stephon said. "Let's take you to the hospital."

CHAPTER 10

Wyatt surveyed Putzi Hanfstaengel's country cottage and its surrounding property through a pair of binoculars he brought with him in the Advanced Lifeboat. They were 10x50 Dienstglas BLC binos he had found in the store room when picking out the clothing he would wear.

The cottage, with two small sheds, was about a mile southwest of the village of Uffing in the shadow of a smallish mountain north of the Staffelsee, an elongated heart-shaped lake. They had parked the Advanced Lifeboat just outside a large grove of trees, a few yards southeast of the cottage. They were observing from a much smaller bunch of trees within spitting distance of the cottage.

Since arriving earlier in the day, Wyatt, Lucy, and Rufus spent some time exploring the area around the village and the road leading to the cottage. They posed as visitors from the United States. Wyatt gave his name as Steve Rogers, Lucy was Peggy Carter, and Rufus was Sam Wilson. Again, Lucy was oblivious to the references, so Wyatt promised they would watch the "Captain America" movies when they returned from the mission.

He had tried to get Lucy and Rufus to stay with the Advanced Lifeboat, where it was hidden from the view of the cottage. But Lucy would have none of it. Mostly, she just wanted to be with him, but she had made the argument that she could be of help from a historical perspective.

Rufus' motivation was that he just didn't want to hang around the Advanced Lifeboat by himself. While he was a little concerned about a black man walking around in Germany, Wyatt realized that in 1923, while black people in Germany were rare, they did exist. Plus, Uffing was sufficiently rural that the team would not run into many crowds. So he decided the risk was minimal.

For his attire, Wyatt had selected a matching brown Bavaria casual outfit, including a second-hand green-gray great coat worn by a German soldier during the First World War. He believed that it would give him an opportunity to be trusted by the person or group bringing Hitler to the cottage. During their walk through the village, the great coat had drawn some stares. But no one spoke to them, so they never even had to use their fake identities.

Lucy wore a one-piece dress that appeared to be a white, short-sleeved blouse under an overall-type green-colored dress with a pink apron. Over it all, for the cold Bavarian weather in November, a fur-lined greenish overcoat with the wide lapels turned up to expose the fur. Rufus was dressed in nondescript civilian clothing, including calf-high leather boots laced up the front, dark brown wool trousers, a tan shirt much like denim, with a light brown heavy wool jacket with a pocket on the left breast and two at the bottom on each front side that extended just below his waist.

As darkness began to fall, they went to the clump of trees they had found earlier that, just inside the tree line, had a picnic table where they could sit. It provided cover from the nearby road to the cottage, but they had a clear view of the road and the structure.

"Are you sure this is going to work?" Rufus asked after they had been alternately chit-chatting and re-discussing the plan. "I mean, after this failed takeover, will Hitler or those with him be trusting anyone?'

Lucy was quick to answer.

"This is a place he feels he has friends," she said. "He and Putzi Hanfstaegel were friends; that is why they brought him here."

"But what happens if they don't believe Wyatt is one of Hitler's supporters?" Rufus asked. "Or that he has been sent here for added protection?"

Wyatt sighed. He had already considered all the scenarios that could go wrong and believed he was prepared for them.

"No plan ever goes completely as planned," he said. "That's why you have to have contingencies."

Rufus was not convinced and was about to express it when Wyatt put his index finger to his lips and became suddenly alert. It was then that the other two heard the faint voices. Wyatt trained the binos on the roadway to their left and saw two figures walking from the village toward the cottage.

"We've got company," he whispered. Lucy and Rufus looked in the direction he was pointing the binoculars.

"Two people," he said almost under his breath. "A man and a woman. I can't make out any facial details."

They all watched as the pair continued up the roadway at a casual pace, not too concerned about what or who may be nearby. As they were nearly adjacent to where the Lifeboat team was hiding about fifty yards away, Wyatt handed the binoculars to Lucy. She looked for a few seconds and handed them back, nodding, indicating to Wyatt that one or both of the newcomers were the ones trying to kill Hitler in 1916.

They remained silent while the two people went past their position.

"They are definitely headed for the cottage," Wyatt whispered.

"What do you think they plan to do?" Lucy asked.

"I don't know," he answered. "But I suspect they think they'll take him by surprise as he enters the house and kill him immediately."

That put Wyatt in contingency mode. His original plan had been to go to the cottage at a time they calculated was shortly before Hitler's arrival and convince anyone inside that he had been sent ahead by Hitler to secure the property to prevent a frontal attack either on the cottage or the road leading to it.

Now he went to plan B.

"We wait for the car that brings Hitler, and we stop it just down the road there and convince them to turn back," Wyatt said. "Then we'll go up to the cottage and confront them."

After about thirty minutes, they saw two more people walking up the road.

Wyatt turned to Lucy and Rufus. "Stay here," he instructed. "If I can't get them to turn back, I'll go up to the cottage with them. You both follow as discreetly as you can." He then darted out of the trees and stood in the roadway.

When the men came to a stop in front of him, Wyatt saw one man pointing an Ortgies pistol at him. He glanced at he other man and recognized Hitler, a pained look on his face as he held his shoulder.

"I am Paul Schmidt," Wyatt said in German, using his alternate, more German-sounding alias. "I was sent by Herrmann Goering to help protect you."

"That can't be," the man holding the pistol answered in German. "I saw Herr Goering shot in the alley."

"That is true," Wyatt said. "But he was able to give me instructions to get here, as this was where Herr Hitler would be taken."

The man didn't seem convinced. But Hitler spoke up.

"I believe that is what Herrmann would have done," he said weakly.

Slowly, the man lowered the pistol, but his facial expression told Wyatt he was not totally convinced.

"I watched two people go into the house a while ago," Wyatt said. "I think it would be best if you go back to the village and find lodging. I will go with you to help protect Herr Hitler."

"What makes you think these people are a threat to him?" the other man asked.

"Herr Goering told me there would be only one person at this cottage," Wyatt said.

"That would be Helene," Hitler uttered. "I trust her."

"So these two others could be anyone, including the Bavarian police to arrest Herr Hitler or someone with more sinister intentions," Wyatt said urgently.

Wyatt was searching for a more persuasive argument. It was going to be difficult since Hitler himself was insisting on going to the cottage. Also, the longer they stood in the roadway, the more the chance they would draw suspicion from the other time travelers. He decided to improvise another contingency.

"Alright," he said. "But I'll go with you."

Both German men agreed, and they began walking toward the cottage.

Watching Wyatt's attempt to turn back Hitler and his companion, Lucy could tell it was not working. Even before the three men began walking toward the cottage, Lucy silently gestured to Rufus that they needed to begin their own journey there.

He vigorously shook his head. Lucy gave him an annoyed look and turned to head for the cottage alone. Rufus rolled his eyes. *"Crap,"* he thought, and followed her.

It was quite dark out, and Lucy pulled the shawl she had around her neck over her head for warmth and spread the ends across the open portion of her coat to help conceal the white portion of her dress. They were far enough away from the road to keep from drawing attention to themselves after they left the clump of trees.

As they half walked, half jogged toward the cottage, Lucy could see they were getting there quicker than the three men. She could see Wyatt walking in front of the other two men, keeping the pace slow as he scanned the area from side to side. The other man was at Hitler's side, appearing to attend to him as they walked.

Lucy and Rufus reached the side of the cottage and flattened themselves against the wall at the corner. Lucy peeked out and saw the men approach the porch, Wyatt still in the lead.

As they neared the cottage's porch, Wyatt held a hand back to indicate the other men should stay where they were. He drew the P08 Luger he had in a holster at his hip and proceeded to the front door. He stopped to listen and heard muffled voices inside. He could tell there was arguing.

He slowly reached out and turned the knob on the door until he heard the light click that indicated the bolt was free of the opening. He pushed the door inward and jumped inside with his weapon at the ready. He quickly took in the scene and saw a woman in traditional Bavarian dress sitting at a table. There was also a woman and a man with their backs to the front door, but turning to face him.

"Freeze," he said firmly in English. "Don't make a move." They complied.

Wyatt slowly moved up to the man and quickly frisked him with his free hand while he kept the weapon at the ready. He found a revolver, a modern Glock 17, in his right pocket, but nothing else. He did the same to the woman and found no weapons.

"Sit down," he instructed the pair. Bobby Anderson and Paulina Howser did as they were told.

Wyatt then motioned the two men standing outside into the cottage.

"Take him upstairs and make him comfortable," Wyatt instructed the man with the gun in German.

Wyatt backed to the doorway and stuck his head out. He saw Lucy looking around the corner of the cottage.

"Come on in," he told her. She did so, followed by Rufus.

The woman sitting at the table registered surprise at seeing a black man come into her home, but not as much as she had at seeing a black woman in her home earlier.

She looked to Wyatt

"Can I go attend to Herr Hitler?" she asked in heavily accented English. He nodded his ascent, and she bounded up the stairs.

"We don't have a lot of time before the Bavarian police get here to arrest him," Lucy told Wyatt as they talked privately in a corner of the cottage while Rufus kept watch over Paulina and Bobby.

"What do we do with them?" he asked, gesturing toward the other time travelers. "They can't be here when the police come."

He glanced at Rufus then back at Lucy.

"For that matter, neither can you two," he said.

"What about you?" she asked.

"I can fit in better than you or Rufus," Wyatt told her.

Lucy did not protest. She knew he was right.

"So what do we do?" she asked.

Wyatt glanced at the pair with Rufus, then upstairs. Despite the risks of their being discovered if the police showed up unexpectedly, he did not want to send Lucy and Rufus away just yet. They could be helpful.

"I'd like you to go upstairs and watch over Hitler, make sure he doesn't do something rash," Wyatt said. "I want to talk to these two and maybe convince them to stop their meddling in time."

He glanced at his watch.

"How much time do we have before the police arrive?" he asked Lucy.

"I'm not exactly sure," she said. "Some accounts say tomorrow and some say three days from now."

"So we go with tomorrow," Wyatt said, and motioned for her to go upstairs.

Not long before that conversation, the man who had accompanied Hitler went to the village to send a doctor to check him out. The man soon returned with the doctor.

The medical man discovered that Hitler had dislocated his shoulder in the fall in the alley. He reset the shoulder, causing Hitler to nearly pass out from the pain. He and the man who had brought Hitler then left the cottage, having done all they could. Now it was just the future dictator, the woman of the house, the Lifeboat team, and the other travelers in the home.

Wyatt sat across from Paulina and Bobby at the table and studied them for a few moments. He judged Paulina to be in her late twenties or early thirties and Bobby to be a few years older. He could also read the confusion on their faces.

"We know who you are and what you are trying to do," Wyatt said. "That cannot happen."

"Then you are condemning millions of people to death," Paulina blurted out.

"We don't know that," Wyatt fibbed.

"Of course we do," she answered. "If he is not allowed to gain power, the world war will not happen."

"No, you're wrong," Rufus interjected. "We've seen what happens when…."

Wyatt held up his hand in front of Rufus' face to silence him. He did not want these two to know everything the Lifeboat team knew. There was no telling whether they had the same capability to see the results of their jumps. In fact, Wyatt doubted they did, or they would have realized their futility after the first jump. But tactically, it was best not to give up too much information to the enemy.

"How do you know someone else may not fill that void?" Wyatt asked. "There are so many factions in Germany right now trying to reverse the effects of the Versailles Treaty. Any one of them could take power, and any one of them could lead to the same – or worse – result than what Hitler brought to the world."

Wyatt could see from Bobby's expression that his argument was taking root with him. But Paulina remained as steadfast as before.

"No, you're wrong," she said. "We can stop it all."

Wyatt sighed. He could see he was getting nowhere with her. He pulled his weapon out of his pocket and set it on the table, keeping his hand on it to indicate to Paulina and Bobby that he was ready to use it.

"Well, one way or another, we can't allow you to keep trying," he said.

Paulina's look of horror told Wyatt she deduced what he wanted her to. But Bobby's expression was one of protection.

"Wyatt, what are you doing?" Rufus asked uneasily.

Wyatt diverted his eyes to Rufus for only a second, and it was in that second that Bobby began to stand. Wyatt pulled the pistol up into a firing position, but Rufus reached out to grab his arm to stop the shot he was sure was coming. Instead of Wyatt's arm, Rufus grabbed the gun and inadvertently jostled it forward, causing Wyatt's finger to press on the trigger.

The shot startled them all, but none more than Bobby as he was thrown backwards onto the floor. Wyatt bolted out of his seat and went around the table to check on him, leaving the weapon on the table in front of his seat. As he neared Bobby, the man jumped to his feet.

In an instant, Wyatt saw he was wounded in his left chest near the armpit. Most likely, Wyatt thought, the bullet went into the fleshy part of the underarm and out the other side.

As they stood there facing each other, Paulina grabbed Wyatt's weapon and pointed it at him.

"Are you OK, Bobby?" she asked. He nodded. "Then we're going upstairs to finish this right now."

She moved to the stairs and started to back up each step slowly, training the gun on Wyatt the whole time. When she got to the halfway point of the stairway, Lucy lunged from above and smacked her with a walking stick on the arm holding the weapon. It fired again and fell from her hand, clattering to the floor below.

Wyatt was closest to it and ran to pick it up. Before he could, Paulina punched Lucy in the nose, and Bobby, who had run past Rufus, standing open-mouthed at the table, grabbed Paulina and half-dragged, half-carried her out the front door. Wyatt ran after them, but they were lost in the darkness.

Shaking off the punch, Lucy ran back upstairs to find the woman of the house standing at the door to the room where Hitler had been taken. She had a Walther PP pistol in her hand.

"Whoa, it's OK," she said. "We just stopped an attempt on Herr Hitler's life."

Reluctantly, the woman lowered the pistol and went back into the room. She laid the weapon on a nightstand by the bed where Hitler lay, still semi-conscious from the shoulder pain.

Downstairs, Wyatt glared at Rufus.

"What the hell did you do that for?" he yelled.

"You were going to kill those people, Wyatt," Rufus answered.

Wyatt rolled his eyes and put the pistol back in his pocket.

"Jesus, Rufus, I wasn't going to kill them," he said. "I was trying to scare them."

"Oh," Rufus said. "Sorry." But he knew it was a hollow apology.

During her time upstairs earlier, Lucy learned the woman they found in the cottage was Helene Hanfstaegel, Putzi's wife. By observing, she could also see that she and Hitler had a bit of affection for each other.

Shortly after midnight, there was a knock at the cottage door. Wyatt answered it to find a man in civilian clothing asking to see Helene. After he spoke to her briefly, she went upstairs, followed by Lucy, to inform Hitler that the police were on their way from Munich and would be there within the hour.

Hitler, sitting on the edge of the bed, stared straight ahead for a few seconds.

"Now all is lost, no use going on," he said, and grabbed for the pistol on the night table. But Lucy jumped in quickly and snatched it away.

"What do you think you are doing?" Lucy shouted in French. "After all your effort and struggle, are you going to leave all the people you've gotten interested in your idea of saving the country by taking your life? They're looking for you to carry on!"

After the words had escaped her lips, she felt nauseous. She turned to Helene.

"You talk to him," she said as she headed for the stairs. She hesitated at the doorway to listen.

Helene urged Hitler to dictate to her his instructions to his followers before the police came to take him away. That way, they would know what to do to keep the movement alive while he was in prison. After a moment's thought, he thanked her for helping him remember his duty to his men.

Lucy descended the stairs and found Wyatt and Rufus standing near the front door.

"It's time to go," Wyatt said.

Paulina was livid when she and Bobby stepped out of the Time Pod. She had been able to stop the bleeding from Bobby's wound before they made the jump back, and except for some residual pain, he was feeling fine.

"Those people were there again," she yelled.

"What people?" Ivan asked.

"Those people who stopped us in 1916," Paulina hollered.

"How could that be?" Glenda asked. "How did they know you even went there?"

Paulina was beginning to gain control of her rage, and she began to think logically.

"They are somehow able to tell when we jump," she said. "We have to figure out how and come up with something that will jam their scanning capability."

Lucy was scanning historical documents to determine if anything changed in history following the last jump. She discovered some minor, insignificant differences. These included the fact that two men accompanied Hitler to the Hanfstangel cottage that night and that there were two maids at the cottage when he arrived.

She could find no explanation for these alterations and had to credit them to chance.

She had been at the task for hours and was just about to give up when a document title caught her eye: "The Woman Who Saved Hitler From Suicide."

She could feel the bile working its way up her throat as it had in the cottage after she told him to buck up and continue his crusade. She felt even sicker as she reluctantly read the story.

It was a brief biography of Helene's life through that fateful night in November 1923. Regarding the incident of Hitler's potential suicide, she claimed credit for all the words that were spoken, and there was no mention of another woman in the room.

She felt two hands begin to caress her neck and looked back to see Wyatt. He could feel the tension in her muscles.

"What's wrong?" he asked.

She just pointed at the computer terminal, and he read the article quickly.

"Yeah, I understand how you feel," he said. "We could have walked away from this whole thing and let Paulina achieve her goal and not feel the guilt."

"But that's only part of this," she said, gesturing to the article. "It wasn't her that took the gun away from him and yelled at him to carry on."

Wyatt turned her chair around and kneeled in front of her. He already knew what she was going to say, so spared her the agony of saying it.

"I know," he said.

He could see the tears forming in her eyes.

"Are we doing the right thing, Wyatt?" she wailed. "Are we so sure that what we're doing is the right thing?"

He took her hands in his and kissed each one.

"With the things we have seen over the last two-plus years, I believe we are," he said. "The things we see after a jump tell us history is taking the path it did before."

She took her hands from his and wiped the tears from her eyes. She leaned forward and wrapped her arms around him.

"I know what you are saying," she said. "And losing Amy tells me the kind of damage that can be done by changing history."

She started sobbing again.

"But keeping a megalomaniac alive is hard to justify," she said. "I don't know how much more I can do to keep doing that."

With that, Wyatt knew his job had become even harder.

CHAPTER 11

As she descended the ladder from the main hatch to the bunker, Agent Christopher could see Connor standing near the bottom, facing back toward the computer terminals at the other end of the corridor.

When he had called her a little more than one hour ago, he sounded excited in a gleeful way. But at the same time, she could detect some concern in his voice. He had said very little in the phone conversation, just that she needed to come as soon as possible.

"Should I assemble the team?" she asked, knowing they had all gone to their respective homes the night before.

"No," he replied quickly. "Just you. I need to talk to you about something very important."

So when she stepped off the last rung of the ladder and he turned to face her, she was a bit leery.

"What is it, Connor?" she asked.

"There is something I need to show you," he said, and beckoned for her to follow him.

They traversed the corridor to the bank of computer terminals, and he settled into the seat in front of the one he usually used. He gestures for her to take a seat.

Agent Christopher's uneasiness remained.

"When we developed the time machines, we had no reason to believe we needed a way to track movements through time," he explained. "We had the only time machines, or so we thought."

Agent Christopher had only mild interest in the conversation. Until now, she had assumed the tracker was always part of the program. But she was struggling to figure out where Connor was going with this discussion.

"It wasn't until Garcia Flynn and his people took the Mother Ship that we discovered the tracking capability," Connor said.

"But if you didn't include tracking in the machines and software, how did it come to be?" Agent Christopher asked, becoming more interested.

"Because the Lifeboat was the prototype, when we built the Mother Ship, we copied all the prototype's systems," Connor explained. "I suspect that since the two machines are linked, any movement by either shows on our instruments the way we have seen it."

"You suspect?" Agent Christopher asked.

Despite his dark skin, Agent Christopher could tell he was blushing a bit.

"Well, when Rittenhouse was in control, they wanted me to find out how the Lifeboat team was able to know when they went back in time," he explained. "That was part of why I agreed to force Rufus to record the team's trips."

He put his face in his hands for a moment before continuing.

"I was hoping to use that against him to get him to help me figure it out," he said. "But when he finally refused to do the recordings, I started having second thoughts about going along with Rittenhouse. So I just went through the motions. After you got control again, it just didn't seem to matter."

Agent Christopher still had no idea what importance this conversation had.

"But what does all that have to do with the here and now?" she asked.

Still a little embarrassed and ashamed of what he had done to Rufus almost two years ago, Connor took a moment to compose himself.

"From what I've heard about the trips so far now, I don't think the other travelers have a way to track our trips," Connor said. "They were surprised both times by our team's appearance."

Agent Christopher was struck by his use of the word "our" when referring to the current Lifeboat team. He was clearly considering himself part of the team now. Her decision to brief him on the 1916 trip and include him in all other briefings since was obviously the right thing to do.

"But the pace at which they have progressed in what they are doing makes me believe they will now try to find a way to jam our scans of their trips," Connor said.

"You don't think they will figure out some way to track us?" she asked before he could go on.

"They might eventually, but without another vehicle, there isn't the link there to do it," he said.

"They might have a prototype," Agent Christopher said.

"I don't think so, the way they only did three test trips and went right into making attempts to change history indicates they are in a hurry," Connor said. "But that's not really the point here."

It was clear to Agent Christopher he was getting a little impatient to get to his point, so she gestured that he continue.

"I developed an algorithm that will jam any jammer they might come up with," he said, then sat back waiting for the praise he was sure was coming.

"How is it going to work since you don't know what they have, or will develop?" Agent Christopher asked.

Connor was a bit irritated that her words contained no praise. But the logical part of his mind took over. A layperson would not understand how computer programming worked.

"It isn't based on what they are doing," he explained. "I've put a jammer on our signal. It's based on the technology that allows police to jam radar detectors."

With that reference, it was easy for Agent Christopher to understand.

"That's great work, Connor," she said. "Thank you for working that out."

She got up, ready to head back home.

"And thank you for letting me know," she said. "I appreciate that you are working with this team. You've earned my trust."

His satisfied look as she turned to walk up the corridor to the hatch told her he was firmly on board with the team.

Wyatt lay on his left side facing Lucy in the master bedroom of her home. He watched her, lying flat on her back, sleeping; he could tell by the heavy breathing and the pained look on her face that she was still struggling with their ongoing mission of "saving" Adolf Hitler.

Not that he didn't have his own uneasiness with their task. Being an active duty military man and having served overseas in a combat zone, he knew the horrors of war. He had seen friends killed in battle. He had seen the strife caused to civilians in a war zone. Wyatt cringed at the thought of so many people dying in World War II, the suffering, the destruction. It turned his stomach.

But he couldn't shake the personal damage he and other team members had dealt with as history was tampered with – Amy's disappearance, Jessica's rebirth, and then eventual death to bring Rufus back to life, Garcia Flynn's decision to kill Jessica, and his eventual sacrifice by stranding himself in his own past.

That, along with his military training, kept him focused on the mission.

But as he watched Lucy in the bed beside him, he was torn in another direction. To stay on mission, he must keep the woman he loved in a position of continued emotional distress and even physical danger.

It was a prospect that made him question his own resolve.

With all that bouncing around in his brain, Wyatt joined Lucy in a very restless sleep.

It had been a week since the 1923 time jump. Rufus and Jiya were spending a rare day together at her apartment. They were working on the tech business they wanted to start and run together.

The project had been put on hold when the time jumping had started up again. But two days earlier, Rufus had told her something that renewed their interest.

"Connor came to me the other day and said he would hand over all his work on rebuilding his company to us," he told Jiya. She was a little shocked and somewhat confused.

"Why would he do that?" she asked.

Rufus put the briefcase he had been carrying on the table and gestured for Jiya to sit down.

"He said he is reconsidering restarting the company," he said. "He is considering another option."

"He's just considering it?" Jiya asked. "Then why give everything to us?"

He shook his head.

"I asked him that, too," he told her. "He said that even though his mind wasn't totally made up, he was pretty sure he didn't want to restart the company. At least not that kind of company."

Jiya thought about the information she had just received. As fanatical as Connor had been about his company, it was hard for her to imagine that he would just give up an opportunity to get it started again. But at the same time, she could see the common sense in it.

What had happened to Connor Mason and his company over the past two-plus years could make a person want to distance themselves from such memories. Moving in another direction, maybe even with a different kind of profession, made sense to her.

"So why didn't he talk to both of us about it?" she asked.

Rufus was a little embarrassed about that question, as he had been, for the same reason, when Connor had spoken to him about it.

"I don't know, Jiya," he said. "I suppose because he has known me longer, I worked for him longer."

The response did not seem logical to her.

"That doesn't make sense," she responded. "If he's handing over his business information to both of us, why wouldn't he want to include me in the conversation?"

Rufus became a little frustrated. He really did not have an answer to the question, and he had not pursued it with Connor to get an answer.

"I don't know," he said a little angrily. "Maybe he feels guilty and can't face you."

"What would he have to feel guilty about?" Jiya asked, a little annoyed at Rufus' tone.

"I don't know, maybe because you got stuck in 1800s San Francisco or got those visions all because of the Lifeboat," Rufus said, adjusting his tone as he recognized her annoyance, and dropping his head to stare at his shoes.

She reached out and took his hand. He lifted his head and looked into her eyes. She could see the sadness there.

"It's okay, I was just curious." It was an innocent little lie to spare his feelings. She remained a little hurt that she had been left out.

"He also said he would help us find financing if we need it," Rufus said, feeling a little better. "He would also be available if we needed to consult with him. He doesn't want anything for it, just to be a silent partner."

It was a lot to take in, and Jiya filed it away to digest later.

"I really don't think he's really looking to start another company at all," Rufus said, since the conversation had taken a less tense track.

"What do you mean?" Jiya asked.

"Well, he seems to be getting along better with Agent Christopher," Rufus said. "And they have been spending a lot of time working together."

"Well, we know it's not some kind of romantic attraction," Jiya said. "She already has someone in her life, and a family," she added after seeing the questioning look on Rufus' face.

"No, no, I didn't mean that," he said quickly. "I just think he is satisfied continuing to be a consultant to Homeland Security."

Jiya nodded. She could see the logic in that as well.

"Well, if this time travel thing continues, his advice will be needed," she said.

Rufus frowned, then turned up his nose like he smelled something nasty.

"What is it?" Jiya asked.

"I'm just not so sure I want to be involved in this time travel stuff anymore," he said.

Jiya had had the same feelings ever since her experience in 1800s San Francisco. But she still felt an obligation to help as much as she could, and she felt a connection with the entire Lifeboat team and wanted that to continue.

"Why not?" she asked. "We're keeping history as it should be. That's important."

Rufus made that face again, and Jiya involuntarily sniffed the air to see what it was he smelt.

"This whole 'saving Hitler to save history' is something I'm having a lot of trouble with," he said.

Jiya understood completely.

"I know," she said. "So far, we've done mostly good things to keep history on track."

"But this man caused millions of deaths, and most of them were so gruesome," he said. "If anyone in history deserves to die, this man does – or did – or should – or whatever."

She squeezed his hand.

"I understand where you are coming from," she said. "But what we are seeing after their jumps is telling us things would be worse."

They both knew well what would have happened if Hitler had died in 1916. Following the 1923 jump, the team learned that the alternate history saw that Rudolf Hess took power in Germany and built the country to be a military might, just as Hitler had in the actual history.

In the altered history, World War II started two years later, and the Germans never invaded the Soviet Union. As a consequence, Germany actually invaded and conquered Great Britain, all of Europe, and the Middle East. But, as in actual history, Germany was overextended, and the Soviets took advantage of it and conquered Germany and all the territory it had taken. Eventually, the USSR invaded and conquered all of North America. From there, the world became a communist world government.

"So we are doing the right thing," Jiya said.

But Rufus had never been very enthusiastic about the time jumps and their missions. He did it because he felt he needed to. With each jump to save Hitler, his enthusiasm was chipped away a little bit more.

"I'm just not sure how much more times I can be a part of saving that lunatic's life," he said, and got up from the table and left the room.

Jiya decided a talk with Agent Christopher was in order.

Agent Christopher received Jiya's call about nine o'clock in the evening, asking to meet about something very important to the team. Jiya did not say what she wanted to talk about, but Agent Christopher had a pretty good idea.

Rufus had been a reluctant participant in this whole project almost from the start, but he went along because he was the only pilot and he felt an obligation. But along the way, he developed a bond with the other team members. In some ways, he actually started to enjoy the work.

His death in 1800s San Francisco could have put a damper on that enjoyment. But since, after his rescue, he had no memory of the incident, only what he was told, he eased back into the routine when they started traveling through time again.

But Agent Christopher had seen a slight change after the 1916 trip and even more after 1923.

While she wasn't exactly sure, Agent Christopher speculated that their overall goal of keeping Hitler alive was eating at him. Hell, it was eating at her. And in private conversations with Connor, she knew it was bothering him as well. She guessed it was a concern for all of them.

She had also noticed a drop in enthusiasm from Lucy following the 1923 trip. For that reason, after Jiya set up the meeting, she called Wyatt to include him as well.

To avoid running into Rufus, Lucy, or Connor, she had arranged to meet with them at her home. When they arrived, she led them into the kitchen and offered them some cake and something to drink. Neither was hungry, but they each asked for water.

"So, Jiya, what did you want to talk about?" Agent Christopher asked after the small talk died out.

She took a slow sip of her ice water while still trying to find the best way to say it.

"I'm not trying to get anyone in trouble," she said sheepishly. As it came out of her mouth, it sounded a bit like she was still a child trying to tell her parents something a sibling had done to upset her.

"I mean, I'm not saying anyone is doing anything wrong," she tried again, still feeling like she was bungling it.

"I understand," Agent Christopher said softly. "Just tell me what's on your mind."

She sipped her water again and, out of the corner of her eye, without turning her head to look directly at him, glanced over at Wyatt, who was sitting patiently.

"I don't think Rufus wants to continue with what we are doing," she blurted out.

Agent Christopher and Wyatt exchanged a look. They each wondered if the other was thinking the same thing they were.

"What do you mean, he doesn't want to continue?" Agent Christopher asked.

"Well, he's not happy that we are going back to make sure Hitler lives," Jiya said.

There it was. It was now out in the open, the same thing that was on everyone's mind. Agent Christopher and Wyatt looked at each other again as a way to confirm that they had the same thought.

"I don't think any of us are real pleased with that," Wyatt said. "But I am convinced it is what we need to do."

Agent Christopher nodded her head in agreement.

"But Rufus told me he's not sure how much longer he can keep doing it," Jiya said.

"Lucy feels the same way," Wyatt admitted.

Now that Jiya and Wyatt were fessing up, Agent Christopher decided she needed to as well.

"This is not something that is all that surprising," she said. "I have kind of guessed that for a while."

She took a deep breath.

"I've had some conversations with Connor, and he and I feel the same about this being the hardest mission to justify that we're ever done yet," she said. "But like Wyatt, I am convinced we need to do this."

For the first time since they arrived, Jiya turned to look Wyatt in the eye.

"I do, too," she said. "As disgusting as it is."

Agent Christopher let out a big sigh of relief. She was worried that the entire team would have second thoughts. It was one thing to not like what one was doing, but yet another to be so against it as to not participate. While Rufus and Lucy, and Connor for that matter, had not balked on a mission yet, it sounded like a real possibility.

"So now it seems possible that we may be moving on without one or two of our team," she said. "Can we go on, and if so, how?"

Wyatt shook his head. He was not ready to write Lucy, or even Rufus, off so quickly.

"I am all for having contingency plans," he said. "But I don't think we are at the point to implement them, at least not with Lucy." He looked over at Jiya with a *What about you with Rufus?* question on his face.

"I agree," she said. "I don't think Rufus will quit on us."

Agent Christopher nodded. She was not as sure as her gesture would indicate, but she did not want to argue the point with Wyatt and Jiya. The two couples' romantic relationships were no secret, and she believed their assessment was somewhat biased because of that.

"Be that as it may, we should talk about what to do in the off chance one or both of them don't go on the next or other jumps," Agent Christopher said.

Wyatt saw Jiya begin to protest, to again come to Rufus' defense. He wanted to defend Lucy as well, but his practical military training told him Agent Christopher was right. He jumped in before Jiya could get the words out.

"You're right," he said.

"So, Jiya, do you feel confident that you could pilot the Advanced Lifeboat in Rufus' absence?" Agent Christopher asked.

At the time that Rittenhouse instructed Connor to have Rufus clandestinely record Lucy and Wyatt's conversations during missions, the pilot's loyalty to Connor came into question when he reluctantly made a few recordings and turned them over, then he suddenly refused to cooperate. That prompted Connor to begin training Jiya to be a backup pilot.

When Rufus was wounded by Flynn in 1931, Jiya joined the team on their next jump, just in case Rufus could not pilot, to 1954. But the trip triggered seizures in which she saw visions of the future. She went on several other jumps with the team and was later abducted by Emma, a Rittenhouse agent, when she stole the Lifeboat.

Jiya was able to escape and, piloting the vehicle alone for the first time, ended up in San Francisco's Chinatown in 1885. She sent a message to Rufus, using the Klingon language from "Star Trek," to reveal the Lifeboat's location so they could find it in the present day. She also urged her friends not to come back for her, which, of course, they ignored. Their mission was only half a success, as in the process, Rufus was killed by Emma.

He is restored, though, by the team in the Advanced Lifeboat they now use, provided by future versions of Wyatt and Lucy.

Remembering all this, Jiya reflected on Agent Christopher's question before answering.

"Rufus has not said he will not pilot the Advanced Lifeboat," she prefaced her answer. "But yes, I'm sure I can do it."

"It's not quite the same one you piloted before," Agent Christopher pressed.

"No, it's not, but the basics are the same," Jiya said. "I have been spending time in it, and Rufus has been showing me how it works."

Agent Christopher and Wyatt both raised eyebrows at that assertion. Jiya knew exactly what they were thinking.

"That does not mean he is planning to quit," she said quickly. "He knows the need to have someone else trained to pilot. He was wounded on two missions and died on another, for Pete's sake."

Wyatt nodded, knowing from his military training how cross-training is essential. Agent Christopher accepted the explanation, but with some reservations.

"That leaves us with Lucy." she said. "What do we do if our historian flakes out?"

Wyatt was a little stung by the question. He did not like the idea of Lucy being viewed as some kind of quitter or traitor to their cause. But the rational side of him also knew it had to be contemplated, especially after the discussions they had had together about her revulsion of doing anything to keep Hitler alive.

"She's not going to quit on us," Wyatt said firmly. "Even if, and this is a big if, she doesn't want to make the jumps with us, she will do everything she can to provide us with all the information we need."

Again, Agent Christopher accepted his assessment, but she didn't fully trust that it would pan out that way.

"But her input can be, and has been, critical to you in the moment," she told Wyatt. "And if she's not on the jump, she can't give you that input."

Wyatt agreed, but was a little offended.

"I have been trained to deal with fluid situations on the battlefield," he shot at her. "And I've proved my worth in those situations in real life, and I'm not talking about these time trips."

Agent Christopher was well aware of his military experience and record. His success overseas was one of the reasons she picked him to work with the Lifeboat team. She regretted offending him, but she could not afford to be unprepared for changes in the team's dynamics.

"I understand, Wyatt. I am just trying to make sure we are covered," she said. "Remember, Jiya came to me about her concerns over Rufus, and you confirmed my own concerns about Lucy."

"But there's another thing you need to consider," Wyatt said. "This period in history comes up a lot in our Delta Force training, and it is of particular interest to me. So I'm sure I'll have enough information, or can find it quickly if I don't, to be well briefed."

He looked over at Jiya before he went on.

"But I don't think it will come to it," he said. "Lucy will be with us, all in."

While Jiya nodded her agreement, she wasn't sure she was that certain of Rufus.

"Alright then," Agent Christopher said with a finality that told the others the meeting was over. "We will plan on things staying the same as always, but if not, we'll plow ahead with you two filling in as needed."

CHAPTER 12

He was not sure if Agent Christopher caught it, but Wyatt saw the hesitation on Jiya's face when she nodded at his assertion that Lucy would be "all in" when the time came to make a time jump. He said nothing until he and Jiya were outside the house, headed for their respective vehicles.

"Are you as sure about Rufus as you wanted us to believe?" he asked. He had followed her to her car, a Honda Civic, and waited until she opened the driver's side door.

She paused for a moment before answering, and then realized it was a moment too long.

"You have to think about it? That doesn't fill me with confidence," Wyatt said. "Please tell me I'm wrong."

This time her response was quick, but it did not address Wyatt's concerns.

"I don't think any of us are thrilled with what we are doing – keeping Hitler alive," she said. "Tell me I'm wrong."

This time it was Wyatt's turn to pause. He knew everyone involved, including Agent Christopher, was having their inner struggles with the goal of keeping who most would consider history's most evil tyrant alive.

"Jiya, I am a soldier. I am trained to follow orders whether I like or believe in them or not," he said. "So I can only imagine what is going through the minds of those who don't have that kind of rigid training."

She narrowed her eyes and cocked her head slightly to one side.

"So the rest of us aren't trained or disciplined?" she asked in a tone that screamed she had been offended.

"I'll have you know that what we do takes a lot of discipline," she said before he could respond. "We may not be soldiers, but we do have training and we know how to get things done."

Wyatt couldn't help but recognize the disdain when she used the word "soldiers." He did his best to keep his emotions in check and not take offense.

"I am not saying you are untrained or undisciplined; I know it takes a lot of both of those things to do what you and Rufus do. I know because it is way above my head," he said. "I'm just trying to tell you that you are not alone in being conflicted with all this."

His words did not seem to change her attitude.

"But you sure are quick to wave your military training out there as a flag of superiority," she said, then began to get into the car. Wyatt shot out his hand to stop her from shutting the door.

"I'm not trying to put myself out there as superior," he said angrily. "But I will tell you this, because I am in the military makes me want to kill that bastard as much, if not more, than any of you."

His response just seemed to reinforce Jiya's growing anger with him. She pulled the door to close it, but he tightened his grip. She pulled harder, and this time he let it close.

"I'll believe that when it happens," she barked through the closed window, put the car in gear, and roared off. Wyatt had to jump back to keep from getting his feet run over.

He cursed his failure to keep his emotions in check.

As he looked away from where Jiya's car had been just seconds before, he saw Agent Christopher standing at a window in her home, looking in his direction. How long she had been there and just what she had heard, he did not know. But it was not his concern right now. He got in his Dodge Ram and left.

Wyatt and Jiya now had personal issues to deal with, on top of everything else buzzing through their heads. Do they talk to Lucy and Rufus about this meeting? Do they clue them in that their commitment and loyalty to the mission were being questioned?

Both were certain that the news would not be received well. But their relationships, in both cases, were dependent on honesty and trust. Neither Wyatt nor Jiya wanted to keep anything from their partners.

It was also not lost on either of them that Agent Christopher had not instructed them to keep the discussion under wraps. Was that deliberate? Did she actually want them to talk to Lucy and Rufus about the meeting to let them know she knew about their doubts?

The bright spot in their self-deliberations was that, as late as it was in the night, they would not have to face the choice right away. Jiya was headed back to her apartment, and Wyatt was on his way to the bunker.

However, they both knew the reprieve would be short-lived. They only had the rest of the night to decide how they would play this latest twist.

Wyatt didn't even have that much time.

When he got into the bunker, he could see that no one was at the computer terminals at the far end of the corridor. That meant Connor and Rufus had gone home. While it was unusual for no one to be there, he was alone.

But when he walked into his quarters, he saw that it was not the case. Lucy was sitting on the edge of his bed.

"Hi," she said. "I called a couple times, but it went right to voicemail."

Wyatt used that to disguise his surprise and uneasiness as he reached for his phone and checked it.

"I had shut the ringer and vibrate off and forgot to turn it back on," he said as he hugged her. "Sorry."

"Where were you?" she asked.

Although he was leaning toward talking to Lucy about the meeting with Agent Christopher, he had not yet fully made up his mind. He hesitated just a second or two.

"I was meeting with Agent Christopher," he said, pulling a chair toward him and sitting in it backwards so he could rest his arms on the back.

"What about?" she asked.

Because he had not completely decided whether to tell Lucy about the meeting, Wyatt had not put much thought into how he would approach Lucy about it or what he would tell her and what would be held back, if anything. He sighed deeply and composed himself.

"She called me to meet," he said cautiously. "Jiya had some concerns about Rufus."

Already curious about Wyatt's whereabouts, Lucy's attention was grabbed even harder.

"She thinks he is having some second thoughts about what we are doing," he said a bit lamely. Knowing that Lucy had her own misgivings, he didn't want to just blurt it out. However, he knew he would have to face it sooner or later.

"I know he hasn't had his whole heart in this project, but I didn't know he didn't believe in us keeping history straight," Lucy said.

Wyatt put his forehead on his crossed arms on the chair back. He had to spell it out for her. But he didn't really want to for fear she would, because of her own doubts about her own commitment under the current circumstances, take it too personally.

Finally, he raised his head to see a look of deep concern on her face.

"It's not that he isn't committed to keeping history straight; it's just this part of history." Wyatt still couldn't bring himself to say it. But he didn't really have to.

"It's about keeping Hitler alive," Lucy said with a bit of sadness in her voice. "Like me."

He reached out and ran his fingertips up and down her cheek. What he had tried to avoid was now reality. Wyatt hoped Lucy was not going to take this so personally that it chipped away at her resolve any more than it was already eroding.

Lucy reached up and gently put her fingers around the wrist of the hand that was caressing her cheek. She took his hand down and grasped his fingers softly with her other hand.

"Wyatt, I know you've been worried about me," she said. He lowered his face to look at his arm draped across the chair back. He was worried for a number of different reasons.

"This thing with Hitler in 1923 hit me pretty hard," she said. "It hit me because I was so close to him that I was the one who talked him out of killing himself."

She released his wrist and took both his hands in hers. He raised his head and looked her in the eye.

"Lucy, I know this is hard on you, on all of us in different ways," he said. "If you want to not be included on future trips, I understand. And I can fill in for you."

Her face blazed with disappointment, but not in him. She was disappointed in herself. As a historian, she knew the devastation that would – did – visit the world because of Adolf Hitler. What historian would not relish the idea of changing history for the better.

But in the last two and a half years, she had seen – especially first-hand – what could happen if history was changed, even in the smallest way. She had lost her sister, her mother, Wyatt got his wife back then had to lose her all over again to make history right. What other damages to the timeline could have been made in history from the minor changes they had caused with their previous trips, no one knew.

Lucy was disappointed – maybe even a little ashamed – at her reluctance to continue the mission they had started. But she could not shake the disgust she felt at what she knew they must do.

"Wyatt, I can, and I will, continue on these missions," she said with a conviction that was taking all she had to maintain. "This is something we have to do."

Wyatt's tension relaxed, but only slightly. Even if he was certain Lucy would not break, and that certainty was by no means complete, there was still Rufus to deal with. Despite Jiya's resentment at what she perceived as a slight to her and Rufus' discipline and resolve, Wyatt knew Rufus was more apt to balk at the main mission than Lucy.

"I believe you," he said. "But I'm not so sure about Rufus."

Agent Christopher had a dilemma.

Over the past two and a half years, she had come to trust the Lifeboat team in a way she had not trusted any others in her life – with the exception of her wife and children. It was more than even trust.

If not for Lucy's help during a time jump to 1980, the young Denise's life would have taken a much different course. She wouldn't even be Denise, and she would have been in an arranged married to a man she did not love. She would not have the loving partner and very satisfying family life she has now. Jiya had also played a part in that turning point in her life. Hell, so had Wyatt and Rufus.

And that was just the personal aspect of their relationship.

Professionally, they had all put their lives on hold to participate in this project. Rufus and Jiya gave up promising professions, and Wyatt and Lucy had lost so much more than that – his wife and her sister and mother.

Even though his obsession with his dead wife had led Wyatt to endanger not only the Lifeboat but the entire team, he had performed flawlessly otherwise. And how could she fault him for the things he did to reclaim the love of his life.

Denise would have done anything for these people.

But Agent Christopher had to keep Denise and her emotional attachments out of the hard decisions she was having to face right now.

Replacing Lifeboat team members was tricky business, as Agent Christopher learned early during the project. While the team was in 1836 at the Alamo, she made plans to replace Wyatt after she ordered him to eliminate Anthony Bruhl, Rufus' colleague with Mason Industries, who helped steal the Mother Ship. Wyatt did not follow her orders and covered up Rufus' protection of Bruhl during a jump to 1962. But Lucy talked her out of replacing him.

Then, when Wyatt and Rufus stole the Mother Ship to travel to 1983 to try to prevent the conception of the man Flynn identified as the man who killed Wyatt's wife, Wyatt was taken into custody upon his return. He was replaced by Master Sergeant Dave Baumgardner, who was promptly killed on the next mission to 1927, the day Charles Lindbergh made his history-making solo trans-Atlantic flight.

Agent Christopher reluctantly welcomed him back to the team after Rufus and Lucy stole the Lifeboat and reunited with Wyatt. Those incidents showed the tight bond the Lifeboat team had at that time.

From then on, Wyatt had her trust again.

Rufus was one of the remaining original trained pilots. Jiya was still learning the task. While there were other historians to choose from, none but Lucy had the knowledge of the importance of the team's work, its trials and tribulations over the last two and a half years, her knowledge of the other team members and how they reacted to one another, or her uncanny intuition for all things history.

So replacing team members was a task too hard to accomplish with the time-sensitive situation they were in.

But at the same time, she had to be prepared for the eventuality that one or more of them would balk on a mission.

So she confided her concerns to Connor. She did so reluctantly, knowing his feelings for Rufus, and got him to agree not to discuss it with Rufus. Agent Christopher then tasked Connor to search out possible replacements for Lucy and to find any feasible replacement pilots who could train quickly.

The decision to involve Connor would come back to haunt her.

Connor Mason was not the type of man to take kindly to being told what or how to do anything.

A man of black British descent, he made his own way in life; there was no silver spoon in his mouth. He studied hard in high school, enough to place him at the top of his class and draw the attention of major universities. He chose the best school for computer engineering, the University of California-Berkley. The San Francisco area school was a pioneer in the subject at the time.

Fresh out of Cal, Connor found opportunities in the then-budding industry of information technology in the Bay Area hard to come by – ironic as it would some day be known as the Silicon Valley, the hub of the industry. So he took a job at a small firm in Chicago. Starting at the entry level, he worked his way up the ladder until he was a vice president of development.

During the climb, Connor saved and invested his money wisely. After a few years leading the development department, it became clear he had gone as far as he would go, as the company CEO had no intention of letting anyone else move into his position until he was cold in the ground, which wasn't going to happen naturally for many years yet.

So Connor decided it was time to strike out on his own. With connections he had made during his days at Cal, he started his own company – Mason Industries – in San Francisco. After the rapid establishment of the company and his reputation as someone who could get things done, he initiated a project that had been rattling around in his brain for some time – a way to travel through time.

During the establishment of Mason Industries, Connor knew he would need good people involved. He hired only the best minds he could find or develop. One of those was Rufus Carlin, a young man he came to know in Chicago who was living on the streets while putting himself through high school. Connor could tell he was a young man of intelligence and admired his tenacity.

So he took Rufus under his wing and financed his education at the Massachusetts Institute of Technology. Upon graduation, Connor hired him as a programmer. After a few months' experience within the company, Rufus was assigned to the time travel project.

Yes, Connor Mason believed his way was the only way, and resented being told what and how to do things.

Okay, so there was the case of the time travel project draining company finances, and the offer from Rittenhouse of $2.5 billion to finance it so he could avoid bankruptcy. But Rittenhouse's interference in the project only proved to him that his way was the better way to do things.

And then there was Connor's loyalty to Rufus. The man had been like the son he never had. He had invested a lot – financially and emotionally – into the young man. While he certainly didn't want to see his financial investment wasted, the emotional side of Connor, the very small side that was not self-centered, also wanted to see someone he believed in so strongly succeed.

So the agreement he made with Agent Christopher not to share their discussions with Rufus was null and void, even as the words "I agree" passed through his lips.

As he pulled out his phone and scrolled through to find Rufus' number, Connor tried to compose how the conversation would go. He wanted to be subtle in what he said to Rufus, but at the same time, phrase things in such a way that he would get some information. But he didn't want Rufus to know he was fishing for information. He wanted to talk to Rufus about the concerns raised about him, but he wanted to somehow preserve the agreement he made with Agent Christopher -- not because he respected her, but because he wanted to avoid a confrontation with her.

The trouble was that being subtle was not part of Connor's makeup.

He was still formulating what he would say when Rufus answered.

"Where are you?" Connor asked. While he thought it was an innocent way to open the conversation, his tone was stern and business-like. It was a dead giveaway to Rufus that this was no social call.

Not that he expected a social call from Connor Mason. In the years they had known each other, he could count the number of social conversations, telephonic, electronic, or in person, they had had using just one hand, with fingers left over.

"I'm at home working on a few things," he said hesitantly. "Why?"

"Are you there alone?" Connor asked. Clearly, he had not been able to find that small – very small – bit of casual conversation ability buried deep in his personality.

"No," Rufus said, rotating his head to the left to look at Jiya working on her laptop. "Jiya's here."

Connor bit his lower lip a little. He had hoped, even expected, Rufus to be alone, wherever he was. He was going to have to be careful how he phrased things from here on.

"I was wondering how you were doing," Connor said. "We haven't had a chance to talk for a while."

"I'm doing fine," Rufus answered. He had turned his head to look away from Jiya, but he suddenly felt her eyes on him. He looked her way and shrugged his shoulders, then turned back to the computer terminal in front of him, trying to work while talking.

"How are you holding up with this time travel?" Connor asked. "It has been six months since you were involved in that. I hope it hasn't been too much of a strain getting back into it."

Rufus stopped what he was working on. He recalled that he and Connor had spoken about this very subject after the first jump to 1916. *"So why does he think he needs to talk to me about it again now?"* Rufus thought.

"I'm OK with it," Rufus said. He shot another glance at Jiya and gave her his best puzzled look.

"Alright, I just wanted to check in on you," Connor said. "Remember that if you need to talk about anything, you can come to me."

"I will, Thanks," Rufus said with a bit of puzzlement in his voice. He cut the connection and stared at the phone for a few seconds. He then looked over to find Jiya staring at him, the question, *"What was that all about?"* clearly etched on her face.

"It was Connor, wanting to know how I was doing with the time travel," Rufus said. His confusion went from Connor's phone call to the changed expression on Jiya's face after his statement. The golden-almond skin in her face took on a lighter tone, almost white. It was brief, but it was enough to tell Rufus that what he said caught her off guard somehow.

"Oh really?" she said, turning back to her computer terminal. "That's weird. What made him want to ask you that?"

Rufus thought her response was a little too casual.

"Am I missing something?" he asked.

Jiya paused before answering.

"What would you be missing?" she asked, still not looking in his direction.

"Well, you seem a little edgy all of a sudden," Rufus said. "And you weren't that way until I told you what Connor said."

Jiya wished he would drop it. She knew she wasn't going to be able to keep up the charade much longer. Not only was she, by nature, a brutally honest person, but her time in 1880s San Francisco had hardened her. She was now a stronger woman than she used to be, and she was not going to allow herself to be pushed around by anyone.

"I'm not 'edgy,' just busy," she said firmly, trying to end the conversation. But Rufus was having none of it.

"You were fine until I told you what Connor was asking me about," he said. "I could see it in your face."

Jiya lowered her head. She wanted to lash out at him, to tell him he was harassing her and he needed to stop it. But, while she had hoped he had not, she knew now that he had seen her reaction. Jiya was not one of those people who could hide their emotions, so her first reactions to things nearly always gave away her thoughts.

Now her mind was racing to find a way to be honest with him, but to do it in such a way that he did not get offended, or resent her for her concerns. Knowing Rufus' sensitive nature, this was not going to be easy.

"Rufus, there was some discussion about commitment to the mission," she said clumsily. There was that brutal honesty, not entirely common for women with ancestors from India, but Rufus could tell it was just the tip of the iceberg.

"Who was doing the discussing?" he asked, although he was sure he already knew. "And about who?"

Jiya could tell by his tone that he was already starting to get a bit offended. Easing into what she had to say next was probably not the best approach, but it was the one she chose.

"Agent Christopher was talking to Wyatt about Lucy," she said. Jiya started to go on, to tell him about her involvement, but the words weren't coming out.

"And?" he prompted accusingly.

The jig was up; she had to come clean.

"I was there talking about you, OK," she said. "I called Agent Christopher and set up the meeting, and she had Wyatt be there, too."

Rufus' body went limp in his chair, and he slumped at the shoulders, his chin dropping into an open-mouth look of disappointment. He had a suspicion this was coming, but in his heart, he hoped that he was wrong. He felt betrayed in a way he hadn't since Connor tried to get him to record the rest of the team on their time jumps in the early months of their original missions.

Jiya felt like her stomach was tied in knots. She knew she had hurt him, and it tore at her inside like a jackhammer on concrete. His silence, with that look of betrayal on his face, made it even worse. She wanted to speak, but was afraid anything she said would just make things worse.

"You went to Agent Christopher about me?"

The question was asked in a way she knew he expected an explanation.

"You told me yourself that you didn't like the idea of keeping Hitler alive, and you said you didn't know how much longer you could be a part of it," she said, almost pleading.

"I was venting, Jiya," he snapped. "That was a conversation between you and me, not one to be shared."

He shook his head, looked away from her, and turned back to face her with such a look of disgust on his face that she felt like he was shooting daggers into her chest.

"And you brought Wyatt into it," he said.

Rufus had come to like and trust Wyatt. He respected him and wanted his respect. He was sure this would mean he would never get it.

"I didn't bring Wyatt into it, Agent Christopher did," she said angrily, now trying to defend herself.

"But now he knows you have doubts about me and that means Lucy knows, too," he said.

Jiya had composed herself and was now less in self-defense mode and more on the offensive.

"Wyatt said he knew we all felt that way, having doubts about keeping Hitler alive," she said. "No one is judging you, dammit!"

"You did, by going to Agent Christopher," Rufus said as he stood up and began walking toward the front door of the apartment.

"Rufus, I believe in you, and so does everyone else," Jiya said to his back as he kept walking.

Without looking back or slowing his step, Rufus gave her a dismissive wave and kept walking toward the front door. He opened it, turned, and threw her another look of disappointment and betrayal, walked through the door, and slammed it shut.

CHAPTER 13

Paulina sat at the desk in the warehouse office, computer in front of her. She had been researching for hours, preparing for the next time jump.

She was frustrated. In two jumps, they had failed to make any changes in history that would have saved her great-grandfather. Each time they returned, and she checked the history of the Red Tails, he was still shot down and killed. The same fate as in the original history befell her other relatives that she hoped to save in and following World War II.

Doubt about whether she would ever succeed began to form in her mind, but her determination overruled. Family was important to her. Restoring hers was the driving force behind all that she had done for so many years. Just like Garcia Flynn had attempted to do during the first year of the Lifeboat team's time travels.

He was unsuccessful in restoring his wife and daughters, who were murdered by Rittenhouse when they learned Flynn discovered they were bankrolling Mason Industries and reported it to his NSA superiors. But during a jump to 1969 to thwart an attempt by Flynn and his team to disrupt the Apollo 11 moon mission, Flynn breaks into a woman's home and injects her son with a shot of epinephrine to counter an anaphylactic reaction, then evades Wyatt's effort to capture him.

When the Lifeboat team returns to the present, they find that the woman whose home Flynn broke into was his mother, and the young boy he saved was his half-brother, Gabriel.

Just why it was that important for Paulina to restore her deceased family members was a little foggy to her.

Bringing her great-grandfather back to life would not affect her that much. By the time she was old enough to know him, he would be nearing his 90s. How would bringing him back have a positive effect on her family? She had no idea.

Because he had died so young, her great-grandfather left no legacy – except his son, and that he had died serving his country.

The same could be said for her uncle, killed in World War II. But other relatives that had been severely wounded in later conflicts had a little different story.

The best she could figure out is that it was important to restore her family, if for nothing else but to just keep it intact. She also believed bringing them back and avoiding their wounds would allow them to live full lives and create their own stories.

But if she saved her great-grandfather, or even all of them, would she even have followed the path she had in life? Would she have even created a time machine in the first place? And with no time machine, how could she go back and save her relatives?

The paradox of time was making her head spin and interfering with her research. She shook her head and tried to concentrate. Just as she did, there was a knock at the partially opened office door. She turned to see Bobby standing in the doorway.

"We've installed the jammer," he said.

Based on radar detector technology, they believed the device they put together should block whatever signal the other time travelers were using to detect their movement through time.

"But I'm not sure we'll know if it is working or not," he continued. "We'll only know if they don't show up. We should make a jump to anywhere just to test it out."

Paulina sighed. She knew he was right, but making a jump to somewhere other than the location and time connected with their established pattern might mean the others would not follow them. They had not done so for their test jumps or the trips to 1943 Italy. They could do a test jump, not see the others, and think the jammer had worked, only to find out on the next real jump that it had not.

"I know, Bobby," she answered. "But we have to assume it will work."

He did not agree. But he also knew arguing with her was a waste of time. Besides, he had other things he wanted to talk to her about. He slowly shut the door and hesitated before looking her way and beginning.

'I'm not so sure our next target time is the best option," he said.

She lowered her head and shook it from side to side.

"I disagree," she said. "This target takes us to a time when there are no recorded assassination attempts or other ways for him to be in danger," Paulina said. "It breaks our pattern. If the jammer doesn't work, it may throw them off because they won't have a clear idea what we're up to."

"But the target will put us in the heart of Germany at a time when security will be at its maximum," he argued. "It will be a lot harder for us to get near him."

Paulina was starting to get irritated. She was not accustomed to having her judgment questioned. But she worked to keep her tone as even as possible.

"We've been to a war zone and were able to get within inches of him," she said. "And there will be so many people from outside Germany there that will help us to blend in a lot better."

Bobby took a few steps toward her.

"Just how are we going to be able to get close enough to kill him in that environment?" he asked.

Paulina stood up from her chair and stepped toward Bobby until she was just a few feet away.

"I have it worked out, Bobby," she said firmly. "You need to trust me."

"You've had it 'worked out' twice before, and we failed both times," he shot back. As soon as he said it, he knew it was a weak argument. He also knew it would upset her.

"And if they had not interfered, we would have succeeded the first time, and if not, the second time," she said, raising her voice. She turned her back on him, trying to decide whether she should say what she wanted to say now. She finally made up her mind and faced him again.

"We're going to do this with or without you," she said. "So make up your mind."

His face went blank, and he stared at her as if he were looking right through her head to the wall behind her.

"And do it quickly, because we'll be going soon," she said, and walked out of the office, leaving him standing there staring blankly at the office's back wall.

The entire lifeboat team was in the bunker, and the tension was thick as molasses and hung in the air like the smog in Los Angeles.

Agent Christopher had called them all in because Connor had monitored the other time travelers as they made another jump. He tracked them to an isolated area in Switzerland, just across the border from Germany, in late July of 1936.

Once this information was passed to everyone, they all set out to prepare for their own jump. Discussion was conducted in a very business-like manner. The trust level between team members was at an all-time low following recent events.

"If they are going after Hitler again, they are nowhere near where he is," Lucy said. "He'll be in Berlin for at least the next month."

"How are you so sure where he'll be and for how long?" Jiya asked.

"Because he'll be at the Olympic Games in Berlin," she answered.

"Why would they be so far from there?" Agent Christopher asked. "Do you think they're after something else?"

Wyatt spoke before Lucy could answer. He said it was doubtful the other travelers' target and goal had changed. With two trips already under their belt with the goal of killing Hitler, they certainly wouldn't change their plans now.

"As to why they are where they are, it stands to reason they don't want to risk taking their time machine into Germany, where security is tight," he explained. "They've gone to an isolated part of a neutral country, and they'll travel to Berlin."

Lucy picked up the narrative.

"There are no known instances of Hitler being in harm's way during this period in time," she said. "Their last two attempts to kill him were at times when he was in harm's way. I think they picked this time, at least partly, to throw us off the track."

"And the other reasons?" Agent Christopher asked.

Lucy pondered the inquiry briefly before answering.

"Going to Berlin during the Olympics means there are a ton of variables for us to consider," she said. "There is no specific event in which he is in danger for us to focus on."

Wyatt chimed in.

"That means there are a number of methods of killing him we need to think about," he said. "We need to come up with the most likely scenarios and be prepared for as many of them as possible."

"That's going to take time," Rufus said. "Do we have that kind of time?"

At that time and in that world environment, travel time between Zurich and Berlin was about 12 hours to go the roughly 600 miles by the best mode at that time – train – Wyatt speculated.

"But they are foreigners and it won't be easy for them to get travel permits through Germany, even if they are prepared with false papers," Wyatt explained. "It could take up to a week, but if they are smart and have the right papers, it could be done in about three or four days."

This was no seat-of-the-pants guess. Being a member of the U.S. Army's Delta Force, Wyatt had experience with such preparations in modern-day Europe on special assignments. He knew that two days was the minimum time it would take in the present day. So he realistically knew it would take the other travelers longer in 1936.

"So let's get to work," Agent Christopher said. "You all do your parts, and let's meet again in four hours."

Wyatt strode over close to Agent Christopher and requested to talk to her privately. The pair moved away from the others, and they talked for just a few moments. Then Wyatt headed down the corridor toward the exit. Lucy glanced in his direction, but he did not look around.

Agent Christopher was angry, frustrated, and worried. She could tell that every Lifeboat team member was on edge more than usual before a mission. She had a pretty good idea why.

It was clear that the meeting between her, Wyatt, and Jiya had been shared with Lucy and Rufus. She knew that Wyatt and Lucy had a romantic relationship going. The ring on her finger was a dead giveaway, and she recalled her conversation with Lucy before the first time jump in which she discussed the relationship and how it might affect her performance.

As it turned out, her performance on missions had not wavered due to her feelings for Wyatt. In fact, settling their feelings for each other made her even stronger.

But Wyatt's revelation about her doubts about the goal of these latest jumps gave Agent Christopher pause. Wyatt assured her Lucy would continue to do her part, but Agent Christopher could not ignore her law enforcement training. She could spot hesitation in people, and she saw it in Lucy this night.

She saw it in Rufus as well, but she had seen it since the team returned from 1916 France. It was reinforced by little things he said and the disgusted look on his face whenever the subject of keeping Hitler alive came up.

This was her real concern in regards to the missions.

For the time being, she had to find a way to keep this team focused and on task. Agent Christopher knew that if history were changed to allow Germany to win World War II, it would have far-reaching impacts on the United States. As an agent of the Department of Homeland Security, it was her job to help protect the country.

And what if there were other changes to history? What would that do to the U.S., and so many other free nations and peoples? The possibilities were too gruesome for Agent Christopher to contemplate.

Once this particular threat was eliminated – if it could be – she could find replacements if necessary. But it was a prospect she also did not want to contemplate. Aside from the fact that the existing team knew the project intimately and training new people would be time-consuming, Denise did not want to lose the friends she had made.

Despite her stiff, business-like demeanor and approach to the task, she had become quite attached to all members of the Lifeboat team – even Connor. The mission in 1980 that changed her life drastically was a large factor in her affection for them. She allowed that bond to show briefly during the gathering following the conclusion of the mission to bring Rufus back. But to maintain a professional attitude about the project, she had kept it hidden most of the time.

She would miss these people if there were a need to replace any or all of them. It was not a possibility she wanted to entertain. But the nature of her job forced her to do so.

All these things were spinning in the back of her mind as she went about the business of preparing the team for their upcoming jump. She had to make sure they could move freely in Hitler's capital and try to make sure they were as safe as possible in that environment.

So she got in touch with her superiors and got the Homeland Security gears rolling. She needed to get the team members' passports, travel permits, identities, money – and it had to be the best forgeries the department could muster on short notice.

The entire Lifeboat team – plus one – was gathered in the common area, wearing the clothing they had selected for the trip, listening as Wyatt briefed them on the upcoming mission.

When he spoke with Agent Christopher briefly before leaving the bunker, he had told her of the team's need to act quickly to stay ahead of the other travelers. To do that, he suggested sending the Lifeboat into the heart of 1936 Berlin so they would be as close to the Olympic activities as they could. To do that, he had an idea of where to go.

He also wanted to get her permission to bring someone else onto the team.

At the beginning of the briefing, he introduced U.S. Army Delta Force Sergeant George Murphy, dressed as a German Army unterfeldwebel, or sergeant. His specialty was as a sniper.

Wyatt's first thought on hearing that the other travelers were in 1936 was that they hoped to kill Hitler using a sniper. Having no knowledge of who was working for the other group, he believed they had to assume there was someone, or more, with military experience.

"A study of the architecture and layout of the city during that time and from this perspective tells me it would be difficult to find a sniper's nest anywhere near the Olympic facilities or in the heart of Berlin that would give an experienced sniper an opportunity to make a successful shot and have the ability to escape," George explained to the team.

He added that his study was limited because looking back through old photos and street layouts available on the Internet did not give him the chance to see the lay of the land first-hand.

"The only way for me to do that is to actually be there," he said.

The impact of that statement was not lost on the team. Wyatt could see that in their faces.

"Are you saying you will be going along on this jump?" Rufus asked the sergeant.

"That's right," Wyatt answered for him. "He will be in the fourth seat of the Advanced Lifeboat."

So far, Flynn and Jiya had been the only other people besides Wyatt, Lucy, and Rufus to be on a Lifeboat mission.

"George will do a recon of the city, of the likely areas where we think something might be attempted, to help make a more strategic plan," Wyatt said. He could read on the faces of the team that they did not believe that would be justification enough to bring along another person, especially one new to the team. After all, Wyatt was also Delta Force trained and had provided plenty of military recon and advice on previous missions.

"That is only part of why George is coming along this time," Wyatt said. "Another one of his tasks is to guard the Advanced Lifeboat while we are away from it."

He paused to look around the room. The others were transfixed, waiting for him to continue.

"To be able to be in a position to act quickly, we have to be as close as possible to the Olympic sites and anywhere else Hitler might be," he said. "To do that, we need some way to secure the Advanced Lifeboat while we're in the city. That's the other part of George's job."

The team had been in situations before in which the Lifeboat was in danger of exposure, including war zones – the Alamo, 1944 Germany, and World War I, just to name a few. So far, there had been no need for protection, Rufus pointed out.

"But this time we are going into one of the most militarized, paranoid police states that we have ever been to," Agent Christopher said. "And we're going to be right in the back yard."

Her words told the others that she gave her sanction to Wyatt's plan.

"We're going to be there over multiple days, so we need to make sure no one discovers the Advanced Lifeboat," Wyatt said. "So we have a cover story and a plan."

Wyatt looked around the room. Normally, there were plenty of questions before a mission. But the tension between the team members remained, and no one was feeling too talkative. Agent Christopher could feel the tension, but did not want to make an issue of it for fear of enflaming it. But she believed she had to say something to keep the team focused.

"This team has been through a lot in the past three years," she said slowly, with a nod to Sergeant Murphy with the silent message, *"except you."* "And no doubt as we continue our missions to keep history straight, we'll go through a lot more." This time, her nod to Sergeant Murphy said, *"Welcome."*

At the beginning of her speech, the attention from team members was somewhat focused. But as the words came deliberately and firmly out of her mouth, their attention seemed to intensify. Seeing this, she warmed to her subject.

"One of the reasons we have come through all the tough times is because we have trusted each other, we've been there for each other,"

Agent Christopher continued. "In the last three years, I believe we have become a family. And good families stick together; they find ways to work together even through their own difficulties with each other."

While there had been personal issues in the previous years, Agent Christopher made that last statement as a reference to the most recent ones. She hoped the team got the reference. Glancing at each face in turn, she knew they each had. But just how they were taking it remained a mystery.

"We have a very important job to do," Agent Christopher began her wrap-up. Again, she looked at each face in turn before going on.

"They don't know it, but the world's people are depending on us to keep their futures safe," she said. "We can only do that if we recapture that feeling of closeness, that feeling of family that we used to have, and know that we can count on each other."

She stood and looked around the room for a few seconds. The somber looks on each face told her they knew how important their tasks were. But whether they had shed the feelings of distrust and betrayal she knew they all had simmering just under the surface was still a wild card.

"If there are no more questions or anything else to say, let's go get this thing done," Agent Christopher said.

Slowly, the Lifeboat team rose from its seats and started to move toward the time travel vehicle. Only the newcomer remained where he stood, until Wyatt motioned with a side nod of his head for the sergeant to follow. Not a word was spoken as Rufus climbed aboard, followed by Lucy, then Wyatt, then Sergeant Murphy.

As he was directed to the fourth seat, George looked out the hatch before it rolled closed. In those seconds, he could have sworn he saw Connor, Agent Christopher, and Jiya disappear, and the bunker filled with men and women in brown uniforms, red trim atop the collars, and red shoulder boards. He was also sure he saw one man with a brown peaked officer's cap with a red band above the visor. His head turned so that it was facing directly at the sergeant. On the front of the cap was a hammer and sickle.

CHAPTER 14

With Lucy and Rufus inside the Advanced Lifeboat, Wyatt and George, standing several feet away from the machine, talked about what was upcoming. They had parked the Advanced Lifeboat in a thick area of the Tegeler Forest on the west side of Lake Tegel. That put them several miles north of the Olympic Stadium and northwest of the government section of Berlin. They had stripped down to their shorts so as not to get their clothing sweaty and put the camouflage netting over the Advanced Lifeboat and fastened it to the ground with stakes. They then cleaned themselves off as best they could with wet wipes and put on each other's clothing.

George needed to do some reconnaissance within the city. He wanted to look over the route they knew from history Hitler would take to and from the Olympic Stadium, an eight-mile stretch beginning at the Reich Chancellery and Wilhemstrasse along the Via Triumphalis along Unter den Linden, through the Brandenburg Gate and onto Charlottenburger Chaussee, commonly known since the previous year as the East-West Axis, to the Reich Sports Field.

George was to go dressed in Wyatt's clothing so Wyatt could wear his German Army uniform while standing guard over the Advanced Lifeboat while the soldier was gone. It was no coincidence that he and Wyatt wore the same size clothing. Wyatt had picked him specifically for that reason, in addition to his Delta Force and sniper skills. They would switch outfits upon his return.

George's forged papers identified him as Unterfeldwebel Jurgen Moeller, attached to an infantry unit Wyatt knew from research was bivouwaced in the city to take part in the Olympic opening ceremonies parade. He would carry those ID documents while in the city; they would show that he belonged there and would give him almost unlimited access to wherever he needed to go.

"From looking at old maps and photos, I don't think there would be much opportunity along that route, but I'll double-check," George said. "It shouldn't take me more than four or five hours, and then I'll be back here."

"Keep as low a profile as possible," Wyatt advised. "Try to avoid too much interaction with people."

George nodded. He had done recon missions in hostile territory before. And, like Wyatt, he spoke fluent German. Wyatt didn't have to tell him how to do his job, but this was a very different situation than he had ever been in, and he appreciated any tidbits Wyatt, or any of the other team members, for that matter, could give him. After all, this was his first trip back in time, while they had made numerous time jumps.

"Got it," he responded. "If I get challenged by the military or government officials, that should at least give us an idea of how good all our documents are."

Wyatt touched the left pocket of his tunic. He would not use his identity papers if challenged at the time machine site while George was gone. They identified him as a civilian newspaper reporter from the United States. That would not do if he were in a German uniform. Instead, he carried a letter with Hitler's forged signature ordering anyone who read it to give the bearer any assistance they needed.

"It worked in 'The Eagle Has Landed,' I sure hope it works here," Wyatt had told Agent Christopher when she gave it to him. She had rolled her eyes and given him a sarcastic smile.

"This isn't a movie," she had said. "But there is evidence that something like this had worked multiple times in real life back then."

George checked his watch. It was eight o'clock in the morning, and he knew it was Friday, July 31, the day before the start of the 1936 summer Olympic Games.

Under an overcast sky, he turned and set out for Berlin, the heart of the most evil empire the world had ever known.

With only brief steps outside to stretch their legs and cool off a little from the humidity inside the all-metal vehicle, always after first getting the all-clear from Wyatt, Lucy, and Rufus, spent their time inside the time vehicle during the day. For the most part, it was silent time. Rufus spent much of the time checking and re-checking the machine's systems.

Lucy, using the thumb drive she brought with her, kept going over information on the events for the first week in August 1936 in Berlin. She wanted to make sure there was nothing she had missed that could affect their efforts.

Except for a few times when they spoke on matters related to what they were doing, the pair said nothing of significance to each other. That changed around midday.

"So, does it bother you that Wyatt doesn't trust you?" Rufus blurted out suddenly.

Lucy was caught off guard, not just because they had not spoken at all for about an hour, but also by the question.

"Why does he think Wyatt doesn't trust me?" she thought as she tried to formulate an answer.

"Wyatt does trust me," she said firmly. "And I trust him."

"Really?" Rufus said in disbelief. "Then why did he go to Agent Christopher to question your commitment to the team and the missions?"

Lucy hesitated only long enough to compose her thoughts. She did not want to create a situation in which Rufus' commitment to the mission at hand would be compromised. She also did not know whether Rufus and Jiya had talked openly about the meeting and, if they had, whether Jiya had told him it was she who initiated the meeting.

"Wyatt went to her because she asked for the meeting," Lucy said calmly. "She wanted his input on issues that had come up."

"You mean Jiya saying she wasn't sure about me?" Rufus said with a touch of disgust in his voice.

"So they have spoken about the meeting," Lucy thought to herself. That allowed her to expand her end of the conversation.

"Yes, she did," Lucy said. "But she did it for a good reason."

Rufus huffed and shook his head.

"If she doesn't trust me, I guess that is a pretty good reason," he said sarcastically. But Lucy detected a bit of hurt feelings in the response.

"I believe she does trust you, Rufus," Lucy said.

The *"Oh really,"* look on his face spoke for him.

"Just because she had concerns about your commitment does not mean she does not trust you," Lucy said.

"That is ridiculous," Rufus said, turning back to the instruments in front of his seat. "She told Agent Christopher I couldn't be trusted on these missions."

Lucy slapped the arm of the chair she was sitting in. The gesture got Rufus' attention.

"According to Wyatt, that is not what she said," Lucy said.

"Not in those words, but that was the message," Rufus replied, staring at her, waiting for a response.

Lucy recapped in her mind the conversation she and Wyatt had after the Agent Christopher meeting. She also remembered her own misgivings about keeping Hitler alive. They remained in her mind, but the rational side of her was overcoming the emotional and telling her that what they were doing was something they must do to keep history on its correct track.

"Rufus, you are forgetting that you are talking to someone who also had the one person in her life who she expected to have total trust in her, talk to Agent Christopher, too, about her commitment," Lucy said, then took a breath before she went on.

"You can trust someone unconditionally but still have concerns about their performance," she said. "Those are two very different things."

Rufus started to respond, but Lucy held up an index finger to stop him.

"And the fact is, if Jiya didn't trust you, her talk with Agent Christopher would have been a demand to have you removed from the team," Lucy said.

Again, Rufus tried to respond, but the index finger came up again. She was on a roll.

"She went to Agent Christopher because she trusts you, she cares about you, and she loves you," Lucy said. "But she also went to her because I'm sure she has her own misgivings about keeping Hitler alive. But she knows what we are doing is the right thing to do."

She paused for a moment, the index finger in her lap. She was ready to hear what Rufus' argument would be. But he only sat looking at her, clearly rolling her words over in his mind.

"We are all struggling with this, Rufus," she said when he did not utter a word. "Every single one of us."

He sat silent for a moment before speaking again.

"I know, I just...."

He broke off in mid-sentence to the sound of a voice he did not recognize from outside the Advanced Lifeboat.

"Was machst sie hier?"

Lucy and Rufus, as quietly and stealthily as they could, moved to either side of the vehicle hatch and stood listening, not daring to peek outside.

Lucy could not help herself and very slowly moved her head so she could see outside for about two seconds, then pulled her head back. In that time, she saw a uniformed soldier confronting Wyatt. Just as she pulled her head back, she saw Wyatt reach into his tunic pocket and take out a piece of paper.

The Hitler letter," she thought.

"Wie heissen Sie?"

"Unterfeldwebel Hans Gruber!" Wyatt replied sharply, clicking his heels and giving the military salute, his right arm straight out, bent at the elbow with his angled hand touching the brim of his field cap.

The soldier read the letter, then re-read it. He then carefully refolded it into the tri-fold and handed it back to Wyatt.

"Weiter mit Ihren aufgaben," the soldier said, turned on his heel, and walked away without looking back. Wyatt stayed at rigid attention until the soldier was out of sight, then turned and walked to the

Advanced Lifeboat hatch, where Lucy and Rufus remained on either side of the opening.

"What was that all about?" Lucy asked.

"I don't know if it was a routine patrol or just some guy wandering around," Wyatt answered. "But at least we know the letter works. He was a major. He went a little green in the gills when he read it."

Rufus poked his head around the edge of the hatch, a smile starting to form at the corners of his mouth.

"Did you just tell that guy your name was Hans Gruber?" he asked, the smile growing.

"It seemed appropriate," Wyatt said deadpan.

Rufus started to giggle, and Wyatt showed the hint of a smile. Lucy stood with a confused look on her face, then held her hands out at her sides, palms up.

"'Die Hard,'" Rufus said, but he got no response from her. "You know, Alan Rickman, the terrorist at Nakatomi Plaza." Still nothing. "Bruce Willis played John McClane, a New York cop who…"

Holding up his hands, palms out, Wyatt stopped him in mid-sentence. He then looked at Lucy.

"Don't give it away," he said. "We'll watch it when we get home."

That made Lucy smile.

"How does someone not know about 'Die Hard'?" Rufus muttered to himself and went back to the Advanced Lifeboat control console.

To make sure they were ready for any more interlopers, George, now back in his German uniform, stood outside the Lifeboat hatch as he briefed Wyatt, sitting on the floor just inside the hatch, and Lucy and Rufus, sitting in the nearest of the four seats inside the time machine.

George had returned to the small clearing in the wooded area about two hours after the German officer had confronted Wyatt. He was careful about his approach, making sure there was no one in the area when he moved toward the time machine. Wyatt had encountered a few civilians wandering in the area, but when they saw a uniformed soldier guarding what was clearly a camouflaged piece of military hardware, they steered clear. No other military officers came to the clearing.

George gave the others a rundown of his day, including walking the route Hitler would take to and from the Olympic Stadium, checking selected buildings, and a brief recon of the Olympic Sports Field itself. He then went into a detailed analysis.

"From a sniper's point of view, this would be a tough nut to crack, even for a seasoned shooter, which, from what you tell me, these people are not," he said.

He explained that the main streets along the route were lined with monuments and tall, red Nazi banners.

"That would make a side or angle shot difficult from street level up to building roofs," he explained.

"What about a shot with the target heading straight to or from the shooter's perch?" Wyatt asked.

"Possible, but hard enough for a pro," George said. "For a less experienced shooter -- impossible."

He also explained that setting up a sniper's position would be tough because of the heightened security. He said guards were everywhere, as it seemed the entire German armed forces were pressed into security duty in the capitol, along with the city police, the Gestapo, and the Ordnungspolizei, the state police.

"They are going through buildings constantly on roving patrols," George said. "Very few of them are in uniform -- the Germans are trying to paint a peaceful picture -- but I had no trouble spotting them."

He did say there were two possible sniper vantage points that would be promising -- a domed building at one end of Unter den Linden and the Olympic bell tower.

"But the Germans surely know how important they are and have them well buttoned up," George said.

"So it's unlikely we're dealing with a sniper attempt," Wyatt said, half asking.

"I wouldn't say it was out of the question," George said. "But damned near."

"What about a bomb?" Lucy asked.

George considered that for a moment.

"I would discount anything being planted on his vehicle or anywhere in the stadium," he said. "The security is too tight."

"There were instances when things were thrown into his car during parades," Lucy said.

During public parades and when he was being taken from place to place, Hitler was driven in a mammoth, armor-plated Mercedes-Benz 770K Grosser. The top was always removed during parades because the dictator often stood up and waved to the crowds. People, mostly adoring women, threw flowers and other gifts at the vehicle, with some actually making it inside.

"That's a possibility," George said. "But I think in this case it is remote."

He explained that even the day before the Olympic opening day, the streets along the route were crowded with people -- both along the sides of the wide boulevards and in the medians.

"I think someone would be extremely lucky to even be in a position to toss something into a car," he said. "And even if they were, they'd have to get by the out runners. Even trying would draw too much attention."

George also said that based on historic photos of Berlin parades in which Hitler was involved, soldiers lined the sides of the streets and, if crowds pushed forward, they locked their arms to form a human barrier fence.

Lifeboat team members looked to one another in turn. It was sounding like they were facing an impossible task -- figure out a method, location, timing, and countermeasures, and more, all without a clue beforehand about the connecting factor. In 1916, it was Hitler's war wound, and in 1923, it was the failed coup attempt. But there were no known assassination attempts on Hitler during the Olympic Games.

"This is like finding a needle in a haystack," Rufus said.

"A needle in a field of haystacks," Wyatt thought, looking at Lucy.

"Is there anything we've overlooked?" he asked her.

She had a pained look on her face when she answered.

"I'm at a loss," she said. "George's arguments against all the things I was thinking make sense."

Wyatt thought for a few moments, looking at everyone in turn. There was no doubt this was the most difficult mission they had been on yet. *The other travelers sure threw us a curveball on this one,* he thought.

But he had been in tougher situations on overseas missions with the Delta Force, and they always found a way. He was certain the Lifeboat team would find a way in these circumstances.

"We're just going to have to be flexible, and very alert," he told everyone. He then climbed out of the Advanced Lifeboat and motioned with his head for George to follow as he headed away from the machine, leaving the others where they were. They stood just inside the camo netting on the opposite side from the hatch and spoke in low volume.

"So, what do you think?" Wyatt asked.

George took a moment to replay his thoughts during the day and the conclusions he developed from his observations.

"Nothing is really off the table," he began. "The things I said were unlikely or difficult, still are, but they are all still possibilities."

The disappointment and frustration were clear on Wyatt's face.

"There is one possibility that I did not touch on," George said. "Through the years leading up to and during World War II, there were myriad opportunities for people to just walk up to Hitler and pull out a pistol and blow his brains out. Even he pointed that out after the July 20 bomb plot failed. He called those who tried to kill him cowards because they did not do that."

This was a possibility that Wyatt had considered. But having seen the other travelers up close, he discounted it. Their previous attempts had shown a desire to make the death of Hitler look as natural to the circumstances, and to history, as possible. Injecting Hitler's wound in World War I would have made it seem that he died of his wound. While he did not know their specific endgame in 1923, whether it was to talk him into suicide or killing him outright, anything they did to kill him then could have been explained away as a natural consequence of the failed coup.

It was also clear to Wyatt that the other travelers were not willing to kill the dictator and be killed themselves in the process. They wanted to survive to see the result of their handy work.

"The only way they could just shoot him and survive the attempt themselves is to get him alone, and I don't think that is very likely at all in this atmosphere," Wyatt said.

George agreed, but still believed the possibility had to be kept on the list of not-so-likely ifs.

"Then there is something else," George said.

Wyatt braced himself for what could come next.

"I gotta wonder why we don't just let this guy die; maybe even help it along," he said. "Just think what we would avoid if he were gone from history."

Wyatt was a little taken aback. That was not a line of thinking he expected from his comrade. He had explained to George the basic concepts of what could happen with a changing timeline. He decided it was time for a more detailed briefing. He gave George all the details of the previous missions by the Lifeboat team, the loss of Lucy's sister, Jessica brought back to life, then having to die again to put the timeline right again, all the small details of history that were changed, even though they were able to correct history so far.

The briefing took a couple of hours, but by the end, George was thoroughly convinced.

They went to the front of the time vehicle to explain to Lucy and Rufus, who had been tempted to go looking for them, what they had discussed.

CHAPTER 15

Wyatt, Lucy, and Rufus were up early from a restless sleep in the Advanced Lifeboat August 1, 1936, opening day for what was even then called the Nazi Olympics. They took a taxi to central Berlin to begin a not-so-leisurely stroll down the city's "main street." George stayed behind to guard the machine in their absence.

The plan was to get as close to the Reich Chancellery as possible and walk the route that Hitler would take just ahead of the car in which he was riding, so they could scan the crowds looking for the faces they had seen on other jumps. It would be a daunting task, as they learned even before the taxi got them to their destination, as the sidewalks along all the streets in the city center were clogged with people.

They could not get any closer to the chancellery than Unter den Linden, just east of the Brandenburg Gate, several blocks away. Wyatt decided that it would not hamper their efforts because if they couldn't get any closer, neither could the other time travelers. The Lifeboat team set itself up on the western end of Unter den Linden, about twenty blocks west of where the River Spree turns south and splits to form an island before turning southeast.

This was a few blocks; they knew from studying German files from the U.S. National Archives, from where the motorcade taking Der Führer to the Olympic Stadium turned onto Unter den Linden. The motorcade would then go through the gate and continue on Charlottenburger Chaussee. They arrived at the location about ten o'clock in the morning, but Hitler was not scheduled to leave the chancellery until three o'clock in the afternoon.

To fill the time, Wyatt suggested they walk the eight-mile route and back to see if they could spot anyone they knew. He was aware that when the motorcade started, the crowds would be larger, if that were even possible. Walking the route now might make it easier to see individual faces in the crowd.

Rufus was skeptical, but went along with the plan.

However, this early in the day, the street was still open to traffic. Lucy, knowing the eight-mile walk would be tough enough one way, suggested they take a streetcar for the first leg and walk back. On the streetcar, they could scan the crowd as they went. It was drizzling, and the streetcar would also help them dry out and not have them already soaked for the walk back.

Wyatt agreed, but though he was thankful for the shorter time spent walking, Rufus remained uncertain that the scouting would bring any results, among other reasons.

When they boarded the streetcar, one of Rufus' worries became reality when the trio -- but mostly Rufus -- became the target of angry stares. Clearly, Hitler's philosophy of Aryan superiority was ever-present on this streetcar.

In an attempt to deflect the German passengers' bigotry, Wyatt spoke in German to those within earshot.

"Hello, we are American journalists here to report on your Olympic games, and your nation," he said. "We're hoping to report that we were well received and welcomed."

He used a polite tone, but it was underlined with a firmness that most Germans, steeped in order and discipline, understood very well. His efforts seemed to bear fruit, as the stares were averted. But the stolen glances here and there showed he had not changed any minds in the long run. It was just Germans putting on a good face for the visitors as they had been instructed to do.

Lucy went to one side of the car to look through the window at the passing crowd, and Wyatt went to the other. Rufus positioned himself a few feet away from Wyatt so he could watch out the back window. But he stayed close enough to his companion to be within his sphere of defense if it was needed.

They made the ride in silence, not speaking to each other or anyone around them. They existed the streetcar at Kaiser Fredrich Strasse, a little more than halfway to the Olympic Stadium from where they started.

For the walk back up the straight line of the street through the Tiergarten, Wyatt took the south side of the street alone while Lucy and Rufus walked the north side. The streetcar ride was more subdued because they were inside a vehicle, and the early bigotry they encountered was stunted after Wyatt's short speech. But on the walk back to their eastern starting point, each Lifeboat team member had a different approach and perspective.

Wyatt strolled along the sidewalk with the bearing of a military man on a mission -- which is exactly what he was. That and his gray suit and thin tie, worn a little loose at the collar, and fedora hat made him appear like any other German man strolling the main street of the capitol city. His pace was steady, but not quick. He took his time surveying the faces around him and trying to look over the crowds in the wide median of the busy boulevard.

He tried to keep the same pace as Lucy and Rufus, dressed much like he was, but his suit was a milk chocolate brown shade over a dark shirt with a thin bow tie, and he wore no hat. He could occasionally see them across the expensive street. Like Wyatt, they tried to walk as close to the roadway as possible so they could look at the people along the sidewalk and in the median. They were easy for Wyatt to spot, partly because Rufus was the only black man in the crowd and partly because of what Lucy was wearing.

She had chosen a bright red blouse with a flowery ruffle on the left breast, with a brown skirt that went down to mid-calf. The skirt had large, round decorative buttons down the left side. She also wore an off-white hat that looked something like a fedora but with a wider, floppy brim with a brown band, matching her skirt, above the brim. The hat was worn jauntily, cocked down to the right, covering the top of her ear.

Her wide smile was also not hard to spot. It was plastered on her face the entire way, with only a few exceptions. The reason was because of her attitude -- she looked upon this opportunity much like a tourist seeing a new place for the first time.

While Lucy kept in her mind the true reason they were there, she could not help but revel in the fact that she was in 1936 Berlin for a very historic occasion. She was a historian at heart. She could not help it.

There was no doubt about the fact that, before it was ravaged by World War II, Berlin was a beautiful city. As they began the walk east, Lucy marveled at the old world architecture mixed with what was then considered more modern buildings. She noticed how clean the building facades and the streets were. That was only partly due to the fact that the Germans, especially those in the seats of power, wanted to present their best for the world during the Olympics. But she knew the spit and polish discipline that was the German way meant not much effort was needed to make that impression.

As their walk took them into the Tiergarten, the magnificent wooded park that was the jewel of the city, she was awed, as were Rufus and Wyatt. They had all been to New York City's Central Park in the 2000s, and all three Lifeboat team members believed the Tiergarten, even from their limited perspective from the street, was better.

Rufus made the walk in fear and almost total paranoia. He was well aware that he was the only black person along the route, and those angry stares met him with every step. He expected to be surrounded at some point by Hitler Youth, Gestapo, or even regular citizens and either beaten or arrested -- or both.

Several times, he was stopped by men in the trademark overcoats of the Gestapo and ordered to show his papers. Agent Christopher had perfect identification papers and passports made for all four Lifeboat team members on this jump. George, of course, was given a different name and IDed as a Wehrmacht soldier. But Lucy, Rufus, and Wyatt, using their real names, were IDed as American journalists there to cover the games.

During each of these stops, Lucy's papers passed muster without even a second look. Rufus, however, was under much more scrutiny. The first time this happened, Rufus stood frozen in terror, expecting to be hauled to the infamous Gestapo headquarters on the Prinz Albrecht Strasse and the feared "interrogation" rooms there.

After it appeared the Gestapo officers were about to do just that, Lucy stepped in as forcefully as she could and demanded Rufus be left alone.

"You leave him alone. We are both American journalists as guests in your country," she said. "If you have problems with his papers, you should contact this man."

Lucy handed the two officers, only one of whom spoke English, a business card for William Dodd, American ambassador to Germany at the time. Agent Christopher had provided each of them a handful of the cards she had made up. They were instructed to use them if they faced imminent arrest or detention.

"He is the American ambassador to your country," she added, in case they didn't understand.

The English-speaking officer spoke to his comrade, frowned at the card, then handed it back to Lucy.

"You can go on your way," he snorted tersely, then added, "But I suggest you be more careful about the men you allow to accompany you. Others may not be as forgiving as we are."

The officers then turned on their heels and walked away. Lucy took a step toward them to get in a few last words, but Rufus caught her arm, which caught the attention of some people standing nearby.

"Oh no, don't push our luck -- or mine," he said, releasing her arm as he saw people giving him a menacing look.

She began to protest, to say he or she did not deserve to be treated like that. But the look of fear on his face reminded her where and when she was, and she relaxed.

The other encounters went about the same, but Rufus was a little more confident. Lucy used the ambassador's card each time, and each time the officers handed it back to her, not wanting to create a scene with an American diplomatic official that would embarrass their Führer.

Lucy was thankful they had given the cards back. Had they followed up with the ambassador's office, a search of the list of accredited American journalists would have revealed they were not on the list, and wouldn't that have made an interesting footnote in history?

As the Lifeboat team was nearly through the Tiergarten, the trio came to a point where they could see the Victory Column through the trees to the north of Charlottenburger Chaussee, with the burned-out Reichstag building directly east of it. The Victory Column was a symbol of the Prussian victory in the Franco-German War in the 19th century. The Reichstag was the German parliament building until it was gutted by fire in February 1933, allegedly by a Communist sympathizer.

From across the street, Wyatt watched Lucy and Rufus staring at the structures. He wondered if either knew the Victory Column had been moved in 1939 to a location on Charlottenburger Chausse in the center of a roundabout that three other streets fed into. The move was part of Hitler's plans to redesign the German capitol city.

They all, Lucy in particular, vowed to themselves not to get distracted on this jump as if they were tourists. But it was a harder task to accomplish than to think about. They were in a very historical period, and things would look so much different in just a decade.

As part of her cover identification, Lucy brought an Exekta VP Type B camera complete with black and white film. She really wanted to get a couple of shots of the column and the Reichstag. Lucy and Rufus fast-walked up a side street about two blocks to get some photos. She tried to get Rufus in one of the shots, but he turned his back when she pointed the camera, and his face was not visible.

After seeing Jiya's photo in 1880s San Francisco, he wasn't sure he wanted to be caught on camera in the past.

Wyatt caught sight of the pair admiring the sites and Lucy taking pictures. He smiled and shook his head. He knew she couldn't resist being a tourist. He waited for them to return to Charlottenburger Chaussee.

The scene was repeated, only a few minutes longer, when they reached the Brandenburg Gate. Built in the 8th century on the orders of Prussian King Frederick William II after the successful restoration of order during the early Batavian Revolution, it was constructed on the site of a former city gate that marked the start of the road from Berlin to the town of Brandenburg an der Havel, which used to be the capitol of the Margraviate of Brandenburg.

The Brandenburg Gate, the Victory Column, and the Reichstag were significant objects for Lucy. They were three German structures that not only survived World War II but also other acts of vandalism or relocation through the years before and after the war.

Lucy finished one roll of film shooting the gate, then reloaded the camera. Just as she was closing the camera, she and Rufus heard a low hum. They looked around for the source and saw others looking up into the sky. On the west side of the gate, they had a clear view down Charlottenburger Chaussee and beyond, and when they looked up, they saw a giant silver airship cruising leisurely parallel to the street above the south portion of the Tiergarten. As it drew closer, they could see the Olympic rings and the inscription "XI Olympiade Berlin 1936" painted on its side. The Olympic flag hung from the huge zeppelin's gondola. Lucy raised the camera and snapped a few photos.

They didn't need to see the swastikas emblazoned on the ship's tail fins to know it was the Hindenburg. In a little more than nine months, the mighty symbol of German air power would burst into flames over the airfield in Lakehurst, New Jersey -- and the Lifeboat team would be there on its first mission.

But the event had two significant differences from the established story when that mission was completed. The airship did not explode at the mooring mast during landing; it was later that night, as the ship left Lakehurst. But the change that had the most personal effect was that somehow, because of the slight change in how things happened, Lucy lost her sister Amy -- she simply disappeared from history.

Rufus saw Lucy's posture sag and watched tears start to roll down her face as she lowered the camera to her chest. He was at a loss as to what to do to comfort her. If he hugged her, or even touched her arm, he knew that because of the time and place in history they were in, he could be arrested, or worse.

"Lucy," he said softly. When she did not react, he said it louder. After a third time at a higher octave, which drew some stares from people around them, she started, as if being brought out of a trance.

She looked at Rufus with some confusion on her face, then she gave the faintest hint of a smile and mouthed, *"I'm okay."*

Lucy then shot a few more pictures of the airship as it floated majestically eastward. Then, with Rufus' urging, they moved on up Unter den Linden to the point where they had started, where Wyatt would join them. It was nearly three o'clock in the afternoon, the time when Hitler and his entourage would leave the Reich Chancellery for the trip to the Olympic Stadium.

Wyatt came strolling across the street, which had been cleared of traffic, and joined them after first being stopped. He was told he could not go into the street. But after showing his documents and explaining his journalist status and that he was joining his colleagues on the other side, they let him pass. He saw Lucy's face with her eyes slightly red and the dried streaks of tears down her cheeks.

"What's wrong?" he asked, taking her hands in his.

"Nothing," Lucy said, dabbing her runny nose with a handkerchief. "I'm fine."

With the fading hum of the Hindenburg in his ears, Wyatt was pretty sure he knew the answer to his own question. He decided there was no need for further discussion about it unless she brought it up. The time had come to focus on the task at hand.

"I didn't see anyone we've seen before, but with this crowd, it's hard to see everyone," Wyatt told the others. They agreed.

"I checked with some people and the motorcade, where the street is divided, will go down the north lanes, just like normal traffic does," Wyatt explained. "So, we'll stay together this time."

He further said he did not believe anyone would make any kind of attempt to assassinate Hitler from the median, as it would be difficult to escape afterward because they would be hemmed in by the crowd and the multitude of soldiers on each side of the wide boulevard. That meant they could concentrate on a smaller crowd.

Wyatt also suggested they be separated by one block as they advanced down the street. Wyatt would stay just ahead of Hitler's vehicle, while Rufus would be a block ahead and Lucy another block ahead of him.

"This will increase our surveillance area," he explained.

As soon as he saw the motorcade approaching the intersection, he sent Lucy and Rufus to their posts ahead of him.

The walk back down the Berlin street leading to the Olympic Stadium had different feels for each Lifeboat team member.

His military training kept Wyatt alert to the mission the entire way. Scanning the crowd for those familiar faces was his priority. But as with the first walking tour of the street, it was difficult to pick out specific faces in such a crowd, especially now that it was larger.

Wyatt tried to stay as close to the street as possible, both to see faces from the front or profile and to watch the motorcade, which was keeping a fairly steady pace of about twenty miles per hour. That speed meant Wyatt had to set a good pace to keep up, but at the same time, it also made it hard for anyone from the crowd to approach the Führer's car without being intercepted by security forces.

Wyatt watched the car intently while scanning the crowd as it made its way around the first corner and traveled the first couple of blocks on Unter den Linden, through the Brandenburg Gate, and onto Charlottenburger Chaussee. Hitler stood up in the front right seat of the car with his left hand, encased in a leather glove, on the windshield frame and and his right hand going up and down in his distinctive salute with the arm straight out in front of him, bent upward at the elbow in what looked like a dismissive wave. This was in opposition to the official Nazi salute -- arm straight out in front, tilted upward at about a forty-five degree angle. He looked from side to side slowly, scanning the crowd, and occasionally looking down and speaking to the driver.

Twice, Wyatt caught Hitler looking in his direction -- it seemed right at him. Both times, Hitler turned to the driver and said a few words, and the driver looked in Wyatt's direction as well.

Rufus, on the other hand, walked further back in the crowd, hoping to avoid prying eyes. It worked to an extent, as some at the back of the crowd gave him long stares as he passed by.

Once he saw the two Gestapo men who had stopped him and Lucy on their first walk up the street. They were at the front of the crowd, and one of them started to thread his way through the throng, but his partner stopped him and said a few words. They both watched him as Rufus continued on his way, still quite self-conscious.

Rufus noticed the pace of the motorcade was faster than they had expected. He quickened his pace, but as they entered the Tiergarten, he decided to catch up to Lucy and warn her. However, he knew she would be near the front of the crowd so she could scan faces. At the next intersection, the start of Charlottenburger Chausse, he found her about three people deep in the crowd.

"We're going to have to go faster to keep pace and stay ahead of Wyatt," he said as he settled in by her side.

"Easy for you to say," she said, looking down at her feet.

To match her outfit, Lucy had chosen a pair of pointed-toe, narrow shoes with two-inch heels.

"I dressed to impress, not for walking," she said as they started to move faster. "Or jogging."

Lucy had begun to feel the effects of so much walking in the heels even before they got back to their starting point. But she was pushing on. She had thought of taking the shoes off, but it was still drizzling and the pavement and sidewalks were damp. Beyond getting her stockings wet, she was concerned the ultra-thin layer of water would be slippery on the nylons, and she risked falling.

The pair worked their way to the back of the crowd as they continued down the street. It was there that they could make better time. Wyatt had come independently to the same conclusion about faster travel.

Lucy and Rufus reached Bismark Strasse and had gained about one block of extra distance between themselves and the motorcade when they heard someone calling their names. They turned to look up the street and saw Wyatt jogging toward them.

"Hitler's car is going fast enough that he'll beat us there if we keep looking at people," Wyatt said as he reached them. "That speed will also keep anyone else from getting to the car."

They walked at a fast pace until they were near the Grosser Stem, where a taxi was parked nearby on Altonear Strasse, pointing northwest. Wyatt spoke to the driver in German, then beckoned the others to get in. As Rufus climbed into the back seat, the driver got a sour look on his face.

"Nein, nicht der Neger," he spat.

Rufus spoke no German, but it was painfully obvious what the driver was saying. Before he could react, Wyatt stepped in.

"Yes, all of us," he snapped in German with his military tone. "We are American journalists here reporting the Olympics. Would it look good for you if we reported in our newspapers and on the radio that we were so discriminated against in your country? We make daily reports. This would get back to your Propaganda Ministry tomorrow."

Lucy, standing near the front left fender, lifted her camera as if to take the driver's photo.

"Geldstrafe," he replied angrily. "Fur das doppelte des fahrprciscs."

Wyatt nodded and motioned for Lucy to get in the cab.

"Just get us there fast," Wyatt said in German and gave the driver their desired destination.

They began to speed down the street. They were at the stadium in fifteen minutes.

CHAPTER 16

The taxi driver dropped the Lifeboat team at the front of the Olympic Stadium, and the light rain they had experienced all morning had finally stopped, and the sun was peeking through the clouds. The nearly one-hundred-thousand paid and complimentary ticket holders were already in their seats, having been entertained since about one o'clock in the afternoon. But there were still a large number of people milling about.

It was clear to all that the German regime was using the Olympic Games as a way to showcase what they had accomplished since being "betrayed" by the Treaty of Versailles. The Nazis also wanted to prove the superiority of the "Aryan race." What better way to do that than to dominate a sporting event that included the majority of nations on Earth?

There was no doubt of the accomplishments of the Nazi regime in the previous three years since Hitler's rise to power. The number of unemployed had been reduced by four million, the Autobahn was initiated, which gave Germany a modern road network unequaled anywhere in Europe, and, like his Italian counterpart, Benito Mussolini, Hitler had the trains running on time.

The summer and winter Olympic Games had been awarded to Germany long before Hitler came to power. But the dictator was determined to use them for his benefit.

The winter games had been conducted the previous February in Gamisch-Partenkirchen, and right away the Nazis were dealt a blow when that area experienced its worst snow drought in a quarter century. But on the eve of the opening ceremonies, snow began to fall, and it turned out to be ideal conditions.

The International Olympic Committee, in a 43-16 vote in May 1931, awarded the 1936 summer games to Berlin. The government at that time revived plans to remodel the national stadium to increase capacity to sixty-five thousand. But when Hitler came to power in January 1933, plans changed to take full advantage of the propaganda opportunities of the games.

Hitler himself decided to use a third design by brothers Werner and Weller March for the Olympic Stadium. The work began in 1934 and was completed in time for the games. The plans called for the demolition of the existing national stadium in favor of a new structure. It was built in the form of a large oval in the monumental Neoclassical style favored by the Nazis, twelve meters below ground level and thirteen above, creating a commanding, highly visible building. In that they succeeded.

Wyatt had visited the stadium on one of his European excursions for the Delta Force. By then, it had been repaired after minor damage sustained during the war and renovated. He was there for a soccer match, and the stands were only about half full, and the seating areas were covered all the way around. It was impressive even with all those empty seats. But it would pale in comparison to what he would see once they were inside in 1936.

Wyatt let Lucy take a few pictures of the twin pillars with the Olympic rings suspended between them that served as the stadium plaza entrance. He then ushered her and Rufus to hurry around the stadium, with its upper seating and two-story colonnade supported by 136 Germanic pillars, to the large Mayfield on the western side of the massive structure. This was where the athletes were positioned for Hitler's entrance. It was where Wyatt now suspected an attempt might be made to kill the dictator.

"With all those people there, it would give someone plenty of places to hide among them," he explained as they fast walked.

Until he was seated in his private box inside the stadium, Hitler would be out in the open and vulnerable.

The trio showed their media IDs and positioned themselves at the edge of the small, flat plaza adjacent to the Marathon Gate at the west end of the stadium. They were facing the bell tower across the Mayfield, from where Hitler would make his appearance.

"This is going to be even worse to spot something happening than the street was," Rufus said.

"Just keep your eyes open," Wyatt said, putting a pair of binoculars, the same ones he had used in Bavaria in 1923, to his eyes.

The procession of International Olympic Committee members, Hitler, and other officials had started across the large field. The athletic teams, in their respective country groups, were lined up on opposite sides of the field, and the group of dignitaries passed between them through an aisle about twenty yards wide. Each national team was identified by a sign and their national flag at the head of the individual nation groups.

When Hitler, in the procession lead, was about halfway through the trek, with the athlete groups lined up on either side of him, Wyatt caught sight of a woman walking out of one national group. She was walking slowly and deliberately, a bouquet of flowers in her hand, toward the aisle. Dressed exactly like the Indian athletes, the woman walked straight ahead at a pace that would have her meet Hitler just as he came even with the Indian team, the second-to-last group he would pass.

The action was so unexpected that only two people noticed at first, and only two reacted. Hitler turned his head to follow her progress, and Wyatt started to jog toward her. Despite her Indian costume, he recognized Paulina.

As the woman reached Hitler, she extended her hand with the bouquet and bowed slightly at the waist. He reached out his right hand and grasped the flowers. But at that moment, he began to feel a familiarity with the woman, as if he had seen her before. Out of the corner of his eye, he saw Wyatt being restrained by two soldiers.

"Halt! Ihn Freizulassen," Hitler shouted, and motioned for Wyatt to come forward. Still holding the flowers, Hitler nodded to Paulina and motioned for her to return to the Indian team, his recollection of her forgotten. Paulina complied, but kept a steady gaze on the pair.

"I know you," Hitler said in German. "Henry, is it not?"

Wyatt was only slightly surprised because he knew of the man's incredible capacity for recall, at least during this period of his life.

"Yes, sir," Wyatt responded in the Fuhrer's language, in his best firm military tome.

Hitler gave a smiling nod.

"Would you join me in my box later, following the opening frivolities?" he asked.

Wyatt hesitated, but only for a second. He turned and held out his arm toward Lucy and Rufus.

"May my companions accompany me?" he asked.

Hitler took a long look. Wyatt saw that same flicker of recognition.

"The woman may accompany you," Hitler said, with a slight hint of annoyance.

Wyatt knew that was meant for Rufus. He was about to reject Hitler's offer unless it included them both, but he didn't get the chance as the dictator continued his march toward the stadium with no further delay.

As he passed the two officers who had restrained Wyatt, Hitler handed the bouquet of flowers to one of them. Paulina watched this with consternation and anger. As the officer accepted the bouquet from his Führer, he bent his face into the flowers to smell the fragrance.

In frustration, Paulina pushed a button on the small remote in her hand. The toxic spores in the tube hidden within the stems of the flowers were released and breathed in by the officer. The odorless poison entered his system as designed -- they just went into the wrong person.

Paulina felt little remorse, even though she knew the man would be dead within a day. When the athletes marched toward the stadium entrance tunnel, she waited until they were inside and she excused herself, ducked into an alcove, removed her Indian costume to reveal the clothing she had underneath, then exited the tunnel and melded into the crowd outside the stadium. Her first plan was to eventually work her way back to her companion at the pre-arranged rendezvous point. But her frustration triggered the impulsive reaction that followed.

As Hitler led the Olympic officials across the ground-level plaza and to the concrete steps down into the stadium bowl, preparing for his grand entry, Wyatt walked up to Lucy and Rufus. Lucy could see a look of irritation on his face she had come to know well. He had a decision or two to make, and he was trying to work it out in his head.

She and Rufus were a bit surprised to see the German dictator single Wyatt out and then speak to him. From the moment Wyatt was called over to him, Lucy and Rufus were eager to know what was said between them.

"What happened?" Lucy asked excitedly as he joined them.

"The woman with the flowers, it was the same woman we've seen before," he answered while motioning for them to follow him along the same path Hitler and the Olympic entourage had taken. When they reached the torch platform that dominated the west entrance to the stadium, they watched in silence for a few minutes while Hitler led the others down the Marathon Steps and onto the red clay running track circling inside the massive stadium.

They took in the sight of the huge venue with every seat filled and heard the tumultuous roar of the crowd as the German dictator strutted slowly along the track to an access point that led to a stairway climb to his private box halfway up the south stands. He stood as still as a statue with his arm extended in the straight-arm Nazi salute. Nearly everyone in the stands returned the gesture.

Nothing more was said between the Lifeboat team members until they found a place outside the track next to the stands to watch the rest of the festivities. But then the barrage of questions began.

"So the woman with the flowers was the same woman on the 1916 battlefield and in Bavaria in 1923?" Rufus asked.

"Yes," Wyatt said. "I know it was her."

"But she seemed to be part of the Indian team," Lucy said. "I saw her come from there. How did she get there?"

"I don't know," Wyatt responded. "She is light-skinned enough to pass for someone from India. But there was something about those flowers."

"A bomb?" Rufus asked.

"I don't know," Wyatt said. "But if it was, why didn't it go off? Hitler had it right in his hand."

Wyatt was scanning the immediate area. He had lost track of the soldier who had the bouquet of flowers. He could not see him in the group of people that followed Hitler down the stadium steps and up to the VIP boxes. Would the bouquet turn up later? Would it still be a threat? Lucy's voice interrupted his thoughts.

"What did Hitler say to you?"

"He invited us to join him in his box," Wyatt said, then looked toward Rufus, trying to find the words to tell him he had been specifically excluded from the invitation.

"Not me. I won't do it," Rufus spat out.

Wyatt was a little relieved that he didn't have to say it, and he could see the anger growing on Lucy's face. He knew she would accept the invitation so she could give Hitler a piece of her mind about the dictator's bigotry, because she knew, just as Rufus knew and Wyatt had guessed, that Hitler would refuse to allow a black man into his private box.

"We are not going unless you are included," Wyatt announced.

That took some of the wind out of Lucy's sails, but she was still steaming.

"No, Wyatt, you guys should go," Rufus said. "There could be another attempt, and even if there isn't, maybe you can find out some things that might be important."

"What will you be doing?" Lucy asked.

"I'll figure something out," he said with a twinkle in his eye that both his friends caught. "You just don't want me up there."

Knowing the intensity of Rufus' feelings about Hitler, Wyatt and Lucy silently agreed.

Wyatt stole a glimpse up to the Führer's box and saw the dictator just arriving there.

"It won't be for a while," Wyatt told the others. "He said after the opening 'frivolities' were over."

The trio turned their attention to the track and infield to watch the 'frivolities.'"

The extra time in the stadium gave the Lifeboat team time to try and figure out if there was more of a threat to Hitler. In their previous dealings with the other time travelers, there had been only one attempt, and then they returned to their own time. But Wyatt knew they had to be prepared for multiple attempts. Having a plan B or C, or more would be something he would have done.

But then again, he was military trained. There was no indication that the other travelers had the same or similar training. But it was best to be prepared.

While they watched for indications of another attempt on Hitler's life, the Lifeboat team took advantage of the opportunity to observe an important part of history.

Now, with no covering over the seating area and someone in every seat, the stadium was overwhelming. Wyatt was fascinated by the flagpoles lining the upper rim of the stadium, set to display the flags of all nations competing in the games.

Lucy and Rufus looked around in open-mouthed amazement. It was the largest arena either had ever been to.

Hitler did not get the domination he had hoped for in either the winter or summer games, but the Nazis made the most of every victory they gained in the competition.

All three Lifeboat team members thought of that as they watched the opening ceremonies of the 1936 Olympic Games play out before them.

After everyone was settled in the Führer's box, Hitler stood and raised his arm, and the German national anthem played. Then naval personnel raised the flags, ringing the upper rim of the stadium on those poles that had fascinated Wyatt earlier, of all the nations competing in the games. Then, on the west end of the Mayfield they had just been on, the Olympic bell high in the bell tower began to toll lightly, then louder and louder, calling forth the youth of the world.

That brought the national teams into the stadium. By virtue of the fact that Greece was the home of the first modern Olympiad, the Greeks led the way, followed by the rest in alphabetical order. However, being the host nation, Germany's national team entered the stadium field last.

Wyatt was most interested in the Indian team, which came about one-third of the way through the team parade. If the woman who had had the flowers was marching with the team, there was cause for concern of another attempt to kill the German dictator.

"If she is there, we have to keep our eyes on her at all times, no matter what," Wyatt said to the others.

"And if she's not?" Rufus asked. "Does that mean she's gone back?"

There was no guarantee, but Wyatt considered it unlikely she would hang around if there was no reason to. He shared that with Lucy and Rufus, but also cautioned that there was no way to guarantee that there might not be another attempt in the coming days.

"I wish I knew for sure, but I don't," he said.

As the lone team member for Haiti approached the Lifeboat team's position, they knew India was coming up. Holland followed Haiti, and then India was in line. As Holland passed, three sets of eyes surveyed the next group. All three had seen the woman on the Mayfield, but because he had jogged toward her, Wyatt had had the best look.

He scanned every face very carefully. The woman with the flowers had a slightly darker skin tone than the others on the Indian team, but she was dressed just like them. Most of the Indian team members were men, so it was easier to scan the faces.

As the last of the group passed by, he turned to his companions.

"She's not there," he said. "Did either of you see her?"

They both shook their heads.

What that meant was uncertain. Did she slip away from the Indian team to move to an alternate plan? Or did she do so to return to her own time? In the time it took the rest of the teams to march in front of them, those were the questions the Lifeboat team could not resolve with any certainty. But Wyatt believed it was prudent to assume the former.

As the American team passed in front of them, dressed in blue blazers and white trousers with straw hats covering their hearts, the Lifeboat trio turned their heads to the west to see the Germans, as the host nation, the last to enter the stadium. After looking over the group, marching sharply in their white naval-style uniforms, something else caught their eyes.

It was missed by everyone else in the stadium, with their attention riveted on the drama on the track, the blaring Frederick the Great's "Hohenfriedberger March" and the thundering roar of the mostly German crowd, but to the Lifeboat team, it superseded everything else around them.

At the top of the Marathon Steps, near the large bronze eternal flame stand, as yet unlit, stood a woman dressed in twenty-first-century attire. Despite being about seventy-five yards away, Wyatt recognized her immediately as the woman with the flowers. He glanced at Lucy and Rufus and nodded to answer their unasked question, *"Is it her?"*

She stood there for a few moments, and Wyatt could see the frustration on her face. He could also see that she seemed to be staring at the Führer's box. Wyatt could see the hate in that stare. Suddenly, the woman's gaze dropped down, and it seemed that she was staring straight at Wyatt. Instead of hate, he read a pleading face.

The encounter was interrupted by a man dressed in civilian clothing, but not as formal as with others in the stadium, who moved to the woman's side. He spoke to her in what seemed like urgent tones. While her gaze toward Wyatt never wavered, the woman spoke to the man, who then grabbed her arm and tried to pull her away. She briefly resisted, but finally went with him across the plaza toward the Mayfield. She continued to look at Wyatt until she was out of his line of sight.

"That didn't look like the same guy we've seen with her before," Lucy observed. "Do you think she was being arrested?"

Wyatt shook his head.

"It's not the same guy," Wyatt said. "And I'm sure she wasn't being arrested."

"How can you be sure?" Rufus asked.

"They were talking like they knew each other," Lucy said. "It seemed like he was trying to get her to leave, and she didn't want to go."

Wyatt was convinced their attempt to kill Hitler in this time period was at an end. But the military training within him told him they needed to stick around for a bit just to make sure.

The Lifeboat team, along with one hundred thousand-plus people in the stadium, listened to Baron Pierre de Coubertin, father of the modern Olympic movement, give a recorded welcoming address, then a rambling fifteen-minute speech by Theodor Lewald, one of the architects of Germany's Olympic bid.

Hitler then opened the games with a brief sentence, "I proclaim open the Olympic Games of Berlin, celebrating the eleventh Olympiad of the modern era." He was then joined by the International Olympic Committee and the Organizing Committee. The Olympic flag was raised on the staff on the west end of the stadium, an artillery regiment fired salutes, and carrier pigeons were released. As the final strains of Richard Strauss' "Olympic Hymn" began to fade, the final torch bearer appeared at the Olympic Gate, the two towers on the eastern end of the stadium with the Olympic interlocking rings suspended between them.

After pausing for effect, German distance runner Fritz Schilgen descended the eastern steps into the stadium and ran along the southern side of the track to the Marathon Steps on the west end and then up to the top. Standing by the bronze altar, just steps from where Wyatt and the others had seen the woman who had handed Hitler the bouquet of flowers, he raised the torch high over his head and held it there for a few seconds before dipping it into the fire basin to ignite the eternal flame.

It was at that moment that a uniformed officer of the Foreign Ministry appeared in front of Wyatt and Lucy.

"Herr and Fraulein, mein Fuhrer requests that you accompany me to the VIP box," he said in a deliberate, formal tone, pointedly ignoring Rufus, who rolled his eyes.

"We'll be back soon," Wyatt made a point to say to Rufus. "We'll meet you right here."

After the officer checked their papers, Wyatt and Lucy followed him to the steps leading upward in the stands. They arrived at the VIP box following the athletes' oath had been administered, and the teams began to leave the field. They were kept in the rear of the VIP box area, away from the dignitaries, but the Foreign Ministry officer whispered in Hitler's ear, to which he nodded once, then returned his attention to the field.

They watched as Hitler, showing a growing disinterest in the proceedings, waited patiently as each team passed. When the German team passed by the Führer's location, Hitler threw up his right arm, straight out at an upward angle, in the Nazi salute. As the German team passed through the Marathon Gate tunnel directly under the eternal flame altar, Hitler turned and headed for the stadium mezzanine.

Catching sight of Wyatt and Lucy, he told those around him to stay where they were. He strode up to the Lifeboat pair, looking intently at each in turn.

"So, it's American journalists Wyatt Logan and Lucy Preston," Hitler finally said in German.

Having not been privy to Wyatt's and Hitler's short conversation earlier, Lucy began to fidget. Wyatt began to respond, but Hitler held up his left hand to stop him.

"Names do not matter to me," he said. "You have both visited me in previous years at critical times in my life."

He looked at Wyatt.

"You saved my life during the war," he said, then turned to Lucy. "You did the same after the putsch."

They both breathed a sigh of relief, but hoped it was not observable.

"I wanted to take this opportunity to express my gratitude and the gratitude of the German people," Hitler said, then paused for a few seconds.

"I suppose this means I needed your protection again?" he asked.

Wyatt only nodded, not wanting to provide any details. Hitler recognized Wyatt's silence for what it was.

"It is not important that I know the details, only the result," he said, looked them over one last time, then motioned for his entourage to follow him as he began to walk away. After three brisk steps, he stopped and looked back at the pair.

"Will I see you again?" he asked.

"I do not know, sir," Wyatt answered.

Hitler nodded once, turned, and continued to leave the stadium.

Paulina had marched with the Indian team from Mayfield to the Marathon Gate tunnel of the stadium. This was where she was to have made her escape after Hitler had inhaled the deadly poison. Ivan, who had made this jump with her rather than Bobby, was waiting nearby. She was to have discreetly stepped away from the Indian team and into a long overcoat left in the tunnel to hide her team attire. She would then meet Ivan near the Olympic Gate, and they would make their way back to Switzerland to the Time Pod and go home.

But just as she was about to put on the coat, she dropped it to the ground, stripped off her team costume, leaving her with her own clothing she had on underneath. She turned and bounded up the steps. From a position near the Eternal Flame stand, she stared at Hitler.

Paulina then lowered her angry gaze to the sidelines on the outside of the track on the southern side. Just as she focused on Wyatt, Lucy, and Rufus standing next to him, he looked in her direction. Their eyes stayed locked for a moment, and her look of anger changed to one of sorrow. She wanted to reach out to him, to beg them to end their efforts to keep her from achieving her goal. She felt a tear start to roll down her cheek, then another.

Ivan noticed from where he was standing Paulina's dash to the Marathon Gate and took off at a dead run toward her. He caught up with her at the top of the gate as she stared down at the Lifeboat trio.

"What's going on?" Ivan asked, a little out of breath both from the rush to catch up with her and the emotion of the moment. "We've got to go. Now!"

She ignored him, just stared straight at Wyatt. Ivan reached out and gently took her arm, but she shook off his hold, without looking away from the target of her stare.

"Paulina, we have to go or we may never get out of here," Ivan said with urgency.

The tone of his voice broke her out of her trance with Wyatt down on the field. She looked over at him and slightly nodded. As they started to cross the small plaza, he threw the overcoat that he had grabbed from the tunnel over her shoulders, and she buttoned up the front. Within thirty minutes, they were in a taxi and headed for the Olympiastadium S-Bahn train station near the southern entrance to the stadium complex, where they would board a train to take them back to the Swiss border.

Following their exit from the Olympic Stadium, the taxi ride for the Lifeboat team was a silent one. Not because there was nothing to say or questions to ask, but because they did not want to voice any of it in front of someone else in that time period. They did not want to risk letting anyone know what they were really doing there. That could have had far-reaching consequences for themselves and the timeline they were trying to protect.

Besides, just about anyone in their present time and location could have been a Gestapo informant. That would have brought a totally new and deadly sort of consequences.

When they were dropped off just yards from the shore of Lake Tegel, there was still a short walk to the Advanced Lifeboat. By now, it was way past sundown, and to be on the alert, they made that walk in silence.

Following the landmarks they had memorized, they got to the machine about nine o'clock in the evening. Despite the darkness, they could make out George standing guard in front of the Advanced Lifeboat, which was still covered with the camouflage netting. Wyatt went ahead of the others and gave the recognition signal they had arranged, and George gave the counter signal.

"We should get this netting down and get back to the bunker as soon as possible," Wyatt said.

"Roger that," George answered and set about the work.

Rufus climbed aboard and checked the machine's instruments. Wyatt stood at the open hatch waiting for him to do his checks.

"There has not been a jump. The best I can tell, the other time machine is still in Switzerland," Rufus said. "But even if they left Berlin right away, it would still take them at least a day to get back there."

Wyatt looked to Lucy for her input.

"Hitler's trips to and from the stadium tomorrow will be much less public, so I'd say their chances of making any kind of attempt tomorrow are slim," she explained. "The same will be true for the rest of the Games, even the closing ceremonies."

Wyatt looked up at Rufus, who was silent for a few moments while he considered it.

"We don't know how advanced their time machine is," he said. "We have to recharge our power source, but we have no way of knowing whether they have unlimited power, or at least a longer power life than we do."

He looked back at the instruments.

"We have enough power to stay a day or two," Rufus said. "Like us, I'm sure they still use power when they're not traveling through time."

"So, you think they won't stay any longer?" Wyatt asked.

"I really don't know for sure, Wyatt," Rufus responded, a little testily.

Wyatt looked at Lucy, who offered no further input.

"Okay, we stay until we know they have jumped," Wyatt said, then went to tell George to keep the netting up.

The Lifeboat team was back in the bunker the following day. They had stayed in Berlin overnight and into the afternoon, when a time jump was detected for the other group. Once back in their own time, Agent Christopher decided they would wait in the bunker for forty-eight hours to see if the others made another jump.

About noon on the second day, Rufus and Jiya were monitoring the equipment for any time movement, Lucy was doing research on another terminal and and Agent Christopher was in the lounge area talking to Connor. Wyatt was in his quarters talking strategy with George.

"There hasn't been any activity," Jiya said. Rufus and Lucy wheeled over to her terminal, and Agent Christopher and Connor walked over to look over their shoulders. There was a collective sigh of relief.

"I'll tell Wyatt and George," Connor said, and headed for the living quarters.

Rufus and Lucy returned to their terminals, but neither continued what they had been doing. They took a few moments to take in the realization that this trip back in time was actually completed.

As Connor, George, and Wyatt returned to the main area of the bunker, Agent Christopher, with the tension of whether they would be returning now gone, wanted to satisfy her curiosity.

"Lucy, have you found out how history was changed if Hitler had been killed?' she asked.

Lucy returned her attention to the computer terminal and clicked a few tabs open.

"From the best I can tell, after Hitler was killed at the Olympics, there was quite a power scramble to replace him, and somehow Rudolf Hess ended up chancellor," she explained. "It looks like, based on decisions made, he was confused without Hitler there to provide guidance."

She moved another tab to the front of the monitor.

"There was no German attack on Poland; instead, Hess signed an agreement with the Russians to allow them to annex the Polish nation,"

Lucy continued. "But after they did, the Russians invaded Germany, then France, then England, and later the United States."

George's barely audible gasp caught everyone's attention. He hesitated as they all looked to him.

"That explains what I saw as we left," he said. George then explained what he had seen through the Advanced Lifeboat hatch as it closed during their departure for Berlin.

"But how could I have seen that?" he asked. "I thought I was imagining it, that's why I didn't say anything about it."

Connor, standing with his hand on his chin in deep thought, finally spoke.

"We were just beginning to understand this when the Mother Ship was stolen by Garcia," he said. "Time is something of a constant, if something is changed in the past, it affects the present simultaneously."

He paused to let that sink in. He saw that all but George understood up to that point. But that was no surprise as they had been dealing with time changes for two and a half years.

"So, what you're saying is, when things changed in 1980 and the team went back and changed my life path, while they were back in the past, I was living that alternate life?" Agent Christopher asked.

"That is correct," Connor said, looking to George, who still had a bewildered look on his face.

"I think I understand that part, but how was I able to see it?" he asked. "And how was that," pointing to the Advanced Lifeboat, "not wiped out of existence when history was changed?"

"That is something not so easy to explain," Connor answered. "We're not sure why, but the Advanced Lifeboat itself, and any people who are in it, are protected from any changes in history."

"At least physically," Wyatt said with a mixture of anger and anguish. Lucy moved close to him and put her arm around his waist in a sign of agreement and support.

Not knowing the full extent of their losses, the gesture was lost on George.

"But if history is changed, Lifeboat protection or not, how do we remember the things we and others did while we're in the past?" he asked, still burning with curiosity. "How do we know we were even there?"

As he spoke those words, Lucy went back to her computer terminal.

"You remember it because you were actually there," Connor said. "You don't lose those memories. That's how you know you were there."

"There are other ways," Lucy said from her terminal. All eyes turned to her, and she motioned for them all to look at the monitor. On it was the photo of Jiya in 1880s San Francisco.

"And then there is this," she said, clicking the mouse.

Now on the screen was a black-and-white photo of the American athletes in the 1936 Berlin Olympics standing in an enclosed space. In the foreground, made more prominent by the camera's flash, was the unmistakable image of Jesse Owens, the man who almost single-handedly embarrassed the Nazis' idea of Aryan superiority by winning four gold medals, including a head-to-head against Germany's Carl Ludwig "Luz" Long in the long jump.

Owens was chatting with another black man in a nondescript jacket over a dark shirt with a thin bow tie. The man held a small notebook in one hand and a pencil in the other. The man was Rufus Carlin.

Slowly, everyone turned their eyes toward Rufus, standing in the back of the group. He did not look surprised.

"I told you I'd find something to do while you were hobnobbing with the Nazis," Rufus said seriously. With every eye in the room boring through him like a drill going through concrete, he began to relate the story.

When Wyatt and Lucy were escorted to the Führer's box by the Nazi official, Rufus began to feel self-conscious, now standing alone among the mostly German bystanders and officials without the relative protection of his comrades. He looked around for areas where he could be apart from other people.

The packed stadium made that impossible. But then he noticed the tunnel under the Marathon Steps. It looked empty, and he began walking toward it. When he got there, he leaned up against the south wall and waited through the remaining speeches.

When it came time for the teams to march out, Rufus wondered whether he should return to his previous spot to see if Wyatt and Lucy had returned there. But something he could not explain kept him rooted to the spot inside the tunnel. As the American team, the second to last to leave the stadium, began to turn into the tunnel, Rufus started to head back to the main stadium, knowing the German team would come through next.

"Hey there," he heard someone call after taking his first step. Rufus froze and looked around him, expecting to find a Gestapo officer with handcuffs at the ready. Then he heard it again from near the mouth of the tunnel. He looked to see a black man among the American athletes motioning him over.

"You look nervous as hell," the athlete said as Rufus walked up and took a position at his side. "Can't say I blame you, the only negro among all those Nazis over there." He motioned with his thumb to indicate Rufus' position near the track during the athlete's march-in.

"Yeah, I guess so," Rufus said, feeling a rush of excitement when he recognized Jesse Owens. Subconsciously, he pulled the small notebook and pencil from his jacket pocket. He felt the need to keep up the appearance of being a journalist as a protective measure. "But you're not nervous."

The team stopped its march for a moment while the team ahead exited onto the Mayfield.

"Not really," Owens said. "It's just another track meet to me."

"Oh no, this is no ordinary track meet," Rufus said.

"I know, it's the Olympics," Owens said. "But if I think of it like that, I will get nervous."

Rufus smiled, and at that instant a camera flash went off.

"Well, then keep that thought," Rufus said. "But when it's all over, you'll know this is no ordinary track meet."

As the American team began to move away, Owens turned back to Rufus and smiled.

"I already know," he said.

Rufus stood in thought for just a few seconds, then turned and hurried back to his previous spot in the stadium. Within minutes, Wyatt and Lucy returned.

CHAPTER 17

Looking through the half-open door of Rufus' quarters, Wyatt saw him standing near the bed looking at a sheet of paper in his hand. While he couldn't see what was on the paper that Rufus was looking at, Wyatt had a pretty good idea what it was.

"What you looking at?" Wyatt asked, still in the corridor.

Rufus looked up slowly and flashed Wyatt a smile. He turned the face of the paper toward Wyatt. On it was a copy of the photo of Rufus and Jesse Owens in the Berlin stadium Lucy had printed out for him.

Rufus laid the paper on the bed and motioned for Wyatt to come into the room.

"Just packing up a few things before I go home," he said.

Wyatt took a few steps into the room.

"Yeah, I'm getting ready to head out," he said. "Want to get a night or two in a comfortable bed."

Rufus put a few pieces of clothing into a small duffel bag.

"So, are you going to the barracks or to Lucy's?" Rufus asked without looking at Wyatt.

"Probably Lucy's, since I did say a comfortable bed," Wyatt answered with a wry smile, wondering where the conversation was headed. "Why do you ask?"

Rufus straightened up and faced his friend. He stood in silence for a moment, organizing his thoughts.

"Well, I was just wondering how you two were getting along after you had that talk with Agent Christopher," he finally said, still not sure how Wyatt would react to the question.

Wyatt thought a moment. He and Lucy had talked about the encounter and seemed to come to an understanding. The question surrounding the meeting with Agent Christopher was about everyone's level of commitment to the Lifeboat missions as they were currently constituted, not just those of Rufus and Lucy.

Because he had his own reservations about saving Hitler's life, Wyatt understood where Lucy and Rufus were coming from. Despite how she felt, Wyatt was confident Lucy would do whatever was necessary to stay focused on the missions.

"We're getting along just fine," Wyatt finally answered.

Rufus slowly shook his head and went back to going through the motions of packing some belongings.

"And how are you and Jiya getting along?" Wyatt asked.

He had an idea what the real answer was. He had seen how Rufus and Jiya hardly spoke to each other since the late-night meeting at Agent Christopher's home. He had also noticed that when they returned from Berlin, there were no signs of affection between the two, no sign of relief from Jiya that Rufus was safe. In fact, they did not even acknowledge each other. They only spoke to each other when they had to.

"Not so good," Rufus said. "But I think you knew that."

Wyatt nodded his head.

"Is it about the meeting with Agent Christopher?" he asked.

"That's part of it," Rufus answered. "When I found out she had gone to Agent Christopher and said she was concerned about my commitment, I admit I was hurt."

He paused for a moment, and Wyatt took the opportunity.

"Was she right?" he asked. He noticed a look of hurt feelings come over Rufus' face, but it was brief.

"I said some things to her that I'm sure contributed to her concerns," Rufus said sheepishly. Then his tone sharpened. "But that was a private conversation, I was just blowing off steam."

Wyatt again nodded, trying to let his friend know he understood before he went on.

"When there is so much at stake as what we are doing, there are no private conversations," Wyatt said, carefully choosing his words. He did not want to offend Rufus. "When you say things that indicate to another team member that you can't or won't do your part, there is a legitimate cause for concern."

Rufus wrinkled his nose and gave Wyatt a disbelieving look.

"That's looking at it from a military perspective," he said. "The rest of us are not military."

"No, you and the rest, except George, are not in the military," Wyatt said. "But what we are doing, we have to approach it that way."

Rufus started to respond, but Wyatt interrupted him.

"What I mean by that is that we are working as a team, and some of the things we do -- and this is certainly one of them -- put us in danger, real danger," he said. "One slip up by any one team member could be fatal for another -- or all of us."

Rufus gave that some thought. It made sense to him. When he said nothing, Wyatt continued.

"You and Jiya are teammates; you depend on each other. Do you remember how concerned you were when she was having her visions?"

"That's different, I was concerned for her welfare because I cared about her personally," Rufus said.

"I agree," Wyatt said. "But two things: I know your concern for her welfare affected your performance on missions, and if you and Jiya did not have the feelings for each other that you do, you would have been able to separate your concern for her from your performance."

"I don't think that's true," Rufus said, but not with full conviction.

Wyatt studied him for a moment, trying to read his emotions, his body language.

"Oh, I do. And I think you do, too," he said. "What I do know for sure is that before you told Jiya how you felt about her, you were more locked into what you were doing."

Try as he might, Rufus could not deny that.

"So how do I do that, separate the personal from the job?" he asked.

Wyatt finally pulled a chair toward himself and sat down.

"It's not something I can give you a step-by-step method to do it," Wyatt said a little wearily. "It's more about focus, getting your mind right, and understanding that there is a difference between personal and the job.”

Seeing the disappointment on Rufus’ face, he continued.

“It’s not something you’re going to pick up overnight,” Wyatt said. “If it’s not there naturally, or pounded into you by training, it’s going to take time.”

“So, are you saying I should not get personal with Jiya?” Rufus asked. There was no sarcasm in the question; he was truly looking for answers.

“Oh hell no,” Wyatt answered quickly. “If you love her, you need to fight to keep that relationship.”

“But maybe I shouldn’t talk to her about the missions, and how I feel about them,” Rufus said.

“Not necessarily,” Wyatt said. “That’s a decision you have to make. But at this point, since you have already confided in her, if you change that, you need to explain to her, not just stop sharing.”

Rufus slowly sat on the corner of the bed. Wyatt could see the conflict in his eyes.

“I want to keep our relationship, but I don’t know how to undo what I’ve done,” Rufus said in a quivering voice. Wyatt knew he wasn’t crying, but he was sure Rufus wanted to let that out. But now was not the time.

“In any relationship, communication is the key to everything,” Wyatt said. It was a lesson he learned the hard way with Jessica and had it reinforced with Lucy. “You’ve got to talk to her, and you have to be honest.”

Rufus nodded his head slowly. He knew it was true. But actually doing it was something he had little confidence he could pull off successfully.

Wyatt stood and went to Rufus’ side. He put a hand on one of his shoulders and gave it a manly squeeze.

“You can do this,” he said. “I know you can.”

The train trip from Berlin to Switzerland was a quiet one between Paulina and Ivan. Except for when they had to communicate, like determining which train they should take at various stops along the way, they did not speak to each other.

Paulina was angry with him. In their brief exchange atop the Marathon Steps in the Olympic Stadium, she had wanted to stay and make another attempt to kill Hitler. However, Ivan argued that they had no contingency plan, and that staying too much longer might deplete the Time Pod's power they would need to return to their own time.

Deep down, she knew he was right on both counts, but that did not diminish her anger at another thwarted attempt.

Changing history to save her family members was consuming Paulina a little more with each trip into the past. It was starting to affect her judgment, but her emotional attachment to the end goal would not allow her analytical mind to recognize it.

But Ivan could see it clearly -- and he was concerned it would interfere with his own plans.

Bobby, Glenda, and Ivan got involved with Paulina and her project for the scientific aspect, but they each had their own desires to fulfill if they found time travel was actually possible. Bobby's and Glenda's goals were similar to Paulina's -- to save some family members or friends who were lost to them.

But Ivan's plans were more ambitious. Like the solution Paulina finally came up with to save her relatives, Ivan's plan was also world-changing -- but it had nothing to do with saving family or friends. Ivan was a closet communist and believed that was the philosophy that would be best for the world.

He never discussed it with Paulina, of course, but he was participating in the project to learn. Once he knew if time travel was possible, and just how to change history in a directed way, he was going to take over the Time Pod and put his plan into motion.

For the time being, he still had a lot to learn. So, keeping Paulina focused on the task at hand was important to his needs.

But like Paulina, he knew time was running out for her to achieve her goals. With each failed attempt, Paulina was becoming more erratic in her thinking and planning.

After the 1916 attempt failed, she refused to make another attempt in that time period. After their experience in their test trips -- the pain felt by Bobby when he traveled back to a time within his own lifetime -- she deduced that it was not possible to travel back to a time in which they had already visited without the side effects. So she believed they had to make any further attempts in different periods as history moved forward.

However, once the Second World War began, it would be more difficult to get close enough to the German dictator to kill him. She also rejected Ivan's suggestion to have contingency plans for each jump in case what they had planned failed. Her confidence, and in later jumps, her arrogance, got the best of her, and she was so certain the one plan they made would be enough.

But Ivan was already hard at work, even as their train click-clacked toward the Swiss border, laying down plans of his own for their next attempt, in whatever time period that would be.

For a good share of the train trip, Paulina's mind was consumed with anger at failing again. The plan had been a good one, and if not for those interlopers who had thwarted her twice before, it could have been successful.

As they approached the area where they had hidden the Time Pod, her mind, fueled by her anger, began running through possible scenarios in the years following the Olympics that would allow for another attempt to kill Hitler, stop the terrible war that was brewing, and save her ancestors.

Rufus stood at Jiya's apartment door. He was determined to speak his mind, but in a way that kept their relationship on track -- or at least idling until he could figure out just where he wanted it to go.

His silence with Jiya since their confrontation in his apartment over the meeting with Agent Christopher was a gut reaction to the situation, not one he really wanted to happen. It went on as long as it did because of the stubborn streak that was part of his personality. Like most people, he did not want to admit that he was wrong.

But if he wanted to retain a relationship of any kind with Jiya -- and he came to realize that he wanted that more than anything -- he had to take that step. And if he was going to be truthful to himself, he had to admit that in this case, he was wrong to have been angry with her.

It had taken a while to sink in, but Rufus came to the realization that if the roles had been reversed, he would have done as Jiya had. What they were doing with these time jumps was important -- and he knew that from the beginning.

Rufus raised his hand and knocked three times on the door -- and suddenly he could not remember the speech he had carefully memorized. In a panic, he turned and started to walk away. He had only taken a few steps when, behind him, he heard the door open.

"Where are you going?" Jiya asked as Rufus was taking another step. He froze in his tracks and remained facing away from her for a few seconds.

"Well?" she said.

Rufus turned to face her, frantically trying to recall even the smallest snippet of what he had planned to say to her. Nothing was coming to his mind.

"Can we talk?" he asked, mostly to fill time while he continued to search his memory.

Jiya, leaning on the door jamb, considered the question for a moment. That gave Rufus a little more time to think, but he was still coming up empty.

"I don't know, can we?" she finally asked. It wasn't a sarcastic remark; she really was wondering if they could have a meaningful conversation. In the days since he stormed out of his apartment while giving her a dismissive wave, their conversations had been limited to technical matters.

But Jiya could see that Rufus was processing her question, trying to figure out whether she was being sarcastic or trying to twist the knife a little. She could tell by the look on his face that he was leaning toward the latter.

"I would like us to talk," she said, and saw the immediate relief on his face.

He took a step forward, but she did not move. He stopped and looked nervously up and down the hallway.

"So, let's talk," Jiya said, still standing in the doorway with her arms crossed in front of her.

Rufus shuffled from one foot to the other and dropped his eyes to the floor. Jiya could tell he was embarrassed. She knew it was difficult for him to talk about personal matters. She was not enjoying his discomfort, but she knew that if he couldn't open up to her, especially now, they may not have a future together.

He finally raised his chin and looked her in the eye.

"I was a bit of an ass, and I am sorry," he said.

Jiya nodded her head but did not respond. Rufus knew she was waiting for more, and in his prepared speech, he believed he had all the right things to say. But those words were still escaping him.

"Look, I know I was wrong to walk out on you about your meeting with Agent Christopher," he said. "I should have heard you out."

Again, she nodded but did not respond.

"I felt like you didn't trust me," Rufus said. "But I know it wasn't that. You were concerned about the missions."

"That was part of it, yes," Jiya said.

He gave her a puzzled look.

"Part of it?" he asked.

Jiya stopped leaning on the door jamb, stood up straight in the doorway, and let her arms drop to her sides.

"Yes, part of it," she said. "I was also concerned about you." He stood there with a look of confusion. "About your wellbeing."

"You didn't need to be," Rufus said when it finally sank in.

"That's entirely possible," Jiya said, rolling her eyes. "But when people are in love, they care about the ones they love."

Rufus took in her words, and they jogged his memory a bit. He remembered part of his speech. But he wasn't going to say that part of it just now because it would seem like he was just tagging onto her words. He would have to find another way to say it.

"I really didn't think about it that way," he said, and that was the truth.

He stood in the hallway, shifting his weight from one foot to the other as they talked, but now he fell silent and stood without motion. But Jiya could tell he had more that he wanted to say. Because he was such a private person, she was certain he would open up if they went inside her apartment to finish the conversation. But she didn't want to make it easy for him.

Since spending so much time in 1880s San Francisco and having to fend for herself, Jiya had become a much stronger woman. She was now capable of taking charge in situations and speaking her mind without fear of facing a confrontation. Her stern talk with Wyatt outside of Agent Christopher's house, following their meeting there, never would have happened prior to San Francisco.

She was happy with the change in her personality. She had much more self-confidence and did not feel the need to hide her feelings.

What she did not want in a relationship -- with Rufus or anyone, personal or professional -- was to be the dominant one, nor did she want to be dominated. She was more interested in an equal partnership. When it came to Rufus, she wanted him to be a stronger personality.

It wasn't that she wanted him to be something he was not; she really just wanted him to be what she knew he could be. He was a smart man with deep feelings. She knew he could go far if he tapped the same self-confidence Jiya had come to find.

Since it wasn't practical to strand him in a time where he had to fend for himself as she had done for herself, she had to find ways to nudge him in that direction. In this instance, she wanted him to spill his beans out in the open, away from the protection of inside her apartment with the door closed.

"So, what did you come here to say?" she asked.

Rufus shifted his weight again and looked up and down the hallway, then turned back to look at her. He wanted to go inside to talk about it, but it was now clear that, for whatever reason she had, Jiya was not going to allow that. He was at a crossroads, and he knew it.

Jiya watched him anxiously. She wanted him to stand his ground and say that he loved her, wanted to be with her the rest of his life, and would do anything to make it happen.

But the longer he stood there in silence, the more she thought it would never happen. And she would survive that. It wouldn't be easy, but she would find a way, because she was a strong woman who could make her own way in life.

Rufus shifted his weight again, in a way that made it appear to Jiya that he was going to walk away down the hall without saying another word. And, in fact, he started to take a step to his left as if he were doing just that. But before he completed the step, he stopped and turned toward her.

After a second's hesitation, Rufus took two steps forward so he was standing within inches of her. Suddenly, he reached out with both arms and encircled her waist, and pulled her against his body. He stared down into her eyes.

They both heard a door open down the hallway. Jiya expected Rufus to disengage the embrace and back away. But he didn't even flinch. It was as if he could hear nothing but the beating of their two hearts so close to each other.

They both looked down the hallway toward the noise they had heard of a door opening. An older woman was standing in front of the door, looking at them, a look of anticipation on her face.

"Move along. Nothing to see here," Rufus said. With a huff, the woman went inside her apartment and slammed the door.

Suddenly, Rufus moved his right hand up to the back of Jiya's head, turned it so they were facing each other again, and held it firmly as he pressed his lips to hers. She responded in kind. The kiss lasted for several seconds, and when he pulled away, she was left wanting more.

Jiya opened her eyes to see Rufus looking down at her with such an expression of desire that it at first frightened her. Was this just lust of the moment, she thought.

"I love you, Jiya," he said, and she could see a tear forming in his eye. "I never want to be without you."

With those words ringing in her ears, Jiya lost all control over her desire to make him work for her love. She grabbed the lapels of his jacket and pulled him into the apartment.

"It's about time, you animal," she said.

Agent Christopher sat at the small desk she had set up in the common area of the bunker. She was going over the latest results of an operation she and Connor had been working on for a while now.

Between the Lifeboat team's jump to 1923 and the 1936 Olympic trip, she had seen the toll this particular mission was taking on the team. The meeting at her home had brought it all to a head. Looking out her window that night at Jiya's and Wyatt's tense confrontation, she resolved to do whatever it took to end this mission as soon as possible.

She harkened back to the days when it was Rittenhouse controlling the Mother Ship, and she worked with Wyatt to conduct a raid on the site they determined the Mother Ship kept jumping back to after each foray into the past. That raid had failed, but she was certain they could pull off a similar attempt to end the other group's interference in past history this time.

For one thing, they had learned some valuable lessons on the raid to stop the Rittenhouse travelers. For another, it appeared Paulina's team was not as sophisticated or as richly funded as Rittenhouse. Finally, there were indications that their technology was not up to the level of what Connor Mason had developed.

For those reasons, she was certain another attempt to end the time jumping at the source would be successful this time.

Following the 1916 jump, an operation of the kind like the Rittenhouse raid was not on her radar, partly because she was not sure just how long this new team would continue its efforts. But after that meeting at her home, she had Connor backtrack and find out where Paulina's time machine went when it returned to its own time.

His research showed they had returned to an industrial area in Los Angeles near the main commercial harbor. Right then, she set a plan in motion for another raid.

Agent Christopher did not involve Wyatt this time. In fact, she did not mention this side operation to the Lifeboat team. She wanted their minds focused for the next jump, if one came. She also did not want to add to their tension.

Instead, she drafted an elite U.S. Navy SEAL team for this effort. The operation was conducted just before the jump to 1936 Berlin. Agent Christopher followed the operation in the SEAL command center.

SEAL platoon leader Lieutenant Allen Brockton, dividing his force into four-man teams, had the location surrounded where Connor's instruments indicated Paulina's team returned. Each team conducted reconnaissance from about fifty yards away under concealment.

They were looking at a three-story warehouse that took up a quarter of a city block of space. It did not look quite like the buildings around it. Unlike the steel and glass structures with modular right-angle box looks, the targeted warehouse was a brick building with few windows, with most at the second and third story levels. It was clearly built years before the ones around it.

Because of the high-level windows, it was difficult for Brockton's recon teams to get a good look inside. But from their perspective, they could see no indications of activity inside the building.

"Prepare for breach," Brockton barked into his communications mic.

His breach team moved toward the door on the east side of the warehouse. A small explosive was placed near the door latch, and when it went off, a team member pushed the door inward and went through the doorway, moving to his right once inside. He was followed by one of his colleagues, who went to the left. The other two team members quickly followed, all four sweeping their laser-sighted M4A1 assault rifles throughout the wide open space.

The soldiers were looking at a dimly lit space encompassed by the four walls of the structure. The ceiling, about fifteen feet above the concrete floor, was supported by flat wood trusses visible to those down below. The trusses had what looked like heavy wooden planks laid atop and bolted to them. That was the second-story floor.

The large warehouse contained nothing except what appeared to be an office in a corner opposite the entry door. On the wall opposite the street-facing wall was a large square door, presumably to allow for large items to be brought into the warehouse. There were two sturdy-looking wood doors, but they were secured shut by chains and heavy-duty modern-looking padlocks.

Illuminated by the light pouring in from the entry door, an orange-colored cat, frozen in place by the sudden activity at the door, stared back at the soldiers in the middle of the floor, its green eyes shining like twin beacons. Suddenly, four red dots appeared on the cat's torso. Recognizing the cat as no threat, the laser dots were then transferred to the office in the corner. Seeing that, the cat ran over to playfully swat at the dots dancing across the wall.

The SEAL team carefully and slowly worked its way across the empty warehouse to the office. Its door was slightly ajar, so one member pushed it open and two others went inside in the same manner they had breached the main door. The office was also empty -- not even a desk or filing cabinet.

The result of the raid was disappointing and puzzling. Connor's computer records indicated that was exactly where Paulina's time machine had returned after the 1923 jump.

When the Lifeboat team returned from 1936, Agent Christopher and Connor again checked for a trace of where the other travelers had returned. The site was the same. But a second raid on the warehouse turned up the same results -- even the orange-colored cat was still there.

While Agent Christopher spent the day reading and re-reading the SEAL team after-action reports from both raids, Connor conducted diagnostics of all the computer equipment and reviewed -- multiple times -- the return traces of Paulina's time machine.

Just as Agent Christopher was re-reading the reports for the umpteenth time that day, Connor came to her desk and sat down on the other side, facing her.

"I have tested the equipment and checked our records of comings and goings of both time machines," he said. "But everything checks out and all the traces are the same over and over again."

"So why can't we find them at that location?" Agent Christopher asked with exasperation.

Connor sat there staring at her for a few minutes, trying to put into words the only thing that made sense to him. She could see the pained look on his face and braced herself for what could be coming. But she wasn't really ready when it finally came.

"The only thing I can deduce is they are operating from a different time than ours," he said.

CHAPTER 18

Peter Wilson was excited by the news of his second child. He was the father of a fine daughter, and now the possibility of a son filled his mind.

As he walked along the sidewalk, he thought of his family in Chicago. How pleased his mother would be to hear the news. She was so delighted when Mary Ann was born that she almost came out to California to live with he and Gwen and their new daughter. Maybe this time she would come.

The world was different than when Peter was born in 1983. Now, children were almost throwaways at just about any age. There were so many children on their own because of broken marriages, divorce and homelessness. When Peter was born, children were welcomed, and in fact, a must in most marriages. The divorce rate was lower, and families worked harder to stay together no matter how tough life became.

It was not quite like when his parents were first married, and certainly not like his grandparents' time. But when he and Gwen decided to start a family, society was still a favorable place for families.

Peter's walk took him through many back alleys. In this day and age, he didn't even need to walk. Streamlined cars zipped everywhere, and nearly anyone could afford one, no matter how financially challenged they were. In fact, Peter owned three of them. But today he wanted to walk and think of the developing child. Would it be a son or another daughter? Would it be healthy? What kind of future was in store for the little one once it was brought into the world?

Thinking about his new child, though, did not take his mind completely away from the true purpose of his adventure out of the house. He was headed to his office. A multi-room, single-story collection of offices in the strip mall about a mile from home.

Peter Wilson was a stockbroker. It was a small investment company he started five years ago when the American economy was booming. He started with just himself and a secretary. But in the first three years, business was so good he added two associates and two more secretaries, who now insisted on being called administrative assistants.

In the past two years, business at Wilson Investments began to level out. He maintained his clients, as did his associates, but new clients were few and far between. On this early Saturday morning, he was on his way to meet with his associates to talk strategy for getting the business back on an upward trend.

Pausing at the office door while pulling the keys out of his pocket, Peter felt a chill. It was a warm June morning, so he wondered if there had been a chilly breeze. But he gave it no more thought as he turned the key and swung the door open.

He expected to see the inside of the lobby, but that is not what he saw. Instead, there was a pile of rubble. The sight was confusing, and Peter shook his head to try and clear his vision. But nothing changed. There was nothing that even gave a hint that this was the lobby of the office he knew so well.

He swiveled his head from side to side to take in the entire area of what had been his office lobby. But all he saw was piles of broken steel, wood, and concrete.

Peter lifted his line of sight a little to check the area past the lobby. But it was much the same. Looking from right to left, there was nothing standing, except small sections of wall here and there, looking like a lower jaw with only a few teeth remaining.

Peter turned his body to face the street behind him. He surveyed the area and saw much the same -- piles of rubble where he knew buildings had been just seconds before. In the distance, he could see some intact structures, and one on the corner of the intersection to his right.

He studied the three-story brick warehouse that he knew well. He passed it on his way to his office daily. The warehouse looked relatively intact, though all the glass was missing from the few windows on the ground floor and the more numerous ones on the second and third floors. There were also large gashes in the brick exterior, as if heavy objects had slammed into the building.

As he stood and studied the scarred warehouse, Peter thought back to a few weeks ago when what he thought was a police SWAT team stormed the warehouse. He had stood in the doorway of his office and watched the goings-on. When it was over, he walked out into the parking lot and caught a close-up glimpse of one of the men who had gone inside the building. His attire was definitely not police; it was more like military. He then saw about a dozen men, dressed in the same military-style gear, walk casually down the street and turn a corner. Minutes later, he watched as a tracked Bradley Fighting Vehicle he recognized from archive news footage of Operation Desert Storm came around the corner and lumber past the strip mall where his office was located.

A few days later, another group -- or the same, Peter couldn't tell -- stormed the building again. Watching from the lobby window this time, he couldn't help noticing the frustration on the faces of the soldiers as they exited the warehouse.

Peter was snapped out of his recollection when a man came out of the warehouse. He was dressed in ragged clothing that was covered with dirt and sweat. The man looked around, then locked eyes with Peter.

"Hey," he yelled. "Get away from there. That's mine."

The man started to advance toward Peter, and in his right hand was a rusted steel rod. Peter looked around to see who the man might be talking to. Surely it couldn't be him, Peter thought. Within seconds, he realized he was, in fact, the man's target.

"Get away, dammit!" the man yelled again. He was halfway to where Peter was standing and still advancing.

Peter turned around to face what had been his office lobby. He heard a voice coming from his right.

"Peter, what is it?"

In the same second, he recognized his associate Candace. Peter shot a quick glance behind him and saw that the industrial area was intact, including the three-story brick warehouse. He saw there was no man with a steel pipe heading toward him.

Peter's knees went weak, and he quickly stepped inside and looked around to reveal the lobby he knew all too well. There was no rubble. The office looked just as it had the day before when he locked up to go home. He sat down in one of the lobby chairs nearest the door.

"I must be hallucinating," he said as he put his face in his hands.

Stephen and Candace looked at each other.

"About what?" Stephen asked.

Peter slowly looked up at them. His look of terror worried his associates.

"It is almost too wild and scary to even think about," he said. "But it seems like this isn't the first time this has happened."

He related all he could remember to his associates.

Paulina sat dejected in the warehouse office. The latest attempt to change history and save her family members from death and disfigurement in the past had failed. It was the most recent in a growing list of failures -- and the last three thwarted by those unknown interlopers.

She was losing hope and enthusiasm for this project. It seemed that there was no way for her to succeed. A part of her was ready to just walk away, let the project die, maybe even destroy the Time Pod. Her sole reason for building it was to restore her family line. What good would come of its existence now that nothing she did was accomplishing her goal?

Another part of her -- the sentimental part -- fought hard to keep her on the task.

As she continued her mental struggle, there was a knock on the half-open door. She looked up with disinterest and saw Ivan peering in at her. She lazily waved her hand to beckon him inside the office.

Ivan stood on the opposite side of the desk, looking down at her for a moment before he spoke. He could see he really didn't have her full attention.

"Do you have another plan in mind?" he asked.

She looked up to face him, but she still seemed miles away in thought.

"For what?" she responded.

Ivan shifted his weight from one foot to the other. He was a little miffed that she seemed to have lost interest in their effort -- the effort that she herself had started and recruited him, and the others, to be a part of.

"To go back and kill that bastard Hitler," he shot back. The hint of anger in his voice caught Paulina's attention.

"What good would that do?" she asked. She was not pleased with his tone. It seemed to her that he was making a demand. This was her project; she was the leader of it. How dare he start making demands of her?

"It would make all the difference in the world," he said, still with the hint of anger, but this time mixed with irritation.

Paulina looked at him for a long few seconds. Had he not been paying attention to the previous attempts? Even before the other time travelers became involved, they were making no changes to history that got the desired results. For all they knew, there were no changes in the established history whatsoever. No matter what they did, the same things they were trying to prevent happened anyway.

"We have made six jumps back and six times we have failed to make even the smallest changes in the way history moved forward," Paulina told him. "Every one of my family members I had hoped to save has died or been maimed as they did before. How do we know another trip will not end the same way?"

Ivan let out a loud and long sigh.

"We don't know," he said. "But if you believe what we are doing is the right thing to do, why does it seem you are so eager to give up?"

Paulina thought about it for a moment. She remembered all her classes in science throughout school, in which multiple attempts were needed to achieve the desired results in experiments. And there were even some that, no matter how many attempts were made, only partial results were accomplished. But in each one, some degree of success was achieved.

She slowly came to the conclusion that Ivan was correct. If something was important enough, there could and should be no end to attempts to make things right. She wanted her family restored, more than anything. But there was a nagging question since she began working with Ivan, Bobby, and Glenda that finally came to the surface for expression.

"What we're trying to change is something for me and me alone," she said. "Why are you so intent on keeping this project going? What's in it for you?"

Ivan did not answer right away. He certainly had a history change he wanted to make, one that might even undo the changes she was hoping to see. But to share it with Paulina would guarantee that he would never get the chance to try. But from conversations he had had with Bobby and Glenda, he knew they had things in the past they wished they could change using the Time Pod. They were small things, not even like Paulina's desire to save family members from death, but they were enough to approach Paulina, once her project came to fruition, to talk her into letting them attempt their own history alterations.

"There are things I, and the others, would like to change in the past," he said cautiously. "I can't speak for Bobby and Glenda, but I'd like to change mistakes that have shaped how my life turned out."

Paulina was silent for a moment. She had wondered whether that was why they had all agreed to take part in the project. And if asked, she would have allowed it, as long as what they wanted would not change history in a detrimental way, after her goal was accomplished. But now it seemed that would never happen.

"Go ahead and try," she said with a dismissive wave. "I've seen too much failure."

"Absolutely not," Ivan said with conviction. "First, we take care of what you want. We all owe you that."

His apparent loyalty found its mark in Paulina's sentimental side. She appreciated their work for her when it seemed they were getting nothing from it. That tipped her mental debate in favor of continuing the effort.

"Okay, but how can we stop the war and save my relatives?" she asked. "We need something that can't fail."

Inwardly, Ivan was delighted, so much so that a small smile began to form on his face.

"I've got an idea," he said.

But before he laid it out for Paulina, he told her he only wanted him and Glenda to make the trip. Paulina flatly refused.

"No. Bobby and I will go with you," she said.

But Ivan pressed his plan for only him and Glenda to make the trip. He knew from talking with him that Bobby was losing confidence in the project. In fact, he had told Ivan just days before that he was thinking of walking away. Ivan shared that with Paulina.

"Unless he is one-hundred percent with the program, he would be a liability," Ivan said.

Paulina had her own doubts about Bobby's commitment. But she had never confronted him about it. He continued to work on the project, and she would not push him out. However, she agreed with Ivan's assessment.

"Alright, Glenda goes on the jump this time," she said. "But I will also go."

Ivan vigorously shook his head.

"No. It would be dangerous for you to be on this jump," he said.

Ivan explained that because she had been seen close-up by Hitler and others at the Olympics, she would surely be recognized. How could they explain an Indian Olympic athlete returning to Germany, especially during the time he had planned to go? Besides, because she was a black woman, that alone would make her stick out like a pig in a cattle herd.

His arguments made sense to Paulina. But she was not giving up on being part of the next time jump.

"No, I will go," she said. "But I will stay with the Time Pod."

Ivan began to protest, but she cut him off.

"It's that or nothing," she said firmly.

That would stifle his plan after the assassination of Hitler was complete. With Hitler out of the way, he would stir things up enough to allow the communists to gain control of the German government. He would do this even if he had to take the Time Pod to different time periods. That meant he would not return to his own time, and that would make Glenda expendable. But Paulina was not going to give in; he could see that clearly. He would have to rethink that part of it.

"So, what do you have in mind?" Paulina asked.

"There is this guy, Georg Elser, who makes the last known credible attempt on Hitler's life before the July 20th plot," Ivan began to explain.

Walking through the streets of Munich, Germany, in early November 1939, Wyatt and Lucy were a bit apprehensive and more than a little on edge. While they had been in Germany twice before, and in a war zone in France, this was much different.

World War II was just more than two months old, and security was amped up from what they experienced in Berlin just three years earlier. That was one of the factors for not taking the Advanced Lifeboat into Germany this time. They followed Paulina's team's lead and went to Switzerland, then traveled to Munich.

They had no idea just where in the neutral country the other time travelers had gone, but based on the proximity to Munich across the border in Germany, they took an educated guess and targeted the Advanced Lifeboat to an area they thought the others might have gone.

The enhanced security and state of war that existed were also factors in leaving Rufus at the Advanced Lifeboat. He did not argue the point. In fact, he relished the idea of not being in the middle of one of the biggest gatherings of Nazis that year.

Wyatt and Lucy were headed for the Buergerbraukeller in the Haldhausen District of Munich. Located on the east side of the Isar River on Rosenheimer Strasse, the establishment was opened in 1885, then called Bürgerliches Brauhaus until it merged with Lowenbrau in

1921. It was the site of the 1923 Beer Hall Putsch, after which the Lifeboat team prevented Hitler from killing himself.

Wyatt was dressed in the uniform of an SS sturmbannführer, and his identity papers listed his name as Kurt Van Hapen. Lucy, dressed as a brau waitress, was identified in her papers as Heidi Schmidt of Dussendorf. Rufus got a kick out of the choice of names from the movie "Where Eagles Dare," a 1968 espionage drama starring Clint Eastwood and Richard Burton in the title roles. Derren Nesbitt played Gestapo officer Van Hapen, and Ingrid Pitt played the role of Heidi Schmidt.

"Nice choice," he told Wyatt with a nudge, then looked at Lucy. "Not quite Heidi, though, more like Maria Schenk." He was referring to the character in the movie named Mary, played by Mary Urie.

Wyatt had looked at Lucy and up and down in her costume, settling his gaze on her chest, which showed less cleavage than Ingrid Pitt had in portraying her role in the movie.

"She'll do," Wyatt responded.

While not really understanding the reference, she certainly guessed by where Wyatt's gaze had held for a few seconds, looking over what was supposedly missing.

"You seem to like it," she said deadpan.

Wyatt and Rufus exchanged glances as she walked away, quite pleased with herself. Wyatt knew there was going to be another movie-watching session once they had time.

As they walked toward the front entrance of the Buergerbraukeller, Wyatt and Lucy smiled at each other, both remembering the breast incident. But they had to conceal their merriment. It was time for some very serious work.

They were challenged at the door by Munich policemen, but Wyatt's uniform and the same letter signed by Hitler giving him carte blanche authority that he had carried in Berlin, and that had worked on the officer in the park who stumbled upon the Advanced Lifeboat, got them inside.

Wyatt and Lucy stood inside the front door and surveyed the room. It was packed with men swilling huge steins of beer. But unlike most beer halls in Germany, there was no tobacco smoke creating a haze in the large room. Hitler would not allow anyone to smoke in his presence. That is how Wyatt and Lucy knew he was already in the building.

Wyatt, with Lucy following almost in his back pocket, began moving toward the other side of the room where a speaker's stand was located. Hitler would be near it. They weaved in between a maze of tables with people crowded around all sides, either sitting or standing. Big-busted waitresses hustled back and forth with up to five full steins in each hand, setting them down on tables and hurrying back to the bar for more.

Ivan and Glenda were watching the main Buergerbraukeller room from one side and slightly behind the speaker's platform. Georg Elser had directed them to an unguarded access to the building leading up to the Fuhrer's speaker podium.

Elser knew how to circumvent security because he had worked in the beer hall for a little less than a year. During that time, he had hidden in the building near closing time, so he was in there all night alone. He used that time to hollow out a portion of a pillar right behind the speaker's platform to place a bomb.

Prior to working at the Buergerbraukeller, Elser worked at an armaments factory. He experimented with some explosives he was able to steal with the idea of making a bomb to kill Hitler himself.

Ivan and Glenda met Elser two days prior to Hitler's planned speech on November 9, the anniversary of the Beer Hall Putsch. The first day was spent convincing him they all had the same goal. It was not an easy task. Elser, despite suspicions after the fact, had hatched and put his plot into action alone. No one else knew.

But Ivan and Glenda were finally able to convince him.

The day before the speech, they accompanied him into the beer hall, hid out with him until closing time, then helped him reset the bomb timer to coincide with the start of Hitler's speech, which was delivered at the same time every year.

On the day of the speech, Ivan and Glenda returned to the beer hall through the route Elser had given them. He was not there. He was already on his way to Switzerland, trying, unsuccessfully as it turned out, to make his escape.

Now Ivan and Glenda watched and waited. They planned to wait until Hitler mounted the platform, about twenty minutes from that moment, then they would hurry out the way they had come. But now, as they watched in seclusion, something caught Ivan's eye.

A man in a black SS officer's uniform was leading a woman toward the area where Hitler was standing, waiting to begin his speech. A woman in the beer hall who was not busy as a waitress was way out of place, and it made the hair on Ivan's neck stick up.

He had devised a contingency plan if the bomb failed to go off. But for it to work, Hitler would have to be at that speaker's lectern. That would put Ivan within twenty yards of the dictator, close enough for a pistol shot to the head. They were also close enough to their escape route to get a head start on anyone who pursued them. Ivan was also ready to sacrifice Glenda if necessary to make his own escape.

But the development playing out in front of his eyes at the moment could eliminate that option.

Using all the military bearing he could muster, Wyatt walked confidently, even a bit arrogantly, which suited the character he was portraying perfectly, up to a small group surrounding Hitler. Lucy had none of Wyatt's confidence or pretended arrogance. She was terrified, which also worked in her favor for what Wyatt had planned.

"Excuse me, mien Führer," Wyatt said in his best and most firm German. "I must speak with you. It is of the utmost importance."

A short, stout man held out his hand, wordlessly demanding his papers and orders. Wyatt looked Martin Bormann up and down with a tilt of his nose slightly upward. He pulled the papers from his tunic and defiantly slapped them into Bormann's hand.

Wyatt glanced at Hitler and saw that he recognized him.

"Stombanfuhrer Kurt Van Hapen of the Special Investigative Service, it says," Bormann spat unbelievingly.

"I know this man," Hitler said, a bit annoyed at his lackey. Bormann took notice of the tone and slinked a little into the background, handing the papers back to Wyatt. "So what is it, Herr Stombanfuhrer?" Hitler asked.

Wyatt pulled Lucy forward. Up until then, Hitler had not seen her clearly. A small smile played across his face.

"This woman has information about an assassination attempt," Wyatt said. "But we must discuss it elsewhere. And quickly."

In his mind, Hitler played back the times he had encountered these two before. Whenever they appeared, his life had been in danger, and they had saved him. There was no way he was even going to question their actions or motives now.

Hitler whispered something into Bormann's ear and then beckoned for Wyatt and Lucy to follow him. They went to a side exit, walked briskly across the street to a storefront, and entered. The shopkeeper was a bit stunned, but Hitler held up his hand and asked if there was an office or other room where they could talk privately. The man pointed to the back of the shop.

Once inside the small office, Hitler looked expectantly at the pair.

"Tell him what you told me," he said to Lucy in French. She hesitated only a moment, then began in French, because she knew Hitler understood that language. They had conversed in it before.

"There was to be an assass..."

She was interrupted by a thunderous, but somewhat muffled, explosion. All three people in the room gave only the slightest acknowledgement of the event.

"It would seem it has just happened," Hitler said, with just a hint of a higher octave in his voice. "And yet, here I am, alive and well, thanks to you again."

Wyatt held his gaze on Hitler. Lucy glanced over to Wyatt, then back to the dictator. He smiled.

"I remember both of you from the Olympics, and Bavaria, and France during the Great War," Hitler said. "Every time you appear, I survive death."

With each incident he mentioned, Lucy could feel the guilt rise in her, and the bile started to creep up her esophagus. She had to fight to keep her remorse from overwhelming her because she knew they were doing the right thing for history's sake. But it was still a difficult reality to face.

Wyatt could feel the anxiety in her and felt a need to protect her. But he was fighting his own internal struggle with what they were preventing from happening.

"It is something we take no joy in doing," he spat at Hitler, the anger in his voice clear.

"Then why do you do it?" Hitler asked.

It was a question Wyatt, Lucy, and the other Lifeboat team members had asked themselves and each other countless times. Each time, the answer lay in the catastrophic -- for them -- changes in history that affected them, directly or indirectly. Lucy's sister, Wyatt's wife, Rufus' death, Denise's life direction, Jiya's visions and stranding in San Francisco, and Garcia's death. Even though on the surface the idea of eliminating Hitler appeared to save so many lives, the team had seen three times now that killing the dictator did not save those lives. In fact, it had made things worse; more lives were lost.

"Because it has to be done," Wyatt said through gritted teeth. He could feel his anger rising.

"How do you know when you are needed to protect me?" Hitler asked.

"We just know," Wyatt said. He could feel Lucy's hand tighten on his left arm. He knew she was trying to keep him from revealing their true identities and mission.

"Perhaps I should just keep you by my side at all times," Hitler suggested, and started to move backward toward the office door. It was the breaking point for Wyatt.

Like a gunfighter in the Old West movies, he plucked the P08 Luger from its holster at his right hip and pointed it right between Hitler's eyes. The dictator did not even flinch, but did stop dead in his tracks.

"You won't pull the trigger," Hitler said steadily to Wyatt. "You yourself have made it clear that is not your mission."

"Maybe it's time to redefine the mission," Wyatt said firmly. He held the pistol without the slightest movement, pointed at Hitler's face as he looked down the barrel. His finger was through the trigger guard, and he began to apply pressure.

"Wyatt, no!" Lucy pleaded beside him and squeezed her arm tighter. He shook her hand loose and placed his left hand under his right to support his aim.

"No, you won't shoot, Wyatt," Hitler said calmly.

The sound of his own name coming out of the dictator's mouth lit the fuse of his simmering emotions. It turned out to be a short fuse. Lucy could see in his face that Wyatt became angrier each time Hitler spoke. She took a step back.

"Please, Wyatt," she said softly. He didn't even glance in her direction.

"Listen to her, Wyatt," Hitler said. "She knows what is best."

The two men stared each other down for a moment, and Lucy looked from one to the other with sickening anticipation and dread.

Then Hitler decided to try another tactic.

"Put the gun down, Herr Stombanfuhrer," he yelled in the almost hysterical tone people would become accustomed to in the years to come.

Lucy gasped with a physical start when she heard the gunshot.

As she stared ahead, she saw Wyatt still holding the Luger at the ready, the wispy blue smoke swirling around the muzzle. She expected to see Hitler slump to the floor with a hole through his face where the bullet passed through to crash into his brain.

Instead, he stood where he had been, raising a hand to his left ear, a brief look of pain on his undamaged face. After a second or two, he pulled the hand away from his ear, his fingertips slightly red with blood.

"So, Wyatt, you are not prepared to see me die," Hitler said. His calm demeanor was a little unsettling. But there was a very slight quiver in his voice that showed there was some fear there.

"No, just staying on mission," Wyatt answered, calm but firm.

He heard Lucy release the breath she had been holding since the pistol fired.

"Now get out of here before I change my mind," Wyatt said, motioning with the pistol toward the door.

Hitler did as he was told, but stopped briefly at the door. He turned back to the pair.

"We will cross paths again," he said in German to Wyatt, then repeated it in French for Lucy.

"Don't count on it, connard," Lucy shot back, surprising Wyatt.

As Hitler exited, a look of disgust glaring back at that, Lucy rushed to Wyatt and threw her arms around him, hugging him so tightly he thought she might break a rib or two. He enjoyed the moment only briefly.

"Connard?" he asked, looking down into her face.

"Asshole," she said.

"And a few other things," he chuckled.

He could feel her giggle for a second.

"We need to go, Lucy, before he gets his goons organized," Wyatt said.

When she pulled away, shaking her head, he could see the tears rolling down her cheeks.

CHAPTER 19

It took less than one hour for Rufus to get bored with sitting around in the Advanced Lifeboat.

George had come along on this jump, but since the time machine was in Switzerland, there was no need for him to stay to guard it. He and Wyatt had set up the camo net, as they had in Berlin, before heading to Munich.

Wyatt brought George along to serve as backup in Munich. He was to stay close enough to Wyatt and Lucy to run interference or offer protection if they needed it. As it turned out, he followed them and Hitler out of the beer hall and stood guard outside the shop they had gone into to talk with Hitler.

But as he waited alone in Switzerland, Rufus needed something to occupy his mind.

The first thing he did was set the Advanced Lifeboat controls for the return trip. He decided it would be best to have it ready in case there needed to be a quick getaway. This was not the first time they had gone into very dangerous circumstances, and this had been the modus operandi in those other situations as well.

With that task completed, Rufus decided to explore the time machine more thoroughly. Since they were now using an enhanced Lifeboat left by the future versions of Wyatt and Lucy, there were aspects of this vehicle, besides the autopilot, that had not been studied. When the future Wyatt and Lucy said Rufus was indeed alive, the two sets went back in time to find and rescue him. When that was accomplished, the future Wyatt and Lucy took the original Lifeboat to return to their own timeline and left the enhanced vehicle with Rufus, Wyatt, and Lucy. But there had been no time to really study it before Agent Christopher put it in mothballs.

Rufus' efforts in Switzerland were limited to studying. He wasn't going to experiment with anything, not knowing exactly how it worked. But he was taking notes for experimentation later when there was time between other trips, if more were necessary.

At the end of a day-long exploration, he came across one monitor that was active, although he had not manipulated any switch to make it so. It showed a map with a balloon marker in the center. He touched the marker on the screen, and it expanded to show a title "Lifeboat" and more text with latitude and longitude, power levels, and a digital clock, counting upwards. Based on the time it showed, Rufus guessed this was the duration of their current jump.

All the information on the screen was displayed in other areas of the Lifeboat's control panel. Since he had never noticed this monitor as active, he had paid it no mind and had not gotten to it in his brief explorations of the multitude of new instruments in the updated Lifeboat.

As he pondered the possible function of this monitor, he noticed another balloon marker on the very edge of the screen. It was only halfway visible; it was that far to the left. Rufus looked for and found a zoom in/zoom out tool and hit the zoom out once. The map expanded to allow the second marker to be seen whole.

He touched the symbol and it, too, expanded to show text. It was labeled "Unknown Power Source." It also included latitude and longitude, power levels, and a running clock. This one was fifty-two hours ahead of the Advanced Lifeboat.

"Is that their time machine?" he said aloud.

Rufus found it hard to believe that of all the places they could have taken their time travel vehicle, they would be in such close proximity to the other time machine. But just how close? He studied the square monitor and found distance markers on all four sides. He was shocked to find the Advanced Lifeboat and the "Unknown Power Source" were just one mile apart.

It took just seconds for Rufus to make his next decision. It was late in the evening and the sun had already gone down. Because he did not want to get lost in the dark forest, he decided to check out the "Unknown Power Source" in the morning.

Leaving the Lifeboat unattended was nothing new for this team. They had done it on numerous jumps. They had parked the Advanced Lifeboat in a wooded area north of the small village of Mettau, so it was isolated enough that few people, if any, would be in the area. So once the sun was high enough to provide good light, Rufus set out in a westerly direction.

To ensure he could find his way back, he activated a homing beacon in the Advanced Lifeboat and took a receiver with him. He then walked to what he estimated to be a mile, then a few yards more. He found nothing. Believing the other travelers would have the knowledge to not park any closer to the border, he started to move south. Rufus had not gone more than the length of a football field when, off to his left, he saw something in the forest that did not seem to belong there.

Rufus moved toward the object, and as he got closer, he was able to make out the details. He saw a large sphere standing on five thick steel legs. The sphere's exterior was a mismatched collection of grays, as if made from spare parts with no concern for aesthetics. From the direction he was approaching, Rufus could see no obvious entry into the sphere.

He slowly made his way up to the machine, studying the construction as he went. He was struck by the realization that it looked somewhat like the early concept sketches of the Mother Ship.

Rufus carefully moved around the object until he could see a hatch opened outward, with the outside edge facing him. He went up to it and peeked around the edge.

"That will be far enough," he heard a female voice say. He looked toward the hatch opening and could see an extended arm, and in the hand was a small pistol, a snub-nosed .38, pointed at him.

George stood outside the shop Wyatt, Lucy, and Hitler had entered just minutes ago. Like Wyatt, he was dressed in an SS officer's uniform.

He had watched them leave the beer hall and discreetly followed them out. Two SS guards started to accompany Hitler with his companions as they crossed the street, but he waved them off. George walked down the street about twenty yards before crossing and doubling back, and taking a station not far from the shop's front door.

When the explosion went off in the beer hall, he watched as people either ran away from the scene or those in uniform went into the building. Shortly after that, he heard the gunshot from inside the shop. Having taken place inside a closed building and with the commotion over the beer hall explosion, no one else seemed to notice. George came out of the alcove he was standing in and moved toward the shop door. It opened, and the shopkeeper ran out. When George was nearly at the shop door, it opened again and Hitler walked out. He saw George and stepped in front of him.

"There is a woman and a man inside that shop," he told George in German. "Take them into custody. I want them in Berlin as soon as possible."

"Jawohl, Mein Führer," George responded as he threw up the Nazi salute and clicked his heels.

Hitler started to turn to leave, then turned back, remembering Wyatt's disguise as an SS officer.

"Give me your papers," Hitler demanded. George complied, Hitler looked them over, and handed them back. "You have your orders," he said and walked away.

As he was stuffing his identification documents back into his tunic, Wyatt and Lucy emerged from the shop.

"We've got to go," George said.

He led the pair a few blocks away, where he had parked a car he had procured by virtue of commandeering it for the state. But there was a Munich policeman looking over the vehicle.

"What's the problem here?" George said in German as he approached.

"Is this your vehicle?" the cop asked. George nodded.

"It was reported stolen an hour ago," the policeman said. "Can you show me proof of ownership?"

George looked to Wyatt, trying to ask the question without speaking it. Wyatt nodded and reached inside his uniform jacket to retrieve the Hitler letter. He handed it to the policeman. His face went as white as the paper the letter was typed upon.

"Do you need my assistance?" the officer asked.

The Lifeboat trio glanced at each other. They had discussed at length the fate of Georg Elser. They decided that if it were possible, they would spare his life. In the original history, the Germans captured him shortly after the explosion, and he freely told them all about his plans. Interestingly, they allowed him to live but put him in a concentration camp. The Germans executed him in 1945.

However, they needed something to throw this policeman off their track and, hopefully, get him out of their hair with no more questions until they could make their escape.

"Are you aware there was an assassination attempt on the Führer this evening?" George asked. The cop said he was aware.

"Give me your notebook," Lucy said. The policeman, looking her over in her waitress getup, was skeptical.

"This woman has information about the plot to kill our Führer," Wyatt snapped.

The policeman took another look at the two SS officers, and the waitress then handed over the notebook. Lucy wrote Elser's name and location on the first empty page and gave it back.

"This is the man who placed the bomb," Lucy told him.

"I need you all to come with me so I can get your statements," the cop said.

"No, you don't," George said. "I am under orders directly from the Führer to get this woman and this officer to Berlin as soon as possible. She has more vital information to provide to the Gestapo, and this officer witnessed the blast and made sure the Führer was safe."

The cop looked dubious, but remembering the letter, he did not question any further. He swiftly walked back to his vehicle and left the area. When he was safely out of sight, Wyatt, Lucy, and George got in the purloined BMW 335 and beat a hasty retreat out of Munich.

After a breakneck drive, the Lifeboat trio ditched the car in the small village of Meiningen on the German side of the Swiss border. Wyatt and George left their SS jackets and caps in the car, and the three then hiked northeast to an area between Swiss border forts, crossed into the country north of Rute to where they had parked the Advanced Lifeboat.

They found Rufus there, who nervously urged them to board so they could leave as soon as possible.

Seeing the gun pointed at him, Rufus took a step back and raised his hands to shoulder height.

"What are you doing here?" the voice asked from inside the machine. It was dark inside, and he could not make out the face of the person behind the firearm, but he recognized the voice.

"I am here to try and stop you from making a huge mistake," Rufus answered.

"You're not going to stop me if I shoot you," Paulina said.

"But you won't do that," Rufus said, not really believing his own words, but putting on his best Denzel Washington performance.

"Why not?" Paulina asked.

"Because you're not that kind of person," Rufus said, hoping he was right.

"And just how do you know that..." Paulina stopped in mid-sentence. She moved forward so she was in the dim light of the sun poking through the thick forest canopy. "I know who you are," she said.

Rufus did not relax. This could still go wrong.

"You have always been in the background, but you have been with those other two the last three times," she said, her face displaying anger.

Rufus knew the next moments were critical, and the thought occurred to him that they could be his last. He needed to tread lightly.

"Where are the other two?" Paulina asked. Rufus did not respond, trying to decide whether telling the truth or lying was the safest choice.

His thought process was interrupted by a loud bang and a flash from the barrel of Paulina's gun.

Rufus waited for death to take him, or at least to feel the pain from a wound. When neither happened, he looked up to see Paulina with an even more angry determination on her face, and the smoking pistol still pointed at him.

"Where are they?" she asked again.

The millisecond he heard the gunshot, Rufus had made up his mind that she could shoot him whether he told the truth or not.

"They are in Munich," he said. "And they'll stop that bomb from killing Hitler."

Paulina slumped to her knees, dropping the arm that held the pistol to her side.

"My people have a contingency plan," she said weakly, not really sure she believed any plan or contingency would succeed, knowing the track record of her opponents. "He'll die anyway."

Rufus knew this was possible. But he was confident that Wyatt and Lucy would find a way to stop any attempt on the dictator's life.

"Changing history is not as easy as you might think," Rufus said, finally dropping his arms to his side. "And even if you do, the results could be worse than what you're trying to change."

"How could there be anything worse than the killing of so many innocents?" Paulina asked, the anger starting to boil back up in her.

"It could mean you lose more than your great-grandfather," Rufus said slowly, hoping it did not anger her further to hear that he knew her ultimate goal.

"How would you know that?" Paulina asked, a bit of shock clouding her gaze. Rufus was sure she was talking about how he knew about her great-grandfather, but he decided to take another tactic.

"I have friends who have lost people because of changes made in time," he said. "And I've been dead because of trying to undo something, and came back because of it."

Paulina looked at him with wonder and curiosity in her eyes.

"You have no idea what can happen when you start messing with what has already happened," he went on.

"But you got brought back from death," Paulina said, grabbing hold of one small thing Rufus had said. "Why can't I bring someone back?"

Despite being happy to be alive again, Rufus had carried some guilt with him after knowing that to achieve that, Jessica had to die all over again. She had died in the original history but, like him, was restored. But her resurrection was engineered by Rittenhouse for their own misguided plans and ambitions. Even though she had caused a great deal of havoc after being brought back to life, Rufus still felt guilty that her life was traded for his.

"The only way I came back is that someone else had to die," he explained to Paulina. "And that death really affected someone I consider a friend. Is that something you want to risk?"

She slumped in the open hatch. Despite her desire and determination to bring her relatives back to life, the thought of sacrificing one life for another had not entered her mind. Now she was questioning whether she could be the person responsible for something like that.

Rufus started to move toward her. He wanted to continue the argument in hopes he could talk her out of her quest. But she suddenly raised the pistol and pointed it at his chest again.

"Go," she said weakly.

Rufus started to say something, but she would not allow it.

"Get out of here!" she yelled, her words echoing among the surrounding trees. She jabbed the gun in his direction.

Rufus slowly backed away and retreated the way he had come. Once back at the Advanced Lifeboat, he sat in the pilot's chair, shaking. He had died before on that San Francisco street in 1885, but if Paulina had actually killed him this time, it was more intimate, more personal, because he would have seen it coming.

Rufus was the last to exit the Advanced Lifeboat. As he climbed down to the bunker floor, Jiya came running forward to him, throwing her arms around him and smothering him with kisses.

The rest of the Lifeboat team, including Agent Christopher, Connor, and George, looked on in surprise. While they had not discussed it with all those present, it was clear to all how they felt about each other. But Jiya had avoided such overt displays of affection when others were around. And, of course, Rufus was not the public display type.

For a few seconds, Rufus and Jiya were caught up in the emotional moment.

"Well, maybe we can put off the debriefing for a short while," Agent Christopher told the others, trying to direct her comments to everyone but Rufus and Jiya. But her words filtered through their passion.

The pair released each other and took a step backward. They tried to physically and emotionally compose themselves, and the embarrassment showed clearly on their faces.

"No," Rufus choked out, his voice a few notes higher than usual. He cleared his throat and continued. "We can talk now."

Everyone giggled when his voice had only lowered one note in pitch. Jiya's face turned a deeper shade of red, and Rufus started to stammer, but no intelligible words emerged. Jiya saved him.

"It's just that I was so worried about him," she said. "And all of you," she added when she saw the mock look of shock on Wyatt's face.

Everyone burst out laughing, including Rufus and Jiya.

Agent Christopher and Jiya had not been idle before, and while the Advanced Lifeboat team was in Germany.

Following Connor's suggestion that Paulina and her time travelers were making their jumps in the past, they set out to do some research. They started with the warehouse in the Los Angeles Harbor industrial area.

Jiya went to the county courthouse to search through ownership records. But that drew a blank as the building was owned by an East

Coast corporation. The company had used it since its purchase in the 1950s to manufacture automobile parts that were shipped to car makers in several locations within the country. When the company's sales dropped in the 1960s, the machine shop was closed.

The building was then leased off and on, but the leases and the specific use for the structure were always identified as legitimate operations. All but the last tenant. That lease was signed by a man named Bobby Anderson. That was a bit disappointing as they had hoped to find Paulina's name connected to the property.

But the warehouse was their best lead, and they had to continue following it.

Connor went to work on a program developed for law enforcement that was designed to find how names fed into the system were connected to each other. The program could be further utilized by connecting names to specific geographic locations.

When Connor searched for connections between Bobby Anderson and Paulina Howser, he found twenty-three hits. When he was able to narrow the search to California, the hits dropped to nine. Finally, he input Los Angeles as the location, and there were two hits. A quick check showed that two people with those names had attended the California Institute of Technology. He also discovered through university records that Paulina and a man named Bobby Anderson had attended multiple classes together.

The next task was to determine from how far in the past Paulina and her team were making their jumps. Jiya found that Bobby Anderson's lease on the warehouse was abandoned about five years ago. No other leases were listed in California under that name since.

"It is possible they went to a facility that would have no records in county or state files, but it's the best we have to go on," Agent Christopher told the entire Lifeboat team gathered in the bunker common area. She had just related their research and conclusions.

"But how are we going to know exactly when five years ago," Rufus asked. "From the time the lease was abandoned, there's about twelve months before that, maybe even longer, in which they could have been making these jumps."

"I believe we can extrapolate the last date based on your own travel pattern," Connor said, continuing when he saw the confused look on the faces of those other than Jiya and Agent Christopher, who had already heard his speculation on the subject.

"What I'm saying is that if you jump back to this warehouse on the same day of the same month you came back from Germany, that is closest to when the building lease was abandoned, it should be the same day for Paulina's group," Connor said.

He explained his theory was based on the experiences of the test pilots in the early days of the project, and the latest cases of the future Wyatt and Lucy, and the present team's jump to Brazil to deliver the diary to Garcia Flynn that set his involvement in the time travel adventure into motion. He also believed travel records from the Advanced Lifeboat Flynn had taken into the past to kill Jessica, to put history right, added weight to his conjecture. The trip cost Flynn his life when, after using the autopilot to send the Advanced Lifeboat back to the present, he spent some time watching his past self with his family outside their home. That stranded him in the past during his own lifetime, and eventually, the ill effects took their toll.

"We know it's risky," Agent Christopher said. "You'll all be going back within your own lifetimes. But if we can either talk her out of these attempts of hers or sabotage her time machine, we can end this."

Wyatt and Lucy looked at each other. They had both lost loved ones through the time travel adventures. Without speaking, each knew the other had the same thought.

"We think it's worth the risk," Lucy said. "And we're willing to take it."

They looked to Rufus, who would have to be the pilot for the Advanced Lifeboat. He knew Wyatt and Lucy could make the jump by themselves with the machine's autopilot. But his loyalty to the team was the overwhelming reason for his response.

"I'm in," he said firmly.

"So am I," Jiya said.

They all looked at her in wonder.

"You're not suggesting you are going with us," Rufus said.

"You bet I am," she said.

"Oh no, that's not going to happen," Rufus said. "I don't want you risking yourself." While she had not had a vision in months, Rufus believed she would be more susceptible than he and the others to the mental damage that could come from trying to have two of the same person occupy the same space in time.

"Screw that," Jiya said. "I'm going, and you or no one else is going to stop me."

"I could," Agent Christopher said. When Jiya started to protest, Agent Christopher cut her off. "But I won't."

She took a breath and continued.

"This team has come to be a family, and I understand the loyalty and commitment of a family," she said. "There is no way I can go against that."

CHAPTER 20

When Ivan and Glenda returned to the Time Pod in Switzerland, they found Paulina sitting in the open hatch. She was clearly upset, but said nothing as they approached. She did not even ask if the mission was successful.

Glenda was quite concerned for her friend. While the last few weeks following the Olympics jump saw Paulina in a down mood, she remained focused on her mission of changing history to save her family members. Or so it seemed to the others. She was able to keep her doubts hidden from them.

"Are you okay?" Glenda asked.

Paulina simply waved her hand weakly at her.

"C'mon, we need to go," Ivan said. But Paulina made no move to get inside the pod, and she was blocking their way inside.

"Let's go," Ivan said a little angrily. Glenda shot him an admonishing look, but he remained determined to be on his way.

"We've got to go, Paulina, so let us inside," Ivan said, slightly moderating his tone.

Paulina slowly looked up, but her eyes had a glazed look. She slowly rolled around from her sitting position and crawled deeper into the pod. Glenda followed her inside. Ivan was right behind her and buttoned up the hatch. Within minutes, the pod was gone.

But unseen by any of them, Ivan's wallet, with the forged ID documents he had made for the trip, had worked its way out of his waist jacket pocket and dropped to the ground at the foot of the ladder.

The four Lifeboat members walked along the street toward the Los Angeles warehouse where they were certain they would find Paulina and her time travel team. They jumped into the later time period about two hours ago into a warehouse a few blocks away that Connor determined would be empty. He knew it because Mason Industries had owned it five years ago and planned to use it on the time travel project as a test landing site once they got to that point.

In the two hours they had been in the later time period, the Lifeboat team had so far felt none of the side effects of occupying the same space in time as their earlier selves. But they were certain it could happen at any moment. Because of that, they had to work fast.

But Wyatt wanted time to recon the warehouse. With few windows on the ground floor, he could not see inside. But he saw signs that indicated people were inside the building.

"We could go in and find only those left behind while they are on the jump," he told the others. "In that case, we won't know how long it will be before they come back."

"But we could find that they have already returned," Lucy said.

"It's a possibility, but I need you all to understand there may be some waiting time," Wyatt said.

They all nodded, indicating they understood.

"That front door is locked, but I can pick it," Wyatt told them. "But they could hear it and be ready when we get in."

Again, three heads nodded in understanding.

"Okay, let's do this," he said, and turned to head for the warehouse, with the other three in a single file behind him as he had instructed before heading to the target.

The Time Pod hatch opened, and Paulina was the first to come out. Bobby knew immediately that something was not right.

Paulina's slow gait was not like her; she usually had a quick pace, as if she were trying to set a record getting to her next destination. She also walked with her head pointed straight at the floor, another trait that just did not fit her confident personality.

As Glenda and Ivan dismounted the pod, Bobby went to Paulina and lifted her chin so he was looking directly at her face. Her eyes had the same glazed look that Glenda and Ivan had witnessed in Switzerland.

"What's wrong?" he asked. But she had no response.

Bobby looked past her to Ivan and Glenda as they approached. They both shrugged. Bobby returned his attention to Paulina, placing his hands on her shoulders.

"Please talk to me, what is going on?" he said.

Getting no response again, he lightly shook her. Slowly, the glaze in her eyes cleared, and she focused on him.

"It's over," she said.

Paulina gently pushed his arms off her shoulders and returned to shuffling toward the office. But Bobby moved in front of her again.

"What do you mean, it's over?" he asked.

"Just that," she said with a little more confidence in her voice. "We're not making any more time jumps."

That was not devastating news to Bobby, nor even to Glenda. They were in this project for the science, but mostly out of loyalty to their friend. If she was ready to give it up, who were they to argue.

They both also realized after the 1916 jump that with another group out there trying to stop them, the task would be more difficult than they had anticipated when they got involved. After the 1923 jump, they also realized there was a pattern of failure due to the other group.

But Ivan had other aspirations that required the use of Paulina's Time Pod. He was not ready to give up on those.

"You can't give up," he said, still a few feet away, as was Glenda, from where Paulina and Bobby stood. "This is too important to you."

"No, Ivan," Paulina said. "We're done."

He began to walk toward her. Bobby moved to her right side and held out his hand, palm out.

"Leave her alone," he said. "It sounds like she has made her decision, and it is her project."

Ivan did not stop, instead going around Paulina on her left side, and he faced her in profile. She did not turn her head to look him in the eye.

"There are things we can do to determine when those other people jump and we can be ready for them," Ivan said, half pleading and half defiantly. "It will just take a little more time. We are so close."

Paulina listened, but the words filtered through her ears and did not take hold in her mind. He was not changing her mind.

"There are other ways to keep them from interfering," Ivan said. "I can take care of them."

Bobby moved between Ivan and Paulina, facing him. Glenda moved forward. She and Bobby feared what Ivan's meaning was.

"Are you talking about harming them?" Bobby asked. "Or worse?" Glenda chimed in.

"I will do what is necessary to secure the success of this project," Ivan said firmly.

"For whom?" Paulina asked, more spark returning to her eyes. She slowly turned her head so she was looking right at Ivan.

He took a step back. He could see he had erred in implying physical violence against the other travelers. Now he needed to stall for time to think of a good argument to extricate himself from the hole he had put himself in. He also needed to be careful, lest he slip again and give away his own plans.

"For you, of course," he said. "Who else would I do it for?"

"For yourself," Paulina said.

Ivan felt a bit of panic enter his thinking. *What does she know?"* he thought.

"What on earth would I want from traveling in time?" he asked.

"I don't know," Paulina responded. "But there's been something bothering me about you."

Ivan fought to control his panic. He had to keep his cool. He had to figure out a way to either keep the project going with these people or to continue it on his own. He knew the latter meant taking drastic action against the others. But he was ready for it if it came to that.

"When I approached you about this, you seemed very eager -- way too eager -- to be involved," Paulina said. "I saw that then, but was too blinded by my own ambitions to see it as a problem."

Ivan raised his hands in a calming gesture.

"All I wanted was to be involved in an interesting project," Ivan said.

"And I thank you for your efforts," Paulina said. "But the project is over now. It was a failure."

For a moment, Ivan lost control over his panic.

"No!" he screamed. "It can't be over."

His change in attitude stunned the others, and they flinched where they stood.

"I agree with the lady," they heard a voice say calmly to their left. "This project needs to be over."

Intent on their own conversation, Paulina and her colleagues did not hear Wyatt's efforts to pick the warehouse lock and did not notice them come through the front entrance. They all jumped slightly at the sound of Wyatt's voice.

"Who the hell are you?" Ivan blasted out.

"Who we are doesn't matter," Lucy said. "Why are we here does."

She looked toward Paulina.

"We need to talk," Lucy said.

"And why do you need to talk to her?" Bobby asked, stepping in between Paulina and the Lifeboat team.

"We're not here to hurt anyone," Wyatt said.

"Then what the hell do you want?" Ivan asked, taking a few steps toward Wyatt, who resisted the instinct to pull his Beretta M9 service sidearm from the shoulder holster hidden under his jacket. He wanted to resolve the situation non-violently if possible.

"We're here to talk to Paulina," Lucy repeated.

"How do you know my name?" Paulina asked. The two had seen each other before in the previous time jumps, and Paulina recognized Lucy. But at no time did either of them divulge their true names.

Lucy confidently strode toward Paulina, trying to bypass Bobby. But he moved in front of her, continuing to stay between the two women.

"It's alright, Bobby," Paulina said. "What is it you want?" she asked Lucy.

Flashing Bobby a satisfied look, Lucy went to within a few feet of Paulina.

"Can we go into that office and talk privately?" she asked.

"Alright," Paulina answered. "But Bobby goes with us."

Ivan began to protest, but a look from Paulina made him choke on the words he was about to say. Paulina turned and walked toward the office, and Bobby followed. Lucy looked back at Rufus, and he also headed for the office.

When the door closed, Ivan looked Wyatt and Jiya over very carefully.

"So what's the story?" he asked.

"We'll let them talk it out," Wyatt said, nodding toward the office.

Inside, Paulina sat behind the desk, and Bobby settled into the only other chair in the room, next to the office door and behind Lucy and Rufus as they stood facing Paulina.

"We have seen each other before," Paulina said, her confidence and focus restored since the familiar strangers walked into the warehouse. "But I'm at a disadvantage. You know who I am, but I don't know you."

Lucy sighed and gave Rufus a side look. They had hoped to remain anonymous. But Lucy decided to go off script and avoid using the names they had discussed before jumping back five years to this period. Rufus guessed her intentions.

"I don't think that would be a good idea," he said.

But Lucy shook her head slowly. She believed they might have better luck if she could establish some thread of trust with Paulina. Trust built on a foundation of deceit is like the Little Pig's house of straw.

"My name is Lucy and this is Rufus," she said, pausing for a beat before going on. "We are from five years in your future."

While it may have sounded like something too preposterous for someone to believe, since Paulina and her team had been jumping through time, it was easier for her and Bobby to accept. Paulina was a bit surprised, however, to learn they were from only five years ahead.

She remembered the side effects they had discovered from being in the same time period as themselves. To this point, she also believed that Lucy, Wyatt, and Rufus were people from the past whom she kept running into by pure coincidence. But it was now dawning on her that their encounters were too specific to be happenstance.

"So why are you here?" Bobby asked.

Again, Lucy hesitated before speaking, trying to make sure she had the right words.

"We're here to keep history on its natural path," she said.

Paulina slowly nodded and glanced at Bobby. In private discussions since the 1923 jump that did not include Glenda and Ivan, it was something they had suspected but discarded as being too bizarre that two groups would be traveling through time. But in an odd way, they both felt comforted that their speculation had turned out to be correct.

"So what are you, some kind of time cops?" Bobby asked.

Rufus smiled, remembering the movie with just that theme. Lucy shot him an unspoken question, and Bobby looked a little irritated.

"Movie reference," was all Rufus said. Recalling the "Hogan's Heroes" reference in France, the "Captain America" reference in Bavaria, the "Die Hard" reference in Berlin and the "Where Eagles Dare" reference in Munich, none of which she got at the time but did when she watched the shows, Lucy felt a smile play across her own face. Wyatt made sure she was introduced to each when they had free time between missions.

Looking behind her and noticing Bobby's continued irritated expression, Lucy was quick to wipe the grin off her face.

"I suppose, in some way, you are right, that is what we have been doing," Lucy said. "Even before we encountered you in 1916."

Paulina leaned forward in her chair and rested her arms on the desk.

"So what you're saying is, you want us to stop going back in time," she said.

Lucy nodded.

"Making changes to history in the past can have serious consequences on history going forward," she said.

"Yes, he told me that, and said people he knew lost loved ones because of it," Paulina said, indicating Rufus.

The shock on Bobby's face was clear for all to see. Paulina had not yet shared with her colleagues her encounter with Rufus in the Swiss forest.

"When the hell did you talk to him?" Bobby shouted as he stood up.

Paulina tried to calm him with a reassuring look.

"He found the Pod while I was waiting for Glenda and Ivan to come back from Munich," she said, then turned her gaze to Lucy. "Are you one of his friends who lost someone?"

Lucy could feel her heart beat a little faster in her chest, and a tear began to form in one eye. She took a deep breath and felt her heartbeat slow toward normal.

"Yes," she said. "I lost my sister; she was erased from existence. After our first trip back in time, she just wasn't there when we got back. Something changed because of our presence in the past, and she was never born. And my mother was killed during one of our earlier jumps."

"And the other one?" Paulina asked, looking out the office window at Wyatt and Jiya in the standoff with Glenda and Ivan.

"His wife was killed years before, but got brought back by the people we were trying to stop from making changes in time to radically change the structure of the United States," Rufus explained when he saw Lucy falter again. "She is the one I told you about who had to die to set history right, and bring me back. We also lost someone else from our team in all that."

"So you are saying you have been going back in time long before you encountered us?" Paulina asked. Rufus and Lucy nodded in affirmation simultaneously.

Paulina and Bobby exchanged unsure looks. The room was silent for a few moments.

"I don't know if I believe all that," Paulina finally said. "We've gone back in time, and nothing has changed with the present."

Lucy moved forward and, still looking a little shaken from reliving Amy's disappearance, her mother's death, and Jessica's double death and all the anguish that brought her and Wyatt, put her hands on the edge of Paulina's desk and leaned in toward her.

"There may be changes you haven't noticed yet," she said sternly. "But I can tell you this. If you had been successful in any one of your attempts to kill Hitler, it would have prolonged World War II, and more people would have died."

Lucy took a breath before spitting out the next words.

"Including your great-grandfather -- every single time."

Paulina jumped up from her chair and got nose to nose with Lucy across the desk.

"You're lying!" she shouted.

At that moment, they all heard Wyatt's shout from the main warehouse floor.

"Stop!"

When Lucy and Paulina led Rufus and Bobby into the office, the other four in the warehouse stood and stared at each other for a few minutes. Initially, they were trying to hear what was being said inside, but they had no luck making out the words clearly.

Finally, the silence outside the office was broken.

"Who are you people?" Glenda asked.

At first, neither Wyatt nor Jiya responded. They glanced at each other, asking the same silent question. *"How much should we tell them?"*

"What's going on?" Why are you here?' Glenda questioned again.

"We're just here to talk," Wyatt said.

"About what?" Glenda was not letting it go.

It wasn't lost on Wyatt that the man wasn't saying anything. He studied him for a few seconds. Wyatt noticed the man was watching him and Jiya intently. Wyatt knew the look. They were being sized up for vulnerabilities. He knew the look because he had done it himself on numerous Special Forces missions.

When Wyatt did not respond to Glenda's inquiries, Jiya jumped in after a few seconds.

"We want to know something about what you are all doing," she said.

As she finished the sentence, Wyatt noticed out of the corner of his eye the slightest flinch from Jiya as she was feeling pain shoot through her entire body. But it passed quickly. However, Wyatt saw that Ivan noticed it also. Wyatt knew the man had found his most vulnerable target.

"What exactly is it you want to know?" Glenda continued her questioning.

Wyatt decided it was time to throw caution to the wind.

"We want to know why you are traveling back in time to save Paulina's great-grandfather," he said.

The surprise was total for both Glenda and Ivan, but he recovered quickly and looked to Jiya for any sign of weakness. They were on opposite sides of the small circle in which they all stood, and Wyatt could easily stop him if he made a direct assault on her.

Then Jiya solved that problem for Ivan. She bent at the waist and put her hands to her head, clearly in pain. Wyatt moved toward her, taking his eyes off Ivan. That was the opening he needed.

Ivan darted to the tables where the computer equipment was located and reached for a backpack at the end of one table. He then turned and started to run toward the Time Pod.

Wyatt immediately yanked the pistol from the shoulder holster and pointed it at Ivan just as he picked up the backpack.

"Stop!"

Ivan took two more steps, and Wyatt fired a shot into the ceiling. Ivan hesitated a split second just as the four in the office emerged in open-mouthed astonishment.

"Stay where you are and drop the pack," Wyatt ordered.

"Ivan, what are you doing?" he heard Paulina scream from behind him.

But neither utterance deterred Ivan as he resumed his run toward the Time Pod about ten yards away. Wyatt repositioned the gun and fired again. The bullet struck Ivan's right arm between the elbow and the shoulder, but only causing a flesh wound. But the impact spun him halfway around and forward. He was now just a few feet away from the Time Pod hatch.

"Wyatt!" Lucy hollered. He did not look back and shouted again for Ivan to halt. Instead, he scrambled up the pod's ladder.

Wyatt fired again, and this time the round missed Ivan as he stumbled at the top of the ladder and crawled inside. They all saw the bullet strike inside the pod, and sparks flew from the control panel. It was the last thing they saw inside as the hatch closed.

"Oh my God, stop him," Paulina yelled. "He'll steal the pod."

Rufus ran forward and directed Wyatt to aim for a point on the side of the pod where there was a small box that looked like a household fuse box. Wyatt took aim, but before he could pull the trigger, there was a familiar flash of light and a "whump," and the pod was gone.

"No!" they all heard Paulina scream behind them.

When the flash of the pod's departure faded, it was Rufus who first realized Jiya was on her knees, bent forward, and still holding her head. He rushed to her and knelt down beside her.

"What is it? Are you alright?" he asked nervously. "Are you having visions again?"

She slowly shook her head, with her hands continuing to cover it. That confused Rufus.

By now, Wyatt and Lucy were also kneeling beside her, with Bobby and Glenda joining Paulina as they stared at the empty space where the Time Pod had been parked.

"Are you alright?" Rufus asked, this time containing himself to one question at a time. Jiya shook her head.

"Is it a vision?" he asked. Again, she shook her head.

Jiya was feeling the pain subside slowly, but she kept her posture as she waited for the throbbing to slow enough to get a few words out. Rufus could find no other questions to ask, and Wyatt and Lucy glanced at each other. Lucy pointed to her own head and uttered one word.

"Brazil." It was a reference to when the team traveled back five years to give Lucy's diary to Garcia Flynn. Lucy had experienced some pain while there because they were in the same time period as their future selves.

They saw Jiya nod, and she started to lower her hands from her head. Slowly, she looked up, first into Rufus' eyes, then at Wyatt and Lucy in turn.

"I'm alright now," she said. "It still tingles a little, but not like before."

Jiya gingerly got to her feet.

"Lucy's right," Jiya said. "It's the effects of being in the same timeline as myself."

While it gave the Lifeboat team a sense of relief to know Jiya was alright, they all knew this was going to happen again -- to any of them -- the longer they stayed. The time was fast approaching to return to their own time.

But there was still something to be done.

"We must go now," Lucy said to Paulina, Bobby, and Glenda.

Paulina slowly turned her head, still a little detached, thinking about the loss of the Time Pod. Glenda and Bobby also turned to look at Lucy. No word was spoken for a few moments.

"Where must you go?" Paulina asked.

"Back to where we came from," Lucy answered. "We can't stay here. It would be harmful to us."

Paulina nodded her head.

"Yes, I know," she said. "We experienced it, too."

Lucy's puzzled look seemed to snap Paulina out of her trance.

"You weren't lying," she said. "I understand now."

Lucy wondered just how much she truly understood. But there wasn't time to find out. She turned to return to the rest of her team, but Paulina's voice stopped her.

"How far ahead of us in time did you say you were?" she asked. "Or are you really from the past?"

Still facing her team, Lucy turned her head toward Paulina.

"We are five years ahead," she said. "We will meet again."

Lucy joined the other Lifeboat team members and walked out of the door of the warehouse.

Epilogue

Jiya, Rufus, and Connor were all hunched over the keyboards in front of their monitors in the bunker. They were searching all the avenues they could think of to track Paulina's Time Pod.

There were no indications the pod had jumped after winking out of the Los Angeles warehouse five years ago -- or as the Lifeboat team saw it, just several hours ago.

Rufus got up from his post and went to the Advanced Lifeboat. He sat at the control console and manipulated the dials to activate the tracker he had discovered in Switzerland. The screen, even at maximum zoom out, was completely blank except for the balloon marking the Advanced Lifeboat.

"There is nothing showing on the tracker," he told the others when he returned to his computer terminal.

Connor and Jiya both registered the same look of disappointment as he had when he saw the blank screen in the time machine.

"But that could also mean that the pod is not near enough to track, or it's back in time and can't be tracked because of that," Jiya said. "Since we don't know anything about that feature of the Advanced Lifeboat, we can't be sure."

"And we can't track it like we did the Mother Ship because the Lifeboat systems are not connected to Paulina's pod like it was with the Mother Ship," Rufus mused.

"We had planned to look into a tracker like that, but didn't think it was really necessary until the Mother Ship was stolen," Connor said. "And I didn't pursue it any further when we discovered we could track the Mother Ship through the shared connection with the Lifeboat."

"I had forgotten until I saw that tracker in Switzerland," Rufus said. "My guess is that the other Lucy and Wyatt must have stumbled across our notes and finished it with the other advancements they made in the future."

Jiya had been tapping a pencil, eraser down, on her tabletop. It made very little sound, but Rufus and Connor saw the motion. Rufus knew she did that when she was deep in thought. He and Connor looked at her until she realized she was being stared at. She bashfully put the pencil down and turned her chair to face them.

"There is another possibility," she said, then paused for a few seconds.

"When Wyatt shot at the guy who took their time machine..."

"Ivan," Rufus interrupted her.

"Yes, Ivan. When Wyatt shot at him, I saw sparks inside the machine at the spot where our control console would have been if it was in that machine," Jiya explained.

Rufus and Connor each gave her a look that silently said, *"And?"*

"I think Wyatt's bullet damaged their machine in some way," she said.

Rufus nodded, and his expression brightened.

"Yeah, I remember seeing that," he said. "I had forgotten until you mentioned it."

He paused a second, then looked at Jiya with concern.

"How did you see that? You were in such pain," Rufus said. "We all saw you go down."

Jiya shuddered with the memory.

"When I heard the first shot, I looked up," she explained.

"Okay, so if there was damage, that could be why we're not able to track it," Connor said, bringing them back to the discussion at hand.

"Or tell if it has jumped to another time period," Rufus said ominously.

"That's not good," Jiya said. "What if he starts to go back to finish what couldn't get done before? We'd never know until it's done."

She saw a wry smile spread across Connor's face. Rufus, still facing her, saw her reaction to it and turned toward Connor.

"I'm usually the guy who sees the worst scenarios," Connor said. "But it's also possible that the bullet damaged their machine in such a way that after he got out of that warehouse, he couldn't jump anymore."

Rufus nodded.

"It could be anything," he said.

Shortly after the Advanced Lifeboat returned from the Los Angeles warehouse in the past, Agent Christopher got a short briefing from Wyatt on what had happened. Jiya was sent to see the Homeland Security doctor assigned to the team, and Rufus was with her. Lucy briefed Connor on the last time jump. Later, all other team members paid a visit to the doctor. No ill effects could be detected in any of them from occupying the same space in time as their past counterparts.

Two days later, the entire team was in the bunker lounge for an expanded discussion. George was not present for this meeting. Agent Christopher explained he had been reassigned to his regular Army unit, but remained on call if needed by the Lifeboat team.

"In the last two days, we have seen no indications Paulina's time machine has made any jumps," she said. "While I take some comfort in that, it is still a little concerning to not know what happened to that vehicle."

She looked to Connor, his cue to continue the discussion.

"There are so many possibilities," he said slowly. "There could have been damage to the machine that kept it from being used again, or it could have just damaged it enough so that we cannot track it."

He paused for a second and thought.

"There are so many things that could have happened," he went on. "But there is one thing we can be fairly certain of. If he were able to go back in history and make the changes they were hoping for, he wouldn't have waited to do it, not knowing if we were able to ascertain his intentions as we had before. So it is highly likely that if he did make any changes, we would have known it by now."

"Or we'd have been wiped from history," Rufus said.

Agent Christopher put up her hands to stop them if they planned to say anything further.

"For all those possibilities and more, we are going to stay active as a team," she said. "I can't force you -- even you, Wyatt -- to remain at our beck and call. I know this has been an ordeal for everyone."

She looked at each face in turn, hoping to get a hint of what they were thinking, how they would respond to her next statement. It was like looking into the faces of expert poker players.

"But I am hoping you will all stay a part of this team," she said, holding her breath a little before she went on. "I believe keeping this team together would be our best hope if we have to face changes in history again."

Each Lifeboat team member looked to the other in turn. They sat quietly for a few minutes. Lucy was the first to speak.

"We have all gone through a lot in the last three years," she said. "Some of us have lost people..."

She hesitated as a lump formed in her throat. She remembered Amy and her mother. Wyatt reached over and took her hand in his. She kept her gaze straight ahead, but she so appreciated his support.

"....and some of us have got them back and lost them again," she went on. "One of us has died and come back again."

Lucy looked at Jiya, then at Rufus. "And we lost someone we'll never get back," she added.

"I know the kind of physical toll this can take on us, and so many dreams have been given up for this," she went on, then looked at Agent Christopher. "Through it all, we've gotten to know and trust each other."

She glanced at Wyatt, and he gave her an approving nod. Clearly, they had discussed this between them privately and come to their own decision.

"We have become like a family," Lucy said proudly, with that lump returning to her throat. She swallowed it and continued. "I don't know what I would do without you all."

She looked at Agent Christopher again.

"We're in," she said, and felt Wyatt squeeze her hand in support.

They heard a little whimper and all turned to Jiya, who had her hand over her mouth. She glanced around at them all.

"Well, this is very interesting from a scientific perspective," Jiya said, lowering her hand from her mouth and showing the slightest hint of a smile playing at the corners of her mouth. "But I'm not all emotional about it."

Everyone but Rufus, for he knew better, nodded their understanding. Rufus sat silent and stone-faced for a few seconds. Then took in a breath, held it briefly, then let it out slowly.

"I'm sure you all know my enthusiasm for this project hasn't been very high from the start, and it has been even less so these last few times," he said. "What we just did -- keeping Hitler alive -- has been the hardest thing I've ever had to do. And it took a toll on me."

The others, including Jiya, sat in fearful anticipation of his answer. Rufus looked slowly around the room at all of them. They were all convinced they would be losing a team member.

Rufus put his head in his hands. Silence filled the room like air in a balloon. After what seemed like an eternity, Agent Christopher spoke.

"I understand," she said. "I think we all do."

Rufus' fingers parted so he could see through them. With his hands still in place, he looked around the small circle of people. He lowered his hands to his knees and leaned back in his chair.

"But how could I walk out on family?" he said, then a grin spread across his face.

Wyatt threw a sofa pillow at him.

Agent Christopher and Connor sat in her car, a hybrid Subaru Forester, in front of a house in Altadena, California, on Alta Pine Drive. It was a medium-sized home, a bit upscale for the neighborhood, but not overly showy. It was just a few blocks from the foothills of the Angeles National Forest.

They had parked there ten minutes previously and for the first five minutes just sat silently and looked over the property. Not looking for anything specific, just perusing the landscape while they each thought over why they had made the two-hour drive to this particular location. They had talked about it plenty on the way. But they were now just making sure in their own minds. Connor was the first to bring his thoughts to voice.

"You still think this is wise, right?' he asked. "I mean the two of us doing this."

They had originally talked about having Wyatt, Lucy, Rufus, and Jiya make first contact. After all, they would be familiar faces. But Agent Christopher believed the last meeting between them all was too traumatic and might scare the target off. Connor understood her thinking, but still argued for letting the active Lifeboat team make the contact. He believed the familiarity would put the target at ease.

The argument -- not really an aggressive argument, more like a firm discussion -- continued just between the two of them for the past twenty-four hours, including the drive down. The idea to make contact at all had been Lucy's. But Agent Christopher simply told her she would think about it, then quietly began her search.

"Am I one-hundred percent sure? No," she finally answered Connor's question. "But we're here now, and it's either go knock on the door or drive away."

Connor gave her the frowning look he reserved for when he was a bit -- sometimes even more than a bit -- peeved at someone.

"I am not at all fond of putting in two hours of my time doing anything, including being cooped up in an automobile, only to have it not accomplish anything," he said.

They sat for another couple of minutes. Finally, Connor gave Agent Christopher a half-questioning, half-demanding look as he grabbed the door handle next to him. She returned his look with a shrug of resignation, and they both exited the vehicle.

They stood in front of the door to the home for a few seconds before Agent Christopher rang the doorbell. It took a second ring before they heard someone turning a deadbolt lock, and then the doorknob. When the door opened, Paulina Howser stood just inside the doorway.

"Yes?" she asked.

"My name is Denise Christopher, and this is Connor Mason. We are with Homeland Security." Agent Christopher made the introductions, then got right to the point of their visit. "We would like to speak with you about what happened five years ago."

Paulina stood in silence for a few seconds. She then motioned for them to come inside the home.

Agent Christopher sat on a chair in the lounge area of the bunker, waiting for the Lifeboat team members to arrive. She had texted each of them an hour ago, telling them she needed to meet with them urgently.

When she heard the hatch open at the other end of the bunker, she wondered who would arrive first. As the feet appeared on the ladder, she knew it was Rufus. As he reached the floor and began walking toward her, she expected Jiya to be right behind him.

But Rufus had come alone.

"What's up?" he asked as he got to the lounge area.

"Let's wait for the others," she responded, motioning for him to sit.

Ten minutes later, Lucy came down the ladder, followed closely by Wyatt. For months, their friends would rarely see one without the other very closely nearby.

Before they could ask, Agent Christopher gestured for them to join Rufus in taking a seat. They exchanged hellos with him and sat facing Agent Christopher, expectant looks on their faces.

"One more, then we'll get started," was all she said.

Jiya came down the ladder just minutes later. With the entire team together, Agent Christopher stood and began to talk.

"As you all know, we've been continuing to monitor time travel activity," she said. "So far, there has been none."

She paused for a moment, then continued.

"We have also continued to try and track Paulina's time machine. Also, with no indication of where and when it is."

Another short pause as she eyed each team member. While their sense of anticipation dulled a bit, they were still expectant. Surely Agent Christopher hadn't called them all in to give them an update that revealed nothing but what they already knew.

"In light of that, we're going into a standby mode," Agent Christopher informed them. "We, meaning Connor and I, will continue to monitor the equipment, but there will be no need for any of you to stand shifts."

The team members looked at each other, trying to soak in the significance of the situation. They had been through this once before, after Rittenhouse had been taken down and the Mother Ship dismantled. They all thought then that life would go back to normal. Then this new wave of being history's watchdog had begun.

Wyatt wasn't buying it.

"You could have let us know all this by text or phone calls," he said. "What's really going on?"

Agent Christopher's only response was to take out her cell phone, send a text, and replace the phone in her pocket. Within seconds, they all heard the bunker hatch open again. They turned to look and see who came down the ladder.

Connor scrambled down and, once at the bottom, looked up and motioned for someone to follow. The person coming down the ladder was clearly a woman. But it was only Lucy who guessed the identity before she reached the floor and turned around.

"Paulina," Lucy whispered.

Connor and the woman walked along the corridor leading to the lounge and the Advanced Lifeboat's parking area. Paulina swiveled her head side to side as she walked, taking in everything as she went, a look of disbelief -- but at the same time recognition -- on her face.

As she came out of the corridor, her eyes were to the right, and she took in the kitchen area. Then she looked directly to the left and saw the four people who looked very familiar, even five years later from her perspective. Those faces were burned into her memory like brands burned into cattle's hides.

Lucy stood and moved toward her.

"You were right," Paulina said.

"Yes, I knew we would see each other again," Lucy responded.

The others stood and joined Lucy to greet Paulina. During the salutations, she caught sight of the Advanced Lifeboat for the first time.

"Oh my God!" she exclaimed, her eyes growing wide with wonder. She took a few steps past the group and continued to stare.

"Rufus, would you like to show our guest the Advanced Lifeboat?" Agent Christopher offered, then added in a mock tone, "That is, if she is interested."

Paulina looked at Agent Christopher, then at Rufus.

"Oh, she is interested," Paulina said. "She is very interested."

Peter Wilson was walking past the warehouse across the street from his office. He had gone on foot to the coffee shop a few blocks away to gather drinks for his staff and himself. Carrying the bag of securely sealed to-go coffee cups stuffed into a four-slot cup holder in his left hand, he was vaguely aware of noises inside the warehouse.

That seemed odd, since he had assumed the building was unused. Only rarely had he seen anyone going into or leaving the structure. There was certainly never any trucks picking up or delivering anything.

He kept walking and had just started to cross the street when he heard a loud bang. It startled him, and he nearly dropped the bag, but was able to maintain his grip on it. He turned toward the warehouse, sure that was the direction from which the sound had come.

Within thirty seconds, he saw a dim flash in the upper windows and simultaneously heard a muffled "whump" sound. It wasn't as loud as the first noise, and not as sharp as the gunshots he had heard in his life, both on television and live during the one time there had been a disturbance in his neighborhood that included gunfire.

Peter turned around again and finished crossing the street. As he reached his office door, he turned and looked at the warehouse again before entering. He saw four people -- a white woman, another woman with darker skin, a black man, and a white man -- leave the warehouse through the main entrance door.

Peter set the carrier filled with coffees at the reception desk and went to his office. He intended to call the police to report the incidents he had witnessed. Just as he got the headset to his ear, he felt dizzy. He fell back in his chair, and his head bowed back onto the high headrest. His eyes rolled back in his head until only small slivers of the irises were visible. Confused scenes played out in his mind. Scenes of uniformed men in his office, being injected with something, the bombed ruins of his office, and the surrounding neighborhood.

Suddenly, he was sitting upright and staring into the faces of his associates who had gathered at his office door.

"Are you alright? We heard you moaning," Candace asked.

Faded memories of what he had just envisioned flickered through his mind.

"I just had the weirdest daydream," he said, and explained what he recalled of it.

In a small clearing in a thick wooded area surrounded by tall pine trees, there was a sudden bright flash of light and a "whump." When the flash faded, there was a spherical machine standing on five thick steel legs, one with a ladder welded to it. What appeared to be a hatch was above the leg with the ladder. The sphere was different shades of gray, as if it were a patchwork quilt of different steel plates.

After about a minute, the hatch opened outward, and a man emerged and looked around. The man's dark blue sleeve on his right arm was wet, and the area had a dark red tint to it. There was a look of horror on the man's face.

"No!" the man yelled, his words echoing through the forest. "No! This is not where I'm supposed to be."

The man slumped forward and sat in the open hatch.

"Not Switzerland," he yelled.

He lowered his head and put his face in his hands.

"This can't be happening," the man said in a lower tone. He then slowly took his hands away from his face and kept his eyes on the ground below the ladder. He saw something and scrambled down the ladder to retrieve it. The man picked up a small, black, bifold leather wallet. He slowly opened it.

Inside the wallet the man held open in his hands was an official-looking document. On the upper left was an eagle with wings spread wide, clutching a wreath in its talons. Inside the wreath was a swastika. A name on the document was Ivan Radinski. The date on the document was November 9, 1939.

About the Author

Rusty Bradshaw is no stranger to writing, having gotten the bug while in junior high school and never gotten over it. Born in California, he grew up in Wyoming and spent 26 years in Oregon before moving to Arizona. He graduated from Dubois High School, attended Northwest Community College in Wyoming, and earned a Bachelor of Science degree from Eastern Oregon State College. He then began what would be a 42-year journalism career that would see him write and photograph for several newspapers in Oregon and more in Arizona. While in Oregon, Rusty won several writing awards from the Oregon Newspaper Publishers Association. He was also named Junior Citizen of the Year in Milton-Freewater, Oregon, where he was active in United Way, was president of a local food bank, and coached youth football.

Rusty retired from journalism in 2023, but continues freelance video reporting on YouTube and other social media, particularly for his home community of Sun City, Arizona. He has two grown children -- Sara in Washington and Evan in Idaho -- and lives in Sun City with his wife, Jeanne, who has a grown son -- Billy in North Carolina. Rusty and his wife enjoy football, bingo, occasional road trips, jigsaw puzzles, and any other activities they can do together.

Rusty also has a large portfolio of scenic photos available for sale.

Visit www.rustythewriter.org for information about Rusty Bradshaw's books and photography.

Other Books by Rusty Bradshaw

> *The Rehabilitation of Miss Little*
> *Moist on the Mountain*
> *Gorge Justice*
> *Battle for Stephanie*
> *Death in Hazard*
> *Murderous Reunion*